LESSON FROM THE MASTER

Remo was worried. He never should have let the aging Chiun go up against the mafia hit squad alone. When Remo heard the gunfire, he raced to the rescue.

"Are you okay, Little Father?" Remo asked anxiously.

"Of course I am all right," said Chiun harshly, bringing down his foot. Pauli (The Maggot) Maggiotto made a cracking sound with his head and a kind of lamb's bleat with his last breath. A combination of blood and brains squirted from each ear. "I am the Reigning Master of Sinanju. Not some doddering ancient. Now see if you can do your part of the job, callow youth."

High-tech computers might make clean kills, but from here on in the action would be down and dirty . . .

The Destroyer

#87

MOB PSYCHOLOGY

Created by
WARREN MURPHY & RICHARD SAPIR

A SIGNET BOOK

SIGNET
Published by the Penguin Group
Penguin Books USA Inc., 375 Hudson Street,
New York, New York 10014, U.S.A.
Penguin Books Ltd, 27 Wrights Lane,
London W8 5TZ, England
Penguin Books Australia Ltd, Ringwood,
Victoria, Australia
Penguin Books Canada Ltd, 10 Alcorn Avenue,
Toronto, Ontario, Canada M4V 3B2
Penguin Books (N.Z.) Ltd, 182–190 Wairau Road,
Auckland 10, New Zealand

Penguin Books Ltd, Registered Offices:
Harmondsworth, Middlesex, England

First published by Signet, an imprint of New American Library,
a division of Penguin Books USA Inc.

First Printing, January, 1992
10 9 8 7 6 5 4 3 2 1

Printed in the United States of America

PUBLISHER'S NOTE
This is a work of fiction. Names, characters, places, and incidents either are the product of the author's imagination or are used fictitiously, and any resemblance to actual persons, living or dead, events, or locales is entirely coincidental.

For Carminc (The Flash) Infantino.

And the Glorious House of Sinanju,
P.O. Box 2505, Quincy, MA 02269.

1

Now that two men were holding him down on the soggy ground and a third had submerged his head in the cranberry bog, Wally Boyajian reluctantly concluded that it had all been too good to be true, after all.

This must be a hazing ritual, Wally thought wildly as he held his breath, his lips compressed to keep out the brackish bog water that was already clogging his nostrils. It was the only explanation.

He had showed up for the job interview bright and early at eight A.M. sharp. Wally had no more stepped up to the reception desk than the blue-blazered security guard immediately buzzed the vice-president in charge of systems outreach.

"Your eight o'clock is here, Mr. Tollini," he said crisply.

"Show him in, quick."

"Mr. Tollini will see you now," the lobby guard had said, pointing down the luxuriously carpeted hallway. "South wing. Last door at the end of the hall."

"Thank you," said Wally Boyajian, fresh out of the Darrigo Computer Institute on his first postgraduate job interview. He straightened his tie as his gray Hush Puppies gathered a charge of static electricity from the carpet.

The door at the end of the south wing was marked "ANTONY TOLLINI, VICE-PRESIDENT IN CHARGE OF SYSTEMS OUTREACH."

Wally hesitated. He was a computer engineer. What was the VP in charge of systems outreach doing screening job applicants for customer service?

But this was International Data Corporation, the Mamaroneck Monster, the company that put the frame in mainframe and a PC in every office. They never made mistakes.

Steeling himself, Wally grasped the doorknob.

"Ouch!" he said, withdrawing his static-stung hand.

The door whipped open and the eager ferretlike face of Antony Tollini greeted him.

"Mr. Boysenberry. Come in. So glad to meet you," Tollini was saying, pumping Wally's tingling hand with both of his. Tollini had a handshake like a cold tuna steak. Wally barely noticed this as he was ushered into the well-appointed office.

"Sit down, sit down," Tollini was saying. His sparse, uneven mustache twitched and bristled as he took his own seat. He wore Brooks Brothers gray. Everyone at IDC wore Brooks Brothers gray. Including the secretaries.

Wally sat down. He cleared his throat. "I want to tell you, Mr. Tollini, that I'm very excited that IDC agreed to interview me for the senior technician job. After all, I just graduated. And I know how tight the job market is right now."

"You're hired," Tollini said quickly.

Wally's eyes jumped wide. His eyebrows retreated into the shaggy shelf of hair above them.

"I am?" he said blankly.

"Can you start today?"

"Today?" blurted Wally, who was having trouble keeping up with the conversation. "Well, I guess so, if you really want—"

"Fantastic," said Antony Tollini, jumping out from behind his desk. He practically gathered Wally Boyajian out of his chair with a friendly arm around his shoulder and piloted him out into the corridor. "You start now."

"Now?" Wally gulped.

The fatherly hand fell away like a deadweight.

"If you can't," Tollini said crisply, "there are other applicants."

"No, no. Now is fine. I just assumed I'd have to be called back for a follow-up interview before—"

"Here at IDC we take pride is recognizing talent early," Antony Tollini said, the warm arm returning to its place across Wally's shoulders like the waterlogged arm of an octopus slipping onto a coral shelf.

"I guess . . ." Wally said as he found himself pushed through a half-open door marked "CUSTOMER SERVICE."

"Hey, everyone," Antony Tollini shouted out, "meet Wally Boysenberry—"

"Boyajian. It's Armenian."

"Wally's our new senior customer engineer," Tollini was saying.

All around the room, grave-faced technicians in white lab smocks perked up. The stony pallor dropped from their faces as if cracked loose by a sculptor's chisel. Smiles lit up the room. There was a smattering of polite applause.

Wally Boyajian smiled weakly. He had never been applauded for his technical knowledge before.

"Oh, when do you start, Wally?" asked a breathy-voiced redhead.

"Wally starts right now, don't you, son?" Tollini said, clapping Wally on the back so hard his horn-rimmed glasses nearly jumped off his narrow-bridged nose.

"That's right," gulped Wally, going with the flow. Going with the flow was very important at IDC, where it was said that when the CEO expired, the entire payroll was promoted and a global search for the perfect office boy was begun.

This time everyone stood up. The applause was unanimous.

They surged in his direction like groupies toward a rock star. Instantly Wally found himself besieged by white lab smocks.

"Oh, that's wonderful, Wally."

"You'll love it at IDC, Wally."

"Here's your LANSCII documentation, Wally."

Blinking, Wally accepted the heavy blue looseleaf notebook embossed with the IDC logo.

"LANSCII?" he said. "That's a language I never heard of."

"It's new," Antony Tollini was saying. "Pilot program stuff. You'll need it to debug our Boston client's system."

"I will?"

Suddenly the stony faces came back. Wounded eyes searched his perplexed face for signs of hope.

The redhead drew close to him, treating Wally Boyajian to a whiff of some indescribably alluring perfume. Since he was allergic to perfumes, he sneezed.

"But," she said worriedly, "you *are* going to Boston, aren't you, Wally?"

Wally sneezed again.

"Oh, no!" a technician moaned. "He's sick!" The technician went three shades paler. "He can't go!"

Stricken looks replaced the worried ones.

"Of course he's going," shouted Antony Tollini, whipping a red travel-agency envelope from inside his coat and shoving it into the vent pocket of Wally's only suit. "We got him booked on a ten-o'clock flight."

"Boston?" Wally said, blowing into a hastily extracted handkerchief.

"First class."

"Oh, you'll love Boston, Wally," a chipper voice said.

"Yes, Boston is so . . . so historical."

"I . . ." Wally sputtered.

Antony Tollini said, "We're putting you in a first-class hotel. A limo will meet you at the airport. Naturally, since you won't have time to go home and pack, we've established a line of credit at the finest men's stores up there. And of course there's the three-hundred-dollar-a-day living allowance."

This reminded Wally Boyajian that the subject of his salary had never come up. In these lean times he was lucky to even have a job, and decided that with a three-hundred-dollar-a-day living allowance, they could keep the damn salary.

"Sounds good to me," said Wally, putting away his handkerchief.

The ring of white lab smocks burst into a ripple of delighted applause. Wally thought of how nice it would be to work here once the Boston job was done. These looked like a super bunch to work with, even if they did go through mood swings pretty fast.

"Okay," said Antony Tollini, "let's get you to the airport, Wally my boy."

The octopus arms urged him around and back out the door. As he left the room, the calls of good luck rang in his ears.

"Oh, good-bye, Wally."

"Nice meeting you, Wally."

"Good luck in Boston, Wally."

"We can't wait to hear how it went, Wally."

They really cared about him, thought Wally Boyajian, twenty-two years old, of Philadelphia, Pennsylvania, never to reach twenty-three, never to see Philadelphia again.

As the company car whisked him away from IDC world headquarters in Mamaroneck, New York, Wally thought breathlessly that it was almost too good to be true. Techies like him dreamed of going to work at IDC the way schoolboys dreamed of pitching in the World Series.

With a lot of passion but minimal expectation.

The flight was short but very pleasant. Wally had never flown first class before. He was a teetotaler, so he passed up the complimentary drinks and settled for a bitter-tasting mineral water.

The stewardess was unfailingly polite but reserved as she served Wally. That was, until he blurted out that he had just joined IDC.

She practically sat in his lap the rest of the way.

Wally Boyajian decided that yessireebob, he was really, really going to enjoy working at IDC.

At Logan Airport there was an honest-to-goodness chauffeur waiting for him. The chauffeur didn't wear livery, only a neat dark sharkskin suit and a cap. He stood nearly seven feet tall and was built like a library bookshelf. Somehow, he seemed more like a chauffeur than if he had worn a uniform, Wally decided.

"You the guy from IDC?" the chauffeur had asked.

"Yes, sir," Wally had said, at a loss for how to address so imposing an individual. Since the Gulf War, he was very respectful of anyone in uniform.

"Come on, then. We're going for a ride."

The limousine was no stretch model, just a long black Cadillac with tinted back windows. The chauffeur opened the door and clicked it shut after Wally had slid in.

The car eased out of the congestion of the airport and into the tiled fluorescent paralysis of the Sumner Tunnel.

"Ever been in Boston before?" the chauffeur called back.

"No. I was reading about it on the plane, though. I hear this is where practically all the cranberries are grown."

"Yeah, there are lots of cranberry bogs out in the sticks."

"Maybe if I have the time, I might visit one. Cranberries remind me of the holidays coming up. This will be the first holiday season I've spent away from my folks. I miss them."

"Pal," said the gruff chauffeur, "if you can fix my boss's computer, I guarantee you all the cranberry bogs you wanna splash around in."

"It's a deal," said Wally Boyajian with the unbridled enthusiasm of a young man to whom all of life's rich possibilities beckoned.

After twenty minutes of stop-and-go riding, Wally noticed they were still in the white-tiled tunnel.

"Is Boston traffic always like this?" Wally asked at one point.

"Only on good days."

Thinking this was a local joke, Wally essayed a timid laugh. He swallowed it when the chauffeur failed to chime in.

Finally they emerged in a section of narrow, twisted streets where the brick apartments crowded one another with suffocating closeness. Almost no sun peeped down past the rooftops.

"By the way," Wally said suddenly, "this company you're taking me to—what is it's name?"

"F and L Importing," the chauffeur said in a bored voice.

"What's the F and L stand for?"

"Fuck 'em and leave 'em," replied the chauffuer. This time he did laugh.

Wally did not. He did not care for profanity or those who resorted to it.

"I never heard of it," Wally admitted.

"It's a wholly owned sub . . . sub . . ."

"Subsidiary?" Wally offered.

"Yeah. That. Of LCN."

"I don't think I've ever heard of LCN. What does it make?"

"Money," the chauffeur grunted. "It makes tons of money."

Before Wally knew it, the car purred to a stop.

"We're here?" he said blankly, looking around. They had pulled into a tiny parking spot behind a dirty brick building.

"This is the place," said the chauffeur.

Wally waited for the door to be opened before stepping out. Almost immediately before him was a blank green-painted door. The air was thick with heavy food smells. Spicy, pleasant food smells. Wally assumed these enticing odors were wafting from the company cafeteria as the tall hulk of a chauffeur opened the blank green door for him.

Wally had only a momentary impression of a cool wood-paneled dimness before he passed through the alcove to a nearly bare room where three very husky men in business suits stood around a tacky Formica-topped card table on which an ordinary IDC-brand personal computer stood like a blind oracle.

"A PC?" Wally said. "I expected a mainframe."

The three husky men in suits tensed.

"But you can fix it, right?"

"Probably," Wally said, laying down his custom leather tool case and testing the cable connections in back of the PC. "What's wrong with it?"

"The whatchcallit—hard-on disk—cracked up."

"Hard disk. Don't you people know that?"

"They're security," said the chauffeur from behind Wally's back.

The room was small and Wally said, "I could use a little elbow room here. Why don't you fellows take a coffee break?"

"We stay," said one of the husky men.

Wally shrugged. "Okay," he said good-naturedly. "Let's see what we got."

Wally got down to work. He tried to initialize the system but it refused to boot on. He next inserted a diagnostic floppy. That got him into the system, but the hard disk remained inaccessible. It was going to be a long first day, he realized. But he was almost happy. He had a job. At IDC. Life was sweet.

By twelve o'clock he started to feel his stomach rumble. No wonder. The close air was redolent with the spicy tang of garlic and tomato sauce. He kept working until one o'clock, imagining that someone would tell him when it was time to break for lunch. Wally didn't want to give an important IDC client the impression that he was more concerned with his stomach than with their hardware problem.

Finally, at one-fifteen, he stood up, stretched his aching back, and said, "I think I need to have a bite to eat."

"Is it fixed?" asked the chauffeur.

"It's a long way from being fixed," Wally said.

"Then you get to eat when the box is fixed."

Wally thought of his three-hundred-dollar-a-day living allowance and the fine dinner it would buy and said, "Okay."

Maybe this was some kind of test, he thought. Getting into IDC entry-level was something. Being promoted to chief customer engineer on the first day was too good to risk rocking the boat.

It was well past eight P.M. when Wally wearily finished his last diagnostic test. He had accomplished nothing more than to activate every error message in the system.

Frowning, he removed his glasses, wiped them clean, and restored them to his thin face.

He looked up to the husky chauffeur and said, "I'm sorry. The data in this system is irrecoverable."

"Speak American," the chauffeur growled.

"I can't fix it. Sorry. I tried."

The chauffeur nodded and went to a door. He opened it a crack and called into the next room. "He said he tried."

"They all fuggin' say that."

"He said he was sorry."

"Tell him not as sorry as he's going to be."

Wally Boyajian felt his heart jump into his throat. The way the three husky security men were glowering at him, he was sure his failure to debug the hard disk meant his job.

Silence. The husky men surrounding him looked at Wally Boyajian as if he had made a flatulent noise. Then the chauffeur asked, "What do we do with him?"

The voice from the other room said, "Scroom."

"Before, he said he wanted to see the cranberry bogs," the chauffeur reported.

"Give him the fuggin' cook's tour," said the voice from the other room.

"Actually," Wally said when the chauffeur had closed the door and was walking in his direction, "they can wait. I just need a decent meal and to be taken to my hotel."

A hand grabbed him by the back of the neck. It was quite a big hand because the fingers and thumb actually met over his Adam's apple, restricting his ability to swallow.

Surrounded by three big F and L security men, Wally was hustled out the side door to the waiting limousine.

Again the chauffeur opened it for him. The trunk this time, not the rear door.

Wally would have protested being stuffed into the car's ample trunk, but the meaty hand kept its inexorable grip on his throat, preventing any outcry louder than a mew.

When the hand let go, Wally's leather tool case was flung in his face and the trunk lid slammed down on his head.

He woke up to the sound of traffic and the limo's quietly humming engine. It sounded like a lion purring.

This, thought Wally Boyajian with the wounded pride of a brand-new senior customer engineer, was not the way to treat an IDC employee.

He informed the F and L security men of this unimpeachable fact of business life after the limo coasted to a stop and the trunk lid was raised.

"Look," Wally had said in an agitated voice as he was bodily hauled out of the trunk and stood on his feet, "I happen to be a valued employee with International Data Corporation, and when I inform Mr. Tollini that you—*mumph*!"

"Have some cranberries," said the chauffeur, jamming a fistful into Wally Boyajian's open, complaining mouth.

Wally bit down. The cranberries were as hard as acorns. His teeth released bitter, acidic juices when they crushed the berries. The taste was not sweet. It was not sweet at all, Wally thought dispiritedly as they walked him, helpless and confused, over to the moon-washed expanse of an actual Massachusetts cranberry bog. It looked like a swamp into which a ton of reddish-brown Trix cereal had been dumped.

None of this, Wally thought, made him think of the holidays at all. In fact, it was inexcusably foreboding.

Crying, he began to spit the foul-tasting cranberries from his mouth.

Wally had almost cleared his mouth of the bitter crushed pulp when they made him kneel at the edge of the bog.

"You were supposed to fix it," a harsh voice said.

"I tried! I really did!" Wally had protested. "You need a media recovery specialist. I'm only a CE."

"You ever hear that saying: the customer is always right?"

"Yes."

"Then you shoulda fixed the box. No questions asked."

Then they pushed his head into the cool foul water. The hand that had been around his throat did this. Wally knew this because he could feel the same strong thumb and fingers putting merciless pressure on his Adam's apple.

Wally did the natural thing. He held his breath. And while he was holding the precious air in his lungs, the others took hold of his ankles and wrists and slammed him spread-eagled on the edge of the bog, whose cold waters were getting into his nose.

He hoped it was a hazing. He prayed it was a hazing. But

it did not feel like a hazing. It felt serious. It felt like he was being drowned for failing to fix a computer.

He held his breath because there was nothing else he could do. His limbs pinioned into helplessness, Wally simply waited for them to release him. He waited for the mean-spirited IDC hazing to be over with.

This did not happen.

By the time Wally Boyajian realized this would never happen, he was tasting the gritty brackish water of the cranberry bog in his gulping mouth. It infiltrated his nose, splashing down his sinuses and into his mouth. Then it was filling his lungs like triple pneumonia. The shock of the cold water made him pass out.

Fear of drowning brought him back around almost at once.

It had been too good to be true, Wally realized, sobbing inwardly. Now it was too unbelievable to comprehend. He was being coldly murdered.

In the last panicky moments of his too-short life, consciousness came and went as he made furious bubbles amid the hard bitter cranberries.

When the last bubble had burst, they consigned Wally Boyajian's limp body to the bog, where his decomposing remains would nourish the ripening cranberries and give flavor to the holidays, which he was destined never to experience again.

2

His name was Remo and he was learning to fly.

"Let's see," Remo said, thinking back to what he knew about airplanes, which was precious little. "To make a plane go down, you gotta crack the flaps. No, that's not it. You lift the elevators. Right, the elevators."

Reaching down with a foot, Remo toed the elevators up just a hair.

The aircraft—it was a gull-winged scarlet-and-cream 1930's-era Barnes Stormer—responded instantly by going into a lop-sided climb.

"Oops! That's not it," Remo muttered, removing his foot. He noticed that only one elevator actually went down.

The Stormer leveled off quickly as Remo tried to retain his balance against the fierce slipstream. When the plane was again on an even pitch, he tried again. This time he pressed down on both elevators with both heels.

The plane slid into a dive. The elevators fought him. Remo increased the pressure.

Up ahead in the Plexiglas cockpit, the pilot fought the controls. He was losing. He couldn't figure out why. Remo imagined it would come to him eventually.

Looking down, Remo realized he was no longer over the airport. He wanted to be over the airport. If he was going to land this thing over the objections of the pilot, he would need an airport underneath him, not a forest.

This part was easy. The plane was steered by the rudder, just like on a boat. Except that the rudder stuck up in the air and not down into the water. The rudder happened to stick up right in front of him, attached to the tail assembly, to which Remo clung with both hands. His feet were planted on the stabilizer.

He removed one hand from the tail fin and used it to nudge the rudder a hair.

The aircraft responded with a slow, ungainly turn. The distant airport came into view like an oasis of asphalt at the edge of the forest.

"I'm starting to get the hang of this," Remo said, pleased with himself. He would have been more pleased had he been able to catch up with the pilot before takeoff. Remo had missed the man at his house. The maid had cheerfully told Remo that her employer was on his way to do some sport flying. Remo had reached the airport just in time to have the taxiing 1930's-era aircraft pointed out to him.

Remo had sprinted after it without pausing to think his actions through. By the time he had caught up, it was lifting its tail preparatory to leaving the ground.

Impulsively Remo leapt aboard. It was an impulse he had begun to regret at twelve thousand feet.

In the cockpit, the pilot was now fighting the stubborn controls like a man possessed. He had no inkling that his tail empennage had acquired a human barnacle as he was taking off. Probably he would have dismissed the thought out of hand if he had.

The pilot, whose name Remo understood to be Digory Lippincott, had her throttled up to five hundred miles per hour, a speed at which no living thing could retain a precarious perch on the tail.

Yet, a mere nineteen feet behind him, Remo straddled the tail like a man wind-surfing. The right foot resting on the right stablizer and the left on the left. He had been holding on to the upright rudder post like a boy hitching a ride on a dolphin's back.

The slipstream plastered his gray chinos against his lean legs. His black T-shirt chattered like a madly wind-worried sail. His dark hair was combed back by the wind, exposing a forehead on which an upraised but colorless bump showed plainly.

Remo's dark eyes were pinched to narrow slits against the onrushing wind. Under the high cheekbones that dominated his strong angular face, his cruel mouth was closed.

He was actually enjoying this. The plane was doing whatever he wanted.

"Look, Ma, I'm flying!" he shouted.

His shout carried right through the Plexiglas of the pilot's cockpit. The pilot look around. His mean eyes became saucers.

Remo saluted him with a friendly little wave.

Furiously the pilot flung back the sliding cockpit.

"You crazy guy! What're you doing on my plane!"

"Trying to land it," Remo called back over the rushing air.

"Is this a hijacking?"

"Nah. You're my assignment."

"I'm your what?"

"Assignment. I gotta kill you."

"By crashing us both?" the pilot sputtered.

"Not if I can help it," Remo said sincerely. "Tell you what. You land this thing yourself and I'll do you on the ground. No muss. No fuss. How's that sound?"

"Like a bad deal."

"Suit yourself," said Remo, bringing the weight of his heels down on both cherry-red elevators.

The aircraft went into a dive. Frantically the pilot fought the bucking controls, attempting to level off.

Remo let him think he was succeeding. After the elevators had righted themselves, he nudged one up with the toe of an Italian loafer.

Instead of fighting, the pilot let the Stormer spiral upward. Its nose strained toward the clear blue bowl of the Connecticut sky.

A notch puckered between Remo's dark eyes. He wondered what the Stormer's ceiling was and if there would be enough air for him to breathe up there.

Remo never found out because the engine began to sputter. It missed a few times, and as gravity drained the last of the aviation fuel from the carburetor, the single propeller just stopped dead.

Like a nose-heavy dart, the Stormer dropped. Its tail, Remo still clinging to it, flipped up like a diving salmon. The plane had gone into what aviators call a tail spin.

Below, the forest turned as if on a giant CD player.

Remo wondered if the pilot was trying to shake him or commit suicide. He asked.

"You trying to crash this thing?" Remo called.

"You figure it out."

The ground was coming up so fast Remo didn't think he had that kind of time. He retained his grip, knowing the centrifugal force of the spin would hold him in place.

He wasn't sure what would happen if the plane stopped spinning. His understanding of his predicament was purely instinctual, not cognitive. That was Sinanju for you. Your body learned but your brain sometimes didn't have a clue.

While Remo was listening to his body, the engine sputtered, coughed an oily ball of exhaust, and roared back to life.

With a wiggle of ailerons, the Stormer came level.

The pilot pushed back the cockpit and said, "Thought we were going to crash, didn't you?"

"Something like that," Remo growled.

"It's an old trick. When you stand her on her tail, the engine stalls out. If you try to restart it yourself, you crash. Have to let gravity do the work."

"Now I know," Remo muttered under his breath.

"If you don't stop screwing around with my aerodynamics, I can do it again."

"No, you won't."

"What's going to stop me? You're way back there."

Remo reached forward, took hold of the rotating beacon bubble mounted atop the rudder post, and exerted the same kind of twisting pressure he would on a stuck mayonnaise-jar lid.

The bubble light assembly groaned and came loose, trailing wires.

Remo gave it a toss. It struck the spinning disk of the propeller. Pieces of the light flew in all directions. One struck the pilot in the face.

"My eyes!" he cried, clutching his face.

"My ass," said Remo, who didn't like to be taunted on the job. As the heir to the five-thousand-year-old House of Sinanju and the next in line to be Master, Remo expected respect. Even from his intended victims.

The pilot was screaming, "I can't see! I can't see!"

"Tell that to your victims," Remo yelled back.

"What victims?"

"The ones you robbed blind when you ran that bank you used to own into the ground."

"That wasn't my fault!"

"My boss says it was."

"He's lying! I'm a sportsman."

"You're a cheap crook who ripped off your despositors. Except one of the depositors happened to be my boss. And he has ways of dealing with financial losses undreamed of by the FDIC."

"I can't see to fly the plane!"

"That's okay," Remo said, pushing down on the right elevator with one foot and lifting the left with the other. "You're about to suffer an abrupt withdrawal from life."

The Barnes Stormer turned around in the air. The pilot, still pawing at his eyes, simply dropped out of the open cockpit, his seat-belt harness ripping free of its anchorage.

"Yaaahh!" he said when he took his eyes from his bleeding face. He still couldn't see, but the absence of the cockpit was hard to miss, as was the precipitous way in which he dropped.

"That," Remo said, "is putting gravity to good use."

The pilot hit a fir tree, impaling himself on his crotch like an ornamental Christmas-tree angel.

Remo righted the Stormer. It responded to his measured foot pressure as if he had been flying all his life.

Now all he had to do was figure out a way to land the aircraft in one piece. Without access to the ailerons and flaps. He knew the flaps functioned as brakes. He had sat over the wing of enough commercial jetliners to grasp that much.

By playing with the rudder and elevators, Remo managed to get the nose of the plane oriented toward the airport. He kept it on course with the occasional nudge and kick.

The forest rolled under him like a marching porcupine. It would not be a good place to ditch, if the pilot's fate was any indication.

When he could see the color of the windsock over the airport operations shack, Remo began his descent.

It was then and only then that he realized he would have to cut the engine if he wanted to survive the landing.

Remo looked around. Not much to work with now that he had used the beacon light, he realized glumly.

He decided that inasmuch as he was nicely on course, he didn't really need the rudder anymore. Not all of it, anyway.

Remo released one hand from the tail fin and used it to chop a piece off the aluminum rudder. Slipstream began to yank it away, but Remo snagged it just in time.

Aiming it like a Frisbee, Remo let fly.

The rudder segment flew true. It sheared off the propeller blades as if they were toothpicks. Remo ducked a gleaming needle of prop shard that skimmed by his head.

There was a lot more to flying, he realized, than just knowing how to work the control surfaces. A person could get hurt.

Without a propeller, the Stormer naturally lost airspeed. Unfortunately it also began to vibrate rather alarmingly.

Remo was not alarmed. He figured that anything that slowed the headlong flight of the disabled craft could only work in his favor, since he would be attempting to land the aircraft without benefit of landing gear.

Remo, nudging what was left of the rudder, lined up on the black and yellow transverse lines at the near end of the runway. He noticed too late that the arrows were pointing toward him, rather than away. He hoped that didn't mean what he thought it meant.

As it turned out, it did.

And at the far end of the runway, a number of candy-colored light planes were revving up for takeoff. Their glittering propellers were pointed in his direction like voracious buzz saws.

"Too late now," Remo muttered. "I'm committed."

He sent the plane into the final leg of its descent. The transverse lines rushed up to meet him like a shark's toothsome mouth.

They flicked by with the fleeting flash of a semaphore signal. And then the hot black asphalt was like a high-speed lava flow.

Remo wrestled to keep the vibrating aircraft level. He did rather well, losing only one wing. The right.

Hissing and sputtering sparks, the undercarriage began to scream in response to contact with the ground. It slewed sideways. The other wing caught and Remo experienced a momentary disorientation not unlike the split second in a roller-coaster ride before everyone screams.

His body told him this would be the perfect time to let go, and so he did.

The Stormer nosed over, which meant that it stubbed its snout and threw its tail up like a bucking stallion.

The plane landed on its back. Pitched into the air, Remo landed on its paint-scraped undercarriage, threw out his arms like a trapeze artist, and said, "Ta-dah!"

The first of several light planes roared only yards over his head. Remo waved them off. He understood how it was to be a pilot now. There was nothing on earth like it.

Next time, he promised himself as he stepped off the crippled plane, he would try soloing the old-fashioned way. From the cockpit.

At a pay phone by the airport restaurant, Remo dialed the code number and put a finger in his free ear to keep out the wail of the crash trucks. He wondered how the FAA would explain finding the plane and its pilot separated by five miles of terrain.

He stopped worrying when a testy voice answered.

"Yes?" it snapped.

"Sorry to interrupt *Jeopardy*," said Remo dryly, "but I'm reporting in as requested."

"I'm sorry, Remo. I didn't mean—"

Suddenly there was another voice on the line, a cracked and aged voice.

"Is that Remo? Let me speak to him at once."

"I—" Smith began.

Remo had a momentary impression of the phone being yanked out of the bloodless hands of Harold W. Smith, his superior.

"Remo," said the aged voice urgently, "you must come right away. All is lost."

"What?"

The phone went abruptly dead.

"What the hell?" Remo muttered, batting the switch-hook bar and redialing.

For the first time in memory, the communications line to Folcroft did not ring. Thinking he had misdialed—which was possible even though the code number had been simplified to a series of ones—Remo tried again. The number did not answer.

Remo dug back into the recesses of his memory for the backup number. He thought there was a five in it. Maybe two.

He tried dialing all fives. That got him a nonworking-number message from AT&T.

"Damn!" Remo said. "I could be here all day trying to remember that freaking number!"

Remo dashed to the operations shack.

"I need a pilot willing to fly me to Rye, New York," he announced.

No one batted an eye.

"Money is no object," Remo said, digging out his wallet.

Still no reply. A reedy man expectorated into the sand of a standing ashtray.

Remo's eyes narrowed.

"Won't anyone help a marine just back from the Gulf?" he wondered aloud.

A small riot broke out as the lounging pleasure pilots fought one another over the privilege of ferrying the heroic marine just back from the Gulf to his destination.

Remo waded in and shattered a lifted chair before it was employed to crown a man. Using just the flats of his hands, Remo immobilized as many as he could without inflicting serious injury.

When he had created a pile of squirming men on the tiled floor, Remo picked through them as if through a rag pile, looking for any pilot who seemed reasonably airworthy.

Remo dragged out a likely candidate.

"I choose you."

"Thanks, mister, but I don't own a plane."

"Then why the hell were you fighting?"

"I got carried away with patriotic fervor."

"There's an airport at Westchester," the reedy man piped up from under a tangle of limbs. "That good enough for you?"

"It'll do," Remo said, extricating him from the pile. "Let's go."

The aircraft was a two-place silver-and-blue monoplane. Remo had to listen to the pilot natter on and on about how this was a home-built job, and once he finished building his wet wing, she'd be as sweet a thing as ever took to the skies.

Remo, who didn't know a wet wing from a wet bar, felt guilty about lying, but only a little. He had actually recently returned from the Gulf, and he had been a marine. Back in Vietnam.

"You know," the pilot was saying as the other aircraft pulled off to the side of the runway to let the plane carrying the war hero go first, "you look familiar to me. I'll bet I caught you on one of those TV news spots, saying hello to the folks back home."

"Yep, that was me," Remo said absently. He wondered why the pilot thought he recognized him.

"You ever think about flying yourself?" the pilot asked after they climbed up over the airport.

Remo looked down at the tangled remains of the vintage Barnes Stormer, now surrounded by crash trucks and fire engines.

"Not in the last half-hour," he said. His tone was worried. He hoped there was nothing wrong Upstairs.

But most of all, he hoped Chiun was all right.

"You fly, then?" asked the pilot.

"I had a plane but it crashed my first time up. How do you think I got this bump?" added Remo, who in fact had no idea how he'd acquired the lump.

3

Remo Williams didn't bother counting out the pilot's money. He just extracted cab fare and handed the man his entire wallet, including ID cards and phony family pictures.

"Hey, don't you want—?"

"Keep it as a war souvenir," Remo said, jumping from the plane. He collared a taxi driver who was sitting in his cab sipping black coffee from a Styrofoam cup.

"Folcroft Sanitarium," Remo called from the back seat.

As if a spring had popped from the cushion, the driver jumped straight up in his seat. His head banged the cab roof and his coffee scalded his lap.

"Hey, what the—"

"I'm in a rush," Remo said, throwing money into the front seat. "Take me there, and no lip. I'm a famous war hero. Only today I brought down a Barnes Stormer flown by a fiscal terrorist."

The driver turned around in his seat and started to protest. He hadn't heard the cab door open or close and had no inkling of how the strange guy in the T-shirt appeared in his back seat. But the dark eyes that looked back at him were so cold and deadly that the driver swallowed his protests.

He peeled out of the cab stand, asking, "Folcroft, where is that exactly?"

Folcroft Sanitarium was exactly situated on the portion of Rye, New York, that overlooked Long Island Sound. It was nestled in a rustic section of the shoreline like a sore tooth in clover.

"Don't drive up to the gate," Remo warned as they drew near. "And kill the engine."

The driver obediently killed the engine, coasting to a stop in a copse of poplars by the side of an unmarked road. He glanced at his fare in the rearview mirror, thinking that the guy looked more like a Vietnam vet than he did a Gulf War hero. He had those thousand-yard-stare kind of eyes. Cold.

"I'll get out here," Remo said quietly, shoving a fifty-dollar bill through the partition slot. "You never brought me here. You never even saw me."

"Tell that to my scalded balls," the cabby muttered.

But he made no other protest as he watched the tall, skinny man in the T-shirt ease soundlessly into the woods. He watched him for several seconds. It was broad daylight, the woods not dark. Just kind of dim, the way thick woods are even at noon under a heavy canopy of foliage.

The man simply disappeared after slipping behind a tree. The driver dawdled ten minutes, and eventually lost interest.

By the time the taxi driver had gotten his cab turned around, Remo Williams was slipping over the perimeter fence surrounding Folcroft Sanitarium, ostensibly a private hospital but in fact the cover for the organization that employed Remo in the service of America.

Breaching Folcroft's gate was no feat, even for someone without Sinanju training. It was simply a matter of slipping up to an unguarded spot and scaling the stone fence. Pausing momentarily, Remo dropped soundlessly to the other side.

Although Folcroft concealed one of America's deepest deep-cover installations, high-profile security—not to mention out-of-the-ordinary secret surveillance equipment—was not present. The very existence of such equipment would have signaled that Folcroft was more than it seemed. And attracted attention.

Attention was the last thing that the director of CURE—the supersecret organization that Folcroft harbored—wanted.

CURE had been set up in the early sixties. A United States President, destined never to complete his term of office, conceived it after he had come to the reluctant realization that his country faced a period of lawlessness and anarchy unequaled in its history.

The President concluded that the sole obstacle to righting the ship of state was its very mainsail. The Constitution. He couldn't repeal it, so he created CURE to work around it. Quietly. Secretly. Deniably.

One man ran CURE. A former CIA analyst named Harold W. Smith. Responsible only to the President, he became the rudder of America, steering the ship of state through political shoals by rooting out crime and corruption and extinguishing them through a variety of subtle methods. At first, by simply alerting traditional law-enforcement agencies and leaving matters in their hands.

But as the years went on, it became obvious that the ship of state needed a secret weapon more powerful than the bank of computers Smith employed to track illicit activity.

And so Remo Williams was recruited to be its enforcement arm.

Remo wasn't thinking of that now as he ghosted around the brick building that was Folcroft Sanitarium. He was working his way down to the apron of grass that sloped gently to the Sound. It was a vista he had seen many times from the window of Harold Smith's office, an office he was about to enter in an unusual way.

Remo stopped in the lee of a ramshackle wharf. He lifted his dark-brown eyes to the building's brick facade, trying to recall which one looked in on Smith's office.

A frown touched his face when he picked it out. The window was easy to spot. It was completely opaque, like a dull mirror. For security reasons it was paned with two-way glass. Not even Remo could see into it.

"Damn Smith and his dippy security," Remo grumbled.

Remo floated up to the building anyway. The facade was brick, which made it easy to scale. Had it been smooth concrete, he could have scaled it just as easily.

Remo went up like a spider and paused at the opaque glass. He set an ear to the pane.

Voices came from within. Pitched low, but charged with urgent emotion.

"Under no circumstances will I allow this!"

Chiun's squeaky voice.

"I must insist."

Smith's lemon-bitter voice. He continued.

"This is Remo's decision, Master Chiun. It will do no good for us to argue it to death. Let Remo decide."

"I will not be ignored. I know how it is with you whites. You have no respect for age or wisdom, both of which I embody in full measure. I will be heard!"

Remo heard Smith's dry, rattly sigh, and expelled one of his own. If they were still arguing like this, there was no danger.

He removed his ear from the glass and knocked twice to get their attention.

He received an instant response.

"*Aaiiee!*" Chiun.

"My God, Remo!" Smith, of course.

Even though he couldn't penetrate the blank glass, Remo knew they could see him plainly. And he knew he wouldn't have long to wait for a reaction.

The sound was a shriek, like a diamond cutter scoring glass at high speed. It started above his head and screeched around the edges. Remo watched a thin silvery line trace a square.

"It is open," Chiun called.

Obligingly Remo gave the pane the heel of his hand. The glass popped out of its frame in one piece.

He climbed in as if stepping through an ordinary doorway.

"Hiya, Smitty." This to the tall, gangling man who had turned in his chair not two feet in front of Remo. He jumped to his feet.

"Remo! What is the meaning of this!" he demanded.

Smith's distended jaw threatened the precise knot of his Dartmouth tie. Behind rimless glasses his gray eyes were aghast. His face was the hue of trout skin. This was normal. Smith always looked ashen and unhealthy.

"You tell me," Remo said, nodding to Chiun, Reigning Master of Sinanju.

Only five feet tall, and looking like the Korean edition of Methuselah, Chiun stood beside Smith's desk holding the large heavy plate glass in his frail arms as if it were mere cellophane. He wore an emerald-and-gold kimono that might have been sewn from a pile of discarded Chinese dragon costumes.

His face was a knot of harsh wrinkles, the skin of his bald head unusually smooth and a translucent nut color. Puffs of wispy hair crowded above each delicate ear. A tendril of identical hair depended from his set chin. It waved under the steady pressure of his exhalations. He was angry.

"Why don't you give me that?" Remo said solicitously, reaching for the heavy pane.

Chiun retreated three short steps, his clear hazel eyes regarding Remo suspiciously.

"Why?" he asked, tight-lipped.

"Because it's heavy. I don't want you to hurt yourself."

"I am the Master of Sinanju!" Chiun thundered.

"Shhh!" Smith said urgently.

"I am no old man to be fawned over and shielded from the harsh realities of life," Chiun continued.

"I didn't mean—" Remo began to say.

Smith said, "Please, please. We can be heard outside this office."

He was ignored.

"I know what you are thinking, Remo Williams," Chiun went on. "You think I am an old man. Go on. Admit this. Speak truly."

Remo folded his arms. "Well, you *are* a hundred now."

"I am not a hundred winters old! I have celebrated no birthdays since my eightieth. Therefore I am eighty. I will always be eighty."

"Fine. Have it your way."

"Do not take that tone with me, pale piece of pig's ear," Chiun retorted. "Eighty is a fine age. Worthy of respect. One hundred winters is an achievement to be revered. Which I would be, had you enabled me to celebrate my *kohi*."

Remo threw up his hands. He didn't want to get into it. It was too tangled. "Fine," he said. "I screwed up. I'm eternally sorry. Now, will you hand me the glass before you break it, please?"

Remo turned to Smith. "Where do you want it?"

Smith's eyes were sick. "My God. First the phone, and now the window. What about security?"

Remo fixed Chiun with his eyes. "Little Father, what did you do to Smith's phone?" Remo spotted the blue telephone on the desk. The coaxial cable linking receiver to base was severed as cleanly as if by bolt cutters. Remo recognized the handiwork of Chiun's long fingernails—the same tools that had scored the glass like a diamond cutter.

"It was an accident," Chiun said dismissively. "In my fear and concern for our future, I mistakenly severed the wire."

"In a pig's ass," Remo said. "You deliberately stampeded me and then cut the wire so I'd come running like a maniac."

"How you come running is your responsibility," Chiun

sniffed. "That you are now here is all that matters. Emperor Smith has placed a terrible choice before me. One I was not prepared to shoulder alone. Not that I am too old to shoulder it," he added hastily. "It is that it is your responsibility too." Chiun looked to Smith. "Emperor, tell Remo all."

"If this is what I think it is about, the answer is no," Remo said firmly. "Just like last time."

Chiun's wizened features softened. His youthful eyes acquired a pleased glow.

"That is what I told Smith, but he insisted upon laying the sordid matter before us both."

"No way, Smitty," Remo said. "I'm shocked you'd try an end run around me like this."

Smith pointed with an anxious finger. "Remo, the glass."

"Where do you want it?"

"Somewhere where I do not have to explain it," Smith said wearily.

Shrugging, Remo stepped up to the Master of Sinanju, who willingly surrendered the glass. Calmly Remo carried it over to the gaping window frame, set it leaning, and scored it to quarters with quick swipes of one diet-hardened fingernail.

Remo cracked the glass into quarters and one by one scaled them out the window into the incoming fall breeze.

The glass squares spun over a mile out into the Sound, actually skipping like flat stones the last five hundred or so yards before sinking without a trace.

"Now," Remo said happily. "Where were we? Oh, yeah. Smith, since you have to be told twice, the answer is a flat no."

"I agree with Remo," Chiun said quickly.

"No," Remo repeated. "Plastic surgery is out."

"Surgery!" Chiun squeaked. "What is this? I have not heard of this request before."

Remo frowned. He turned. "Isn't that what you were arguing about just now?"

"No," said Chiun.

"No," said Smith.

"No?" asked Remo, suddenly sensing that he was on uncertain ground.

"I was discussing with Master Chiun the urgent need to relocate you both in the wake of your participation in the Gulf crisis," Smith explained.

"Relocate? You mean sell my house?"

"*Our* house," Chiun put in.

"I think it's in *my* name," Remo pointed out.

"My lawyer will call your lawyer," Chiun snapped.

"Not unless he's taking you on contingency," Remo remarked. To Smith he said flatly, "We're not moving."

"But you must. Remo, as a result of your activities during the Gulf War, your face was telecast to the world. You were identified as the President's personal assassin."

"What is wrong with that?" Chiun wanted to know. "Let the world know this undeniable fact. Your President is safer if tyrants everywhere understand he is protected by the House of Sinanju."

Smith pressed on. "We must take immediate steps to cover all traces of Remo's recent existence. This involves relocating you from Rye and fixing your face."

Folding his arms decisively, Remo said, "No way. Right, Little Father?"

When the Master of Sinanju did not answer, Remo undertoned, "I said, 'Right, Little Father.' That's your cue."

"Emperor," Chiun said slowly, "when you refer to fixing Remo's face, do you mean changing it, as was formerly done in the days when it was necessary to do so often due to Remo's unforgivable carelessness?"

Smith nodded. "Yes. Only I expect once more will suffice. If we have no further . . . incidents of exposure."

Chiun's smooth brow wrinkled, making it match his spidery web of a face. He glided close to Remo and stared elaborately.

At length he asked, "Can you do something with his nose?"

"Such as?"

"Make it normal. Like my nose."

"I will not have a button nose!" Remo shouted, seeing where the conversation was about to go.

"His nose can be reduced," Smith said, unperturbed.

"You stay out of this, Smith!" Remo shouted. He looked down at Chiun, matching the Master of Sinanju's curious regard with a cold stare of his own. "Both of you listen to me. I'm not going to say it again. This is my face—or at least as close as we could get to my original face after all those old face lifts. And a couple of miles from here is my house. It may not have a white picket fence. It may not be inhabited by a loving wife and children, but it's as close to a normal home as I ever expect to get. And I'm keeping it. Is that clear?"

Remo glared down at the Master of Sinanju. Chiun looked up at him with a grim mien. Smith looked at the ceiling.

When no one spoke for half a minute, Remo pressed his advantage.

"I didn't ask for this life," Remo said evenly, a glitter of steel in his tone. "I was happy as a patrolman. I would have made sergeant one day. Probably. I didn't ask to be recruited to the organization. I didn't ask to be trained in Sinanju. I was dragooned into it. Okay, it worked out. I'm Sinanju now. I accept that. Remo Williams may be dead to the rest of the world, but to me, I'm still him. I mean, he's still me."

Remo blinked. Chiun's dry lips curled with pleasure.

"I mean I'm still Remo Williams," Remo said testily. "And I'm keeping this face and I'm keeping the house. Screw security. A million U.S. troops had their faces telecast from over there. No one's going to remember mine."

Remo paused for breath.

"Very well," Smith said tightly. Remo could tell by his tone that he was seething. He was used to absolute obedience. After twenty years of working with Remo, he should have gotten over that by now. He had not.

Chiun spoke up. "Emperor, what about the eyes?"

"The point is moot," Smith said thinly.

"So are the eyes. I do not want a Remo with moot eyes. Can you give him proper eyes? Like mine." Chiun's hazel orbs wrinkled into wise slits, the better to impress the dull whites with their undeniable magnificence.

"I will not go around looking like a Korean!" Remo shouted.

"I am insulted," Chiun said huffily, shaking a tiny fist in the air.

"You are dreaming," Remo snapped.

"Could you both moderate your voices?" Smith said wearily.

"I will if he will," Remo said flatly.

Chiun made a face. "I will. But only if Remo does first."

"I already started. Your turn."

Chiun compressed his papery lips. His long-nailed hands sought one another. He took hold of his wrists and the belling sleeves of his emerald-and-gold kimono slid together, concealing them.

"Let me propose a compromise," Smith said when the silence was both thick and cold.

"I'm listening," Remo said, not taking his eyes off the Master of Sinanju, who had trained him in the discipline called Sinanju, legendary for centuries as the sun source of the martial arts. Trained him until no feat achievable by the human biological machine was beyond his abilities.

"At least will you, Remo, agree to take an extended vacation?" Smith pleaded. "Until memories fade?"

"I'll consider it."

"I will consider it too," Chiun allowed. "If Remo's face can be fixed to my exact specifications," he added.

"I am not—repeat, never—giving up this face!" Remo said hotly. "I'm comfortable wearing it. It's like an old shoe."

"Ha!" Chiun crowed. "Now he admits its ugliness."

"I give up!" Remo groaned, throwing up his hands.

"I accept your graceless surrender," retorted Chiun. "Emperor, bring on the powerful surgeons of plastic. I will sketch for them Remo's magnificent new countenance."

Smith cleared his throat. He had remained standing through the heated exchange. Now he settled into the cracked leather executive's chair he had broken in when CURE began three long decades before and which he expected to occupy until the day he died. There would be no retirement for the head of CURE.

Smith straightened his gray vest, which matched his suit, his hair, and his pallor in a way that looked calculated but was not. His rimless glasses had slid down his patrician nose. He pushed them back with a finger, taking care not to smudge either lens.

"If this has been settled, I would like you both to find lodgings in Mamaroneck."

"An excellent suggestion, Emperor," said Chiun. "We will not be recognized in so remote a place and I have always wished to sojourn among native Mamaroneckians, despite their primitive ways."

"Mamaroneck," Smith explained patiently, "is just south of here."

"Why Mamaroneck?" Remo asked over Chiun's inarticulate sputtering.

"Because that is where IDC is headquartered."

"Oh, not them again," Remo complained.

"CURE is not connected with the trouble at International Data Corporation," Smith said quickly. "The situation is this: several IDC employees have disappeared. All customer service technicians. Almost all of them on their first day of employment. The company claims to have no knowledge of these disappearances, but the pattern is highly suspicious."

"Want me to go in as the FBI?" Remo asked.

"No, Remo. I want you to apply for the job of field technician."

"I don't know squat about computers."

"The last man hired to subsequently disappear did not either," Smith said. "At least by IDC standards. That alone makes his disappearance suspicious. IDC can have their pick of applicants. But their most recent field personnel hirings have been grossly underqualified. They hire them, send them out into the field. And they disappear. Find out why."

"Is this big enough for us?" Remo wanted to know.

"IDC is not only the leading computer company in the world today, it is perhaps America's premier business. Over the last year the stock market has been depressed by its lackluster quarterly earnings. If something is amiss at IDC, the misfortune may spread to American business as a whole."

"I get it," Remo said.

"I do not," said Chiun. "Is this not the villainous clique which once unseated you, Emperor?"

"That was many years ago," Smith said, wincing at the memory. "And was only one IDC executive. A renegade."

Chiun stroked his wisp of a beard thoughtfully. "Perhaps this time we will eliminate the entire treacherous tribe."

Smith raised a warning hand. "Please. Initiate no violence, either of you. This is a delicate matter. I want answers, not bodies."

"We'll get on it, Smitty."

Remo started for the door. Smith's fearful voice stopped him.

"Remo!"

Remo turned, raising an eyebrow.

"Did I forget to say 'May I?' " he asked.

"My secretary is stationed outside that door," Smith

hissed. "She did not see you enter. She cannot see you leave."

Remo and Chiun exchanged quizzical looks.

"Please," Smith said. "Leave as you came. By the window."

"I refuse," Chiun said tightly.

"Not you, Master Chiun. You must be seen leaving the normal way, otherwise my secretary will wonder how you left the building."

"Are you insinuating that I am too old to depart as Remo has entered?" Chiun sniffed.

"No, I am not."

"I will leave by the door, but only because it befits my dignified station as Master of Sinanju," Chiun said loftily.

Chiun pushed past Remo, flung open the door, turned dramatically, and announced, "Farewell, Smith. I have enjoyed our private conversation, to which no outsiders were a party."

The door was drawn closed with such speed the papers in Smith's out basket fluttered like nervous white hands.

"Better get the phone fixed," Remo said, putting one leg out the empty window frame. "In case I have to report soon. This doesn't sound like much of an assigment."

"The last time you said that," Smith reminded him, "we nearly lost Chiun."

"Point taken," Remo said, bringing his other foot outside and dropping out of the frame so fast that Smith had to blink the stubborn Cheshire-cat afterimage of Remo's grin from his retina.

He regarded the empty frame and the severed phone line by turns. After several long, difficult months, in which Chiun was presumed dead and later Remo had fallen into the hands of the enemy, things were back to normal.

Harold Smith didn't know whether to laugh or cry.

4

Antony Tollini had joined International Data Corporation in 1971 as a salesman. He had been promoted to head of sales in 1973 when the CEO of IDC, T. L. Broon, had died. When Broon's successor, Blake Corbish, had passed away after the shortest tenure as company president, Antony Tollini had found himself director of marketing.

It was like being on an elevator that moved up one step at a time, according to a halting mechanism. Through most of the seventies and eighties, Antony Tollini had been stuck in neutral, a vice-president in an ocean of gray-suited vice-presidents, all serene in the knowledge that they worked for the finest corporation in the world. A corporation so advanced that after World War II the Japanese had come to study it and appropriated its corporate model to create the economic powerhouse now called Japan Inc. A corporation so insular that U.S. business leaders were studying the second-generation Japanese model in order to compete in the global marketplace, unaware that the first-generation model was prototyped under the big blue logo IDC. A corporation so on the cutting edge of information services that no rival firm contemplated going head-to-head with it. They either went plug-compatible or they went their own way—usually out of business. Cloning IDC PC's and mainframes was the sole survival strategy in the field of information systems.

But in the early nineties, when the marketplace was going as soft as a candle stored in a July attic, mainframes were outdated. Any small company could compete in the new era of linked PC's and networking. IDC, bloated and arrogant, had found itself on the verge of becoming a dinosaur.

In these hard times, Antony Tollini almost wished he was

working for one of the also-rans. He had been Peter Principled up to the level of director of marketing, a solid steppingstone to the stratospheric IDC boardroom, and suddenly there was no market.

That alone was enough to make a grown man cry. Antony Tollini refused to cry, however. He was a comer. He put his capped teeth together and his nose to the grindstone and set about the heroic task of identifying new markets, chipping away at the computer industry's diminishing market share.

He was polished. He was direct. He was everything an IDC employee should be. But the economy had been disintegrating faster than he had been innovating.

Then he had had a vision. One that would give IDC a brand-new client base none of the little guys could touch.

He would just have to work out a few minor bugs first.

As he drove in from his White Plains home, soothing New Age music on the sound system of his red Miata, Antony Tollini decided that the bugs warranted laying the entire matter before the board. The time had come. Definitely.

Yes, Antony Tollini thought as be guided his Miata into the parking slot in the south wing of the IDC parking lot, in the very shadow of Bold Blue—as IDC was affectionately called—he would make no excuses. He would stand up and be a man in the true IDC tradition. No more evasions. No more ducking the issue. If IDC was to get out from under this dark cloud, the board would have to be notified.

Why, this was IDC. Presidents listened when IDC men talked. Cabinet members, once their public-service careers were completed, often found seats on the IDC board—and then had to prove their business worth or be terminated like any common inventory-control person.

Who were these new clients to make unreasonable demands of International Data Corporation?

Squaring his Brooks Brothers shoulders, Antony Tollini strode past his personal secretary and asked, "Any messages?"

"Just . . . the Boston client."

Tollini felt his heart squeeze in his chest like a spongy fist. His resolve melted.

"What . . . did . . . they . . . say?" he asked, going ashen.

"They wanted to know where the new repairman was. They sounded impatient."

"Did they say what happened to the old one?"

"Generally. It had something to do with a cranberry bog."

Tony felt a stab of fear in his stomach. "Did they sound angry?"

"They always sound angry. This time they sounded impatient too."

"I seeee . . ." Antony Tollini said slowly, his eyes acquiring a hazy glaze. "Any new résumés come in today?"

The secretary pulled open a drawer and extracted a sheaf of employee résumés only a little less thick than the Manhattan phone book. When IDC placed want ads, millionaires applied just for the thrill of being able to tell their friends they had been granted preliminary interviews.

Bent double with the weight of the latest batch of IDC aspirants, Antony Tollini bore himself into his office and collapsed behind his polished mahogany desk.

His eyes, if anything, glazed over even more. It would take forever to go through all these. Then there was the hard—no, agonizing—selection process. In the old days it had been easy to hire for IDC. One merely skimmed the cream and chose the pearls one found floating in it.

For the position of senior customer engineer newly created to deal with IDC's latest crisis, Tollini had at first looked for the pearls. When the best simply never returned, Tollini knew it was hopeless.

So he began to send the halt and the lame out into the field. It made the most sense. It bought the company time, and in a curious, almost fitting way, it was like survival of the fittest.

But it could not go on forever, he knew.

"Just one more," he murmured under his breath. "One more sacrificial lamb and we'll have worked out a solution."

He rejected the married applicants. He did not wish to widow anyone. Princeton graduates—his alma mater—were likewise spared as a gesture to sentiment. The hopelessly unqualified were also discarded from consideration. Hard times compelled people to apply for positions they could never hope to fulfill, and Tollini recognized these as hardship cases.

He was looking for a middle ground. Someone who could at least put forth a creditable effort. Maybe if enough technicians told the Boston client the same thing, they would realize it was hopeless and stop bothering him.

Thirty-some applicants into the thick pile, Antony Tollini ran across a name that stuck out.

The name was Remo Mercurio.

"Remo," he said aloud, tasting the name. "Remo. I like the sound of it. Remo."

He skimmed the résumé. It was lackluster. There were even a few misspelled words. But at the bottom of the page, in red felt pen, was scrawled a postscript:

"I AM THE ANSWER TO YOUR PROBLEMS."

Normally such a crass deviation from the rigid formalities of business etiquette was cause for summary rejection. But if there was anything Antony Tollini had been praying to Saint Theresa for these last few weeks, it was someone to solve this, his greatest problem since joining IDC as a starry-eyed twenty-three-year-old.

"Remo," he said, tasting the vowels. He picked up the desk phone.

"Nancy. I want you to call an applicant named Remo Mercurio."

"Are you sure, Mr. Tollini? I mean, are you certain you want to do this?"

"Nancy, I'm positive."

Antony Tollini replaced the receiver, a welling of hope rising in his throat. Maybe this time it would work. Maybe this one would be the person. And maybe, just maybe, he could sleep soundly again.

He was sick to death of dreaming of decapitated horses, their dead equine eyes staring back at him accusingly.

5

"I'm on," Remo said, replacing the telephone in the Mamaroneck hotel where he had taken a room.

"*We* are on, you mean," said Chiun stiffly.

"Sorry, Little Father. This is a job interview. No hangers-on. It wouldn't look right."

"You think I am too old to accompany you now?" said the Master of Sinanju, not looking away from the television. It was down on the rug. Chiun sat, lotus-style, not three feet from the screen. The voices coming from the TV had British accents the way a stray mutt has fleas.

"No, I don't," Remo said quickly, checking his face in the mirror. The lump was still there, no bigger, no smaller.

"Ha! Then you admit thinking me old!"

"No, of course you aren't old."

Chiun hit the VCR pause button and turned his cold face in Remo's direction. "Then what am I, if not old? To your round white unseeing eyes?"

"Young?"

Chiun frowned. "You insult me."

"Seasoned?"

"In my native land the aged are venerated. With great age comes accompanying respect."

"Okay, okay. You're old as the hills and twice as respected. Satisfied?"

The Master of Sinanju puffed up his cheeks. This was a warning sign roughly equivalent to a cobra spreading its hood, so Remo thought fast.

"We gotta keep you in reserve," Remo said hastily. "Just in case I blow it."

The distended cheeks collapsed slowly as the Master of

Sinanju slowly released the air held in his mouth in lieu of an explosive retort.

The possibility that Remo would blow it loomed very large in Chiun's mind. As Remo knew it would.

"This is good," said Chiun, nodding seriously. "I accept this." He tapped the play button and the VCR resumed.

"Good," said Remo, heading for the door. "Stick by the phone. Once I land this job, I'll let you know what's what."

Chiun cocked his head to one side, puppy-dog-style. "This is your promise?"

Remo raised two fingers. "Scout's honor," he promised.

On his way out the door, Remo tried to remember if the Boy Scout salute was actually three fingers. It had been a long time since he had seen an actual Boy Scout, never mind one saluting.

Still, he thought as he jumped into his blue Buick coupe, he intended to keep his promise regardless of technicalities such as digit count.

At the world headquaters of International Data Corporation, Remo created quite a stir as he entered the cathedrallike stainless-steel-and-granite lobby.

The desk security man looked him up and down once coolly and said, "Have you the wrong address?"

"This IDC?" asked Remo, rotating his abnormally thick wrists impatiently.

"It is, sir."

"Then this is the right address. I have a job interview."

"We employ outside contractors for maintenance services," the security guard said with level politeness. "You must be mistaken."

Remo realized then and only then that he was wearing his white T-shirt over a pair of black chinos. He had forgotten to dress for the interview.

Too late now, he thought glumly. He decided to go for broke.

"I have an appointment with Mr. Tollini in about five minutes."

"Name?"

"Remo Mercurio."

The guard checked his log, found the name, and leaned across the counter. "Interested in a word of advice?"

"If it'll get me the job," Remo said truthfully.

"Forget it. The company has a strict dress code. I can't allow you past the desk without a suit and tie."

"Why don't we ask Mr. Tollini?" Remo asked, leaning across the counter to meet the security man halfway. "Maybe he'll take me as I am."

"The rule is inflexible."

Remo frowned. While they were nose-to-nose, he asked, "What size suit do you wear?"

While the man was hesitating, Remo reached over and took his muscular neck in his lean fingers. He squeezed a nerve and the security man blew out a gusty Listerine-tainted breath in Remo's face.

Remo jumped the desk and appropriated the security man's blue blazer. It was not a perfect fit, but the dark tie went with Remo's eyes.

It was enough to get him to the elevator unchallenged.

When he stepped off on Mr. Tollini's floor, Remo had shucked the blazer and stuffed it up the ceiling trap of the elevator. He decided that he would look more like a fool in a three-sizes-too-big blue blazer than none at all.

He found the office at the very end of a long austere corridor. It reminded him of his orphanage days when he would have to report to Sister Mary Margaret, the mother superior. Her office had been at the end of a long corridor too.

Remo went through the glass door marked "VICE-PRESIDENT IN CHARGE OF SYSTEMS OUTREACH."

The too-cool secretary gave Remo a disapproving look that made her resemble a distant cousin to the unconscious guard.

"You are . . . ?" she began.

"Remo Mercurio," Remo said.

"Mr. Tollin's ten-o'clock?"

"The very same."

The secretary hesitated, ran a pert pink tongue around the subdued lipstick of her mouth indecisively, and finally buzzed Antony Tollini.

"Mr. Tollini. Mr. Mercurio is here."

"Show him in," said the bright voice of Antony Tollini.

Remo smiled confidently at the secretary as he breezed past, saying, "Don't bother. I'll help myself."

Remo didn't know what to expect when he walked in. He would have to talk around the lack of a suit. That much was for sure. He might even have to strong-arm the man. He hoped his faked history and references—all rigged by Harold Smith—would get him over the hump.

Antony Tollini looked up from the paperwork on his desk. His light brown eyes acquired a stung expression as they alighted on Remo's bare arms and fresh T-shirt.

I blew it, Remo thought.

The stung expression lasted only a moment. Antony Tollini's mouth twiched, his nostrils flared.

Then a slow pleased smile stretched his mustache like a miniature accordion, to reveal gleaming white teeth like a row of tiny tombstones.

"Why, you're perfect!" Antony Tollini said in awe.

Remo blinked. Something was not right here.

"I am?"

"Sit down, sit down," Antony Tollini said, gesturing to a comfortable black leather chair.

When Remo had settled in, Tollini said, "It says here you grew up in Detroit."

"If that's what it says," said Remo, who never bothered with the details.

"From a good *family* neighborhood, am I right?"

"I remember it that way, yeah," said Remo, who had grown up in Newark, New Jersey, an orphan and ward of the state.

"Great. My family is from the Old Country. I'm second-generation. On my mother's side."

"I'm Irish too," lied Remo, who was finding this easier than he had thought. So far, none of the questions had been hard. He had boned up on computer terminology while waiting for his application to be processed. He hoped it would get him through.

"Irish? With a name like Remo?"

"Half-Irish," Remo said quickly, realizing the man meant some other Old Country.

"Great, great," Tollini was saying. He looked at the résumé again. His head lifted and met Remo's eyes with a shine that was almost worshipful. "You're hired."

"I am?" said Remo, eyebrows quirking upward.

"Can you start today?"

"Sure."

"Right now?"

"Yeah."

"Good. You're on the next flight to Boston. The car is waiting."

"Boston? What's up there?"

"Our most important client. Their system is down."

"Down where?" asked Remo, frowning.

"Broken," said Antony Tollini. "Don't you know what down means?"

Remo suddenly remembered what "down" meant in the world of data proccessing. It had been on the list. Right under CPU.

"Where I come from, we don't say 'down,' we say 'flat.' "

" 'Flat'?"

"Yeah, like a tire. All computer talk is like that in Detroit. When our computers crash, people get glass in their faces."

"Now that you're with IDC," Antony Tollini said, rising from his desk, "you say 'down.' Can you say 'down'?"

"Down," said Remo, suddenly noticing Tollini's arm across his shoulder. Remo allowed himself to be hustled from the office. This was happening awfully fast, he thought.

"Good. I can see you have a bright future with us, Mr. Mercurio."

Out by the secretary's desk, Antony Tollini was simultaneously congratulating Remo with a frantic two-handed handshake and telling his secretary to provide Remo with the proper documentation.

It was under his arm when Remo was hustled into a waiting company car. They had to wait while the paramedics finished loading a gurney into the back of an ambulance.

"Someone get hurt?" Remo asked the company driver.

"Lobby security guard. Fainted."

"Imagine that."

"Yeah, and they found him in his shorts. No sign of his clothes. Poor bastard will be reassigned to Siberia."

"IDC have a Russian office?"

"Siberia," the driver explained, getting the car going, "is defined at IDC as anyplace other than Mamaroneck."

"What does that make Boston?" Remo wondered.

"You going to Boston?" the driver asked sharply, looking up into the rearview mirror.

"That's what my airline ticket says."

"I've driven a lot of new employees to the Boston gate,"

said the driver thoughtfully. "I can't remember ever picking one up again."

"I'm the exception that proves the rule," Remo told him smugly.

"I'll bet you are. I've been with IDC going on twenty years. I've never seen a new man dressed like you."

"Didn't you hear? They've relaxed the dress code. All they expect now is clean underwear."

"Who told you that?"

"That security guard, as a matter of fact. Guess the shock was too much for him."

At the airport, Remo checked in and sought a pay phone. He called his hotel and got a busy signal.

"Dammit," Remo said, hanging up. He walked the waiting area impatiently and tried again. The line remained busy. He couldn't understand it. Chiun hated telephones.

When they called for final boarding on his flight, Remo was listening to another busy signal.

He was the last one on the plane. What the hell was Chiun doing on the phone all this time? Remo wondered as he took his seat.

Then he remembered. During the months when Chiun had been presumed dead, Harold Smith had stopped taping Chiun's latest passion, British soap operas. The Master of Sinanju had hectored Smith unmercifully until he had promised to acquire the complete backlog.

No doubt a fresh shipment had arrived and Chiun was catching up. He usually left the phone off the hook while he watched his soaps. When he didn't rip it out of the wall entirely, that was.

"I hope they're especially good episodes," Remo muttered as the 727 engines began to whine preparatory to takeoff, "because when I get back, Chiun's going to kill me."

6

At Boston's Logan Airport terminal, Remo looked around for a payphone.

He was halfway there when an upright hulk in a sharkskin suit got in front of him and asked, "You the guy from IDC?"

"How'd you guess?" Remo asked.

"You got the blue book. They all come with the blue book. We got a lot of blue books now, and we still got our problem."

"Yeah," Remo said, looking around the terminal distractedly. "And if I don't make a quick call, I'm going to have a problem."

"It can wait," the chauffeur said, placing a meaty paw on Remo's shoulder.

"No, it can't," Remo said, heading for the pay phone. The chauffeur was stubborn. He refused to release Remo. And so he found himself being frog-marched to the pay phone, his expression a mixture of surprise and respect.

Casually Remo dropped a quarter into the pay-phone slot and punched in the number. While he was waiting, he absently reached up to pry the heavy hand off his shoulder.

Remo got another busy signal. He hung up. "Okay, lead me to the car."

"You know," the chauffeur said, looking at his numb hand with vague disbelief, "you're not like the stiffs they sent before."

"The classified I answered specifically said 'No Stiffs.' "

The chauffeur's thick features brightened. "I got a good feeling about you. What'd you say your name was?"

"Remo."

The chauffeur's broad face broke out into a broad grin. "No

kiddin'? Remo. I'm Bruno. Come on, Remo. You might be just what the doctor ordered."

"That's what Tollini said."

"That Tollini, now there's a stiff. Keeps sending us stiffs, even though we keep tellin' him not to."

"I think he got the message," said Remo.

"I think he did, at that."

The car was a black Cadillac, Remo saw. It was parked in the middle of a line of cabs. None of the cabbies seemed to mind.

"Hey, Remo," the driver said once they were in traffic.

"Yeah?"

"Do yourself a big favor."

"What's that?"

"If you can't fix the boss's box, don't come out and say so right away. Know what I mean?"

"No."

"Don't give up so easy. We don't like quitters in our outfit. Catch me?"

"What happens if I can't fix it?" Remo asked.

"Never say never. That's all I got to say."

At the offices of F and L Importing, Remo took one look at the lonely personal computer sitting on the Formica card table in the dim room surrounded by husky security men in sharkskin suits and without preamble broke the bad news.

"It's hopeless."

"What'd I tell you!" Bruno the chauffeur moaned. "Ain't you got ears? Don't you listen?" He got between Remo and the three security men, and waving his arms, said, "He's kiddin' us. He's a kidder, see? I was talking to him on the ride over, gettin' him wise." The chauffeur turned to Remo and said, "Tell them you're kiddin', Remo. His name is Remo, see?" he called over his shoulder.

"I'm not kidding," Remo said firmly. "I'm a professional. I can tell by looking that this computer is broken beyond repair."

"None of the other guys said that."

"None of them have my background. I'm a certified genius. I invented the world's first Korean keyboard."

"Korean? What's that got to do with this?"

"You ever see Korean? They got a million characters for

everything. Forget the twenty-six letters. A Korean keyboard, even a small one, is twenty feet long and has thirty rows of keys. To operate it you need roller skates and a photographic memory."

"He's kiddin'," the chauffeur said, his eyes going sick. "Tell them you're kiddin'."

"I am not kidding," Remo said, folding his arms. He made no move toward the keyboard.

His back to the three security men, the chauffeur mouthed a single word. The word was "Try." To which he added a silent "Please."

Because he was getting tired waiting for something to happen, Remo shrugged and said, "Okay, I guess a quick look-see won't hurt anything. Who knows? I might get lucky."

"What'd I tell you?" the chauffeur said, facing the security team once more. He grinned nervously. "He was kiddin'. A little joke. To relieve the tension. He's a good guy. I like him. Go to it, Remo. Show us your stuff."

Remo addressed the silent PC terminal, lifted it in both strong hands, examined his own reflection for a moment, and then brought the screen to his ear. He began shaking the terminal briskly.

"Hey, none of the other guys done that," one of the security men pointed out.

"This is an advanced technique," Remo told him. "We shake until we hear something rattling around in here. You'd be surprised how often the trouble is a paperclip that got in through a vent."

This made perfect sense to the assembled F and L Importing employees. They all went very quiet, listening.

Soon, something rattled.

"Hey, I heard it!" the chauffeur cried. "You hear that? Remo found it. Attaboy, Remo."

"Shhhh," said Remo, still shaking the PC terminal.

Another element began to rattle. Then a third. Pretty soon, under his relentless shaking, the PC began to sound like a majolica rattle.

Remo stopped.

"What's the verdict?" Bruno the chauffeur asked.

Balancing the PC in one hand experimentally, Remo frowned. Then he lofted the PC over their heads. It seemed to float in a shallow arc. Every eye in the room followed it like ball bearings drawn to a horseshoe magnet.

"Hey!" one yelled.

The four men lunged for the floating PC like startled linebackers. They were too late. The PC landed in a wastebasket in one corner, where its picture tube shattered.

The quartet froze in place, looking at the shattered PC in disbelief.

Only when Remo coolly said, "What'd I tell you? Beyond repair."

Slowly they turned around. Their faces were bone-white. Their eyes were hard and glittering. Their limp-with-helplessness fingers made slow, determined fists.

Mechanically three of the men surrounded Remo. The fourth—the chauffeur—lurched to a plain door as if his legs had turned to wood.

"The box is broke," he called in.

A raspy voice said, "I *know* it's broke."

"Now it's really, really broke."

"What happened?"

"Guy broke it."

"Break *him*."

"He's a *paisan*."

"I don't care if he's Frank fuggin' Sinatra! Get rid of him. And get on the phone to that Tollini. Tell him no more screwups. Send me a Jap. I heard Japs are good at computertry. I want a Jap."

"You got it, boss."

The chauffeur came back. Woodenly he said, "The boss says you gotta go."

Remo shrugged unconcernedly. "So I go."

They went. Remo didn't bother to wait for the car door to be opened for him. He got ahead of the escort and opened the rear door himself.

The others hesitated. One said, "What the fuck. From the look of him he'd probably just pee in the trunk." Two of them got in on either side, sandwiching Remo between them.

The remaining pair took the front seat. The car backed out of the alley.

"You know," Remo said, "this kinda reminds me of Little Italy, down in New York."

"It should," said one of the security men.

"Too bad about that computer," Remo said sympathetically. "But broke is broke."

"Yeah," a second man growled. "I'll always remember you for sayin' that."

They didn't take him back to the airport. Not that Remo expected that. Remo didn't know where they were taking him and he didn't care. He hoped it was secluded, wherever it was.

He assumed it would be. They weren't about to try to kill him on Boston Common. And he didn't want their screams to attract attention.

The exit said: East Boston.

Remo knew they were close to the airport because the thunder of jet engines came with monotonous regularity.

As the black Cadillac pulled into the back lot of a Ramada Inn, Remo asked innocently, "What's this?"

"Your lodgings," said the man at Remo's right.

"Where you're going to sleep tonight," said the man to Remo's left.

They both laughed with the humorless rattle of windup toys.

"I expected better accommodations," Remo remarked. "After all, I am a treasured IDC employee."

"You wait here," said the man to Remo's right. "We gotta make sure the accommodations are satisfactory."

All three security men left the car. Bruno the chauffeur turned around in his seat with a sad look in his eyes. Remo could tell by the way his right-shoulder-muscle group was bunched under his tight coat that his hand was wrapped around a pistol. In case Remo tried to escape.

Remo had no intention of escaping. The Ramada Inn would do just fine. He waited.

"Why'd you go and do that, Remo?" Bruno asked mournfully.

"Do what?" Remo asked, his face innocent.

The door opened and one of the trio waved for them to come in.

"Guess my room's ready," Remo said, sliding out of the car.

The man who had waved fell in behind Remo as he approached the partly ajar door.

Remo whistled amiably. This was ridiculously obvious. The only question in his mind was whether they were going to shoot, stab, or bludgeon him to death.

They did none of those.

The moment Remo stepped across the threshold, the third man wrapped his thick arms around Remo's torso, pinioning his arms.

That told Remo that they were going to use the infamous Italian rope trick on him.

Confidently Remo walked in.

The rope was held loose in the hands of the man standing off to the left of the open door. He looped the heavy coil around Remo's exposed neck. It felt like a scratchy python.

The other end was caught by the man standing behind the door. He kicked the door closed with his foot as he hauled back on his end of the rope like a sailor securing a docked boat.

The other man did the same.

As the loose loop of heavy hemp tightened around Remo's throat, he tensed his throat muscles. He didn't bother fighting back. He just held his breath.

"Arggh!" Remo said in a choking rush of air.

"Tighter," a voice hissed. "Don't let him get a peep out."

The hemp constricted like a noose around Remo's throat muscles. It was strong, but his training was stronger.

"Arrghh!" Remo repeated, forcing blood up his carotid artery so his face turned an appropriate shade of red.

"Tighter," the voice repeated. "This ain't no fuckin' taffy pull."

Remo said "Urggg" this time, for variety.

"Jeez, this guy's stubborn," the third man said at Remo's ear, digging his chin into Remo's shoulder. The smell of garlic was enough to make a man pass out—even one who was not allowing air to enter his nostrils.

The man on the left started to pant. His face was going purple, making Remo wonder who was strangling whom.

The opposite man, straining on his end of the rope, kept losing his grip.

"I'm gettin' friggin' rope burns," he said through clenched teeth.

"How're we doin', Frank?"

The man called Frank lifted his chin and said, "His face is turning red. I think he's almost done."

At that moment the room phone rang.

"I'll get it," Remo said in a crystal clear voice. He strode toward the nightstand, dragging the three men with him. One man lost his grip on the rope and snarled a curse as his palms were singed by the sudden friction.

When Remo casually reached out for the receiver, the one called Frank was forced to relinquish his bear hug.

"Hello?" Remo said into the phone. "Yes, everything's just dandy. Thank you." He hung up.

"The guy in the next room complained about the noise," Remo told the one thug still holding on to his end of the rope and what was left of his composure. "Said it sounded like someone was being strangled. Imagine that."

That brought out the guns. The rope dropped to the floor. Frank gathered Remo up into another bear hug.

Remo swept one foot up and around. Corkscrewing, he left the floor, taking Frank with him. The man was stubborn. He held on.

It happened so fast it didn't seem to happen at all. One second Remo was in the cross hairs of two revolvers, and the next, the revolvers were embedded in the cracked plaster of the ceiling like misplaced doorknobs.

The two thugs stared at their stung hands, blinking the way people blink when something is not quite right.

Frank landed on the bed and went "Whoof!" gustily. He didn't get up immediately. His head had somehow gotten jammed in a pillowcase with a pillow.

Remo let him be. His perpendicular toe returned to the rug, braking his spin. His kicking foot joined it smartly.

Then he had both thugs by the throat and his fingers dug in like blunt drill bits.

"Let's see if you can do red," Remo said airily.

He squeezed.

The faces above Remo's hands became like thermometers in August. The red color just suffused upward like mercury.

"Nice healthy shades," Remo said, changing his grip. "How's your purple?"

The man in Remo's right hand could manage only a pale smoky lavender. But the one on his left achieved true purple.

"Fair enough," said Remo. He made his voice sound like Mr. Rogers. "Now, can we say 'Argghh'?"

Neither man could, it seemed. One did leak a little drool out of his mouth in trying, which Remo thought unacceptable.

He broke the man's neck with a sharp leftward twist. It was easier than it looked. Remo could feel the flexing of his neck vertebrae, felt the pulsing of his carotid, and sensed the cartilage of his larynx as it struggled to make sounds. He knew exactly where to apply the pressure that would turn the two adjacent vertebrae into exploding bone fragments.

Remo let go when he sensed the lack of electrical current running down the man's severed spinal cord.

"Now you," Remo said, turning to the other man. "Who do you work for?" He let the man get a tiny sip of air.

"Don't . . . do . . . this," the man said. It was a warning, not a plea.

"I asked a question," Remo said, clamping down with both hands. He lifted the man straight off the rug, even though the man was a half-foot taller than Remo. Just to drive home the point.

"You're . . . making a . . . mistake," the man wheezed.

"Give me a name."

"Talk . . . to the boss. He'll . . . straighten it all . . . out."

"Who's the boss?"

"Talk . . . to . . . Fuggin," the man gasped.

"Who's Fuggin?" asked Remo, giving him a little air.

"What are you, stupid? Fuggin is Fuggin."

Since an answer that made no sense was just as useless as no answer at all, Remo suddenly released the man from his two-handed throat grip.

Gravity took hold of the man. He started to fall. Before he got an eighteenth of an inch closer to the rug, Remo's hands came back, open and fast.

The sound was like a single sharp clap.

When the man's feet hit the rug, the top of his head struck the ceiling. Since the distance between the two was eight feet, and the man just under six-foot-four, there was about one and a half feet of distance unaccounted for.

When the man's head struck the rug, it bounced twice and stopped suddenly. It would have kept rolling but was stopped by a two-foot length of stretched matter that resembled chewed bubble gum after it had been drawn between two hands.

Of course, it was not bubble gum. It was the man's limp, shock-compressed neck.

Remo turned away and helped the one called Frank to his feet.

The man allowed himself to be set on his feet in front of the bed. He allowed this despite outweighing Remo by almost eighty pounds because he had seen the fate that had befallen his coworkers after he had extracted his head from the pillowcase.

"What'd you do to Guido?" the man asked, pointing to the pink taffylike mass that connected the dead man's trunk and head.

"The same thing I'm going to do to your balls if you don't answer my question," Remo warned.

"Look, I don't know who you are or what you want, but you really, really want to talk to Fuggin. Get me?"

"Who's Fuggin?"

"The boss. My boss. The boss of the guys you just croaked. Fuggin don't like for his guys to be croaked."

"Tough."

"This is a big mistake," the thug said in an agitated voice. "I want you to know that."

"What's your connection to IDC?" Remo demanded.

"None."

"I believe you. Now, what happened to the IDC technicians who came to fix that computer?"

"Can I take the Fifth on that?"

"Are your testicles made of brass?"

"No."

"Shall I repeat the question, or do you want proof of that immutable quirk of biology?"

"They got whacked," the man said dispiritedly.

"Why?"

"They screwed up."

"What's so important about the computer?"

"Ask Fuggin. I don't know nothin'. Honest."

"Is that the best answer you can give me?"

"It's the only one I got."

"It's not good enough," returned Remo, feinting toward

the man's neck. The man grabbed his own throat with both hands in order to protect it from Remo's terrible fingers.

So Remo took hold of the man's head with both hands and inserted his thumbs in his eye sockets. He pushed. The sound was like two grapes being squished. The man fell back on the bed with his eyes pushed all the way to the back of his skull and two spongy tunnels through the brain.

Whistling, Remo recovered the rope and, looping it through the ceiling fixture and around the throats of the three dead thugs, created a scene that eventually went down in the annals of Boston homicide as a first.

As the homicide detective asked when he first viewed the macabre scene, "How could three guys hang themselves from the same rope like garlic cloves?"

Remo left the motel room surreptitiously.

The chauffeur was still behind the wheel, his nose buried in a racing form. He tried to look casual, but his face was like a stone chopped out of a granite outcropping.

Remo figured he knew less than the three dead thugs, so he left the man alone as he slipped away in search of a pay phone.

He wondered what Harold Smith was going to say when he informed him that International Data Corporation, the largest company in American, had somehow become embroiled with the Mafia.

Most of all, he wondered who the hell this Fuggin was.

7

From an early age, Carmine (Fuggin) Imbruglia had only one burning ambition in life. To become an arch-criminal.

"Someday," he would boast, "I'm gonna be a kingpin. You'll see."

Carmine had worked his way up from mere hanger-on to proud soldier in the Scubisci crime family of Brooklyn in only thirty years. No crime was too heinous. No infraction of the law too petty. Dock pilferage was as sweet to him as payroll robberies.

All through the heady days of scams and heists, Carmine Imbruglia had never done a day in jail. His first brush with the justice system came one day in the summer of 1953, when he was arrested for having taken part in stealing a newsstand vendor's cash belt.

Carmine and two Brooklyn boys had executed the robbery. Carmine had pretended interest in a copy of *Playboy* that the newsstand vendor was keeping under the counter. He refused to sell it to Carmine, who, despite looking like a beetle-browed tree ape, was underage.

"Aw, c'mon, mister, please," Carmine wheedled, as Freaking Frasca and Angelo (Slob) Sloboni slipped up behind the angry news vendor.

The vendor said, "Get lost, punk!" and Freaking Frasca popped his gravity blade and sliced free the heavy canvas belt. The Slob caught it.

They cut out like thieves.

Carmine tried to run. He would have made it except that he made the mistake of trying to filch that copy of *Playboy* on the fly. The vendor caught him by the scruff of his neck and hollered for a cop.

"I can't believe I got pinched on my first heist," Carmine muttered from the cell he discovered himself sharing with a freckle-faced Irish kid named O'Leary.

"What'd you do?" asked O'Leary.

"I didn't do nothin'," Carmine snarled. "They think I did a robbery. What about you?"

"I didn't open a fire hydrant so I couldn't take a shower," said O'Leary.

"They pinch you for that?" Carmine said, figuring O'Leary for shanty Irish.

"They pinched *me*."

"What do you get for opening a fire hydrant, anyways?"

"Probation."

"I'm looking at three years in Elmira," Carmine said morosely.

"If you can't do the time, don't do the crime," O'Leary recited, turning over in his bunk.

When the court officers came for O'Leary, he was sound asleep.

"Hey, O'Leary," the court officer shouted. "Bag and baggage. Let's go."

"Shh," Carmine hissed. "You'll wake up Carmine."

"You O'Leary?" the court officer asked suspiciously.

"You sayin' I don't look Irish, copper?"

"No, I'm sayin' you don't look clean enough for a punk what got himself pinched for showering in the gutter."

"It's summer," said Carmine. "I sweat easy in the summer. Old dirt must come outta my pores or somethin'."

The court officer shrugged as he opened the cell with a dull brass key. "Come along, then," he said.

Standing with a contrite expression on his broad face, Aloysius X. O'Leary *né* Carmine Imbruglia attempted to explain himself before Judge Terrance Doyle.

"I was mizzled, your honor. I'm askin' for prohibition."

"What's that?" asked the bored judge.

"Them other two guys, they mizzled me. I didn't wanta do it, but I was mizzled."

"Mizzled?" said the judge.

"That's right, your honor."

"Spell that," requested the judge, now very interested, because he surreptitiously worked the *Times* crossword puzzle during the long, boring hours of testimony.

"Mizzled. M-i-s-l-e-d," said Carmine Imbruglia, spelling the word exactly as he had seen it in the morning newspaper, wherein a made guy had defended his participation in a bank robbery, putting the blame on his confederates, thereby getting a reduced sentence.

"Who . . . er . . . mizzled you?" asked the disappointed judge.

"The other two what was with me. Freaking Frasca and the Slob."

"Slob?"

"Sloboni. His real moniker is Angelo. He didn't like 'Angelo' so we kinda call him Slob to keep him happy." Carmine cracked a lopsided grin. "What do you expect from a guinea?" He winked.

"I see," said the judge, frowning to keep from laughing. He banged his gavel once and announced that Aloysius X. O'Leary was free to go. He put out an order to pick up those notorious Italian punks Frasca and Sloboni.

The next day, Aloysius X. O'Leary, protesting that his name was not Carmine Imbruglia, had the book thrown at him.

"Six months for the robbery," pronounced the judge in a grave voice. "And another two for impersonating an Irishman."

After that, Carmine Imbruglia became a legend on the corner of Utica and Sterling in the Brownsville section of Brooklyn.

It wasn't long before a string of car thefts and house invasions brought a summons from Don Pietro Scubisci himself.

Carmine had entered the old man's august presence trembling. The scene was the back of the Neighborhood Improvement Society in Manhattan's Little Italy. It was a dim alcove paneled in black walnut, the walls covered with the sepia-toned pictures of obscure saints.

Don Pietro was eating fried peppers out of a simple brown paper bag so spotted with grease it looked like a faded leopard skin.

"I'm honored to meet you," said Carmine sincerely.

"You been doing crime in my territory," said Don Pietro.

"You heard of me?" Carmine blurted, pleased.

Don Pietro glowered. "I heard you owe me money."

"Me?"

"You steal in Brooklyn, you give thirty percent to me."

"But . . . but that's robbery!" Carmine had spluttered.

"You rob from others. I rob from you. It is a dog-eat-dog world."

"All I got is five hundred bucks to my name," Carmine had protested. "If I give it to you, I got nothing left."

"So? You go rob again. Around and around goes the music, but thirty percent always ends up here," said Don Pietro, smacking a greasy hand on the worn black walnut table. He left a palm print that could be fried and served up whole.

Having no choice, Carmine Imbruglia did as he was ordered. The more he brought to Don Pietro, the more Don Pietro asked for. The percentage jumped from thirty to thirty-five and then to forty.

"This is fuggin' worse than inflation," Carmine complained to his wife, Camilla, one day.

"Then get a job."

"How'm I gonna fuggin' become an *amico nostro* if I bail out now?" had demanded Carmine, who had a dream. And was terrified of physical labor to boot.

One day, as Carmine dumped a pile of bills and loose change on the dark greasy table in the back room, Don Pietro spoke up with his hand deep in the ever-present grease-stained bag of green peppers.

"I'm gonna make you, Carmine," he intoned.

"You're already making me," said Carmine sullenly.

"No, I'm gonna make you one of the guys."

"Will it cost me?" asked Carmine suspiciously.

Don Pietro popped a fried pepper into his mouth and casually indicated the money on the table. "What you just paid is the final installment."

Carmine perked up. "Does that mean I don't gotta pay you a percentage no more?"

"No," returned Don Pietro. "It means that from now on you, Carmine Imbruglia, steal when I say you steal, from who I say you steal from, and you give me all the swag you steal. I, in turn, give you a percentage."

Carmine squinted in the dimness of the alcove. "How much?"

"Twenty."

"That's fuggin' highway robbery!" shouted Carmine Imbruglia, who was instantly surrounded by a dry moat of pinstripes.

"Or I can have you shot in the face and stuffed into the

trunk of a crummy Willys," said Don Pietro casually. "You make the choice."

"Twenty sounds fair," Carmine mumbled.

The next day in a house in Flatbush where the curtains were drawn to create a kind of sad gloom, Carmine Imbruglia was officially inducted into the Mafia.

The induction was done in Sicilian, which Carmine did not understand. For all he knew, they were inducting him into the Portuguese navy.

When they pierced his trigger finger with a needle, he cried at the sight of his own blood. Laughing, they lifted Carmine's bleeding finger to Don Pietro's pierced trigger finger. Their blood mingled.

When it was over, Don Pietro asked, "What is your street name?"

Since Carmine didn't have a street name, he made one up.

"Cadillac. Cadillac Carmine Imbruglia," said Carmine proudly.

Don Pietro considered this for some moments. "No, no good."

"What's fuggin' wrong with 'Cadillac Carmine'? It's a fine car."

"I own a Cadillac," explained Don Pietro, patting his pockets absently. "How will it sound if I'm asking for you, and they bring around the car? Or vice versa. I ask for my car and I get you. No, this will not work. You must have a more fitting name."

"Why don't you fuggin' get another fuggin' car, then?"

"Fuggin," said Don Pietro thoughtfully. "I like the sound of this. Yes. You will be known henceforth as Fuggin."

"I don't fuggin' wanna be called Fuggin. What kinda name is that for a fuggin' wise guy?"

"You can accept 'Fuggin' as your name or you can accept only ten percent of all the money you steal for me," said Don Pietro, looking around for his greasy paper sack. He found it in the vent pocket of his suit, which was mysteriously spotless, if hopelessly wrinkled.

" 'Fuggin' is fuggin' spelled with two fuggin' G's, not three," said Carmine (Fuggin) Imbruglia in a sour voice. "Everybody remember that."

"That is good, Fuggin," said Don Pietro. "Now, the first

thing I ask of you as a soldier in this thing of ours is to get me a few shrimp cocktails."

"What do I look like, a fuggin' waiter?" exploded Carmine.

"No, you look to me like a man who has respect for his capo," Don Pietro said evenly.

Listening to the steel in his capo's voice, Carmine Imbruglia swallowed once and asked, "How many shrimp cocktails you want?"

"One truckload. I understand there is one leaving Baltimore for the Fulton Fish Market at two o'clock this afternoon."

"Oh, swag," said Carmine. "Why dincha say so? I can handle this."

It was not easy. The truck was a sixteen-wheeler and Carmine's aging Volkswagen Beetle was not up to forcing a sixteen-wheeler over to the side of Interstate 95.

So Carmine executed the only strategy available to him. With the driver's door open, he cut in front of the truck, jammed on the brakes, and dived for the shoulder of the road.

In a grinding cacophony, the Beetle disappeared under the truck's front grille and bumper, lodging under the cab like a bone in a rottweiler's throat. The sixteen-wheeler jackknifed to a stop, rubber burning and smoking.

"Okay, stick 'em up," said Carmine to the driver.

The driver was obliging. He got out of the cab and stood white-faced as Carmine climbed behind the wheel. He got the engine started. He pressed the gas.

The truck lurched ahead and stopped amid a squealing of tormented metal.

"What the fug's wrong with this pile of junk?" demanded Carmine.

"The pile of junk under the cab," said the white-faced driver.

Carmine remembered his Volkswagen, which he had intended replacing with his share of the shrimp. Without the shrimp, there would be no replacement. And without wheels, his career as a wise guy was finished.

Rescue in the form of a tow truck happened along then.

Brandishing his Saturday-night special, Carmine made the

hapless truck driver get in front of the tow truck. The wrecker screeched to a halt. Carmine jumped into view.

"You!" he told the wrecker driver. "You hook this wrecker up to that truck there."

"You crazy?" demanded the driver. "I can't haul a sixteen-wheeler. It'll bust my rig."

"You fuggin' do as I say, cogsugger, or I'll give you a lead fuggin' eye."

The driver didn't understand all of it, but the part about the lead eye was clear enough. He lifted the cab, and as cars whizzed by without pause or interest, Carmine made the two drivers haul the remains of his Beetle out of the way.

Then he made the driver of the wrecker tie up the truck driver. Carmine then bound the latter.

Carmine Imbruglia left them by the side of the road saying, "I hope yous jerks rot." It all had been too much like work.

After Carmine had gotten through telling Don Pietro Scubisci the whole story, Don Pietro paused to extract a toothpick from between his teeth and casually inspected a fragment of cold pink shrimp meat impaled on it.

"You left the wrecker?" he asked, unimpressed.

"What was I to do? You wanted shrimp. I brought you shrimp. When do I get my cut?"

Don Pietro snapped his fingers once.

Soldiers began bringing in cases of bottled shrimp cocktails and set them beside Carmine.

"What's this?" he asked.

"Your percentage," said Don Pietro.

"I expected money!"

"You are a smart boy, Carmine. I will let you sell your share of the shrimp for whatever price you see fit. This is only fair, since I will be moving volume at a very low price."

"You are very kind, Don Pietro," said Carmine sincerely, touched by the consideration of his capo.

He was a happy man as he carried the shrimp, one case at a time, on the IRT back to Brownsville.

"We're gonna make a fortune," he told his wife. "Restaurants will be fallin' all over themselves for quality shrimp like these!"

"At least you got work, you bum," Camilla had said.

The next evening, Carmine Imbruglia dragged himself home with a solitary case of shrimp under his arm. It was the same case he had started the day with. The others remained stuffed in his refrigerator and in the cool air of his basement.

"I got no takers," he complained to his wife.

"What're you talking? No takers?"

"Somebody got to every fuggin' restaurant first. I got undercut. Except the last guy, who still wouldn't buy."

"Why not?"

"The stuff had spoiled by then," said Carmine, setting the case on the kitchen linoleum and kicking it methodically.

Carmine and Camilla had a rough next month, but as Carmine explained it to his wife over breakfast once morning, "At least we ain't fuggin' starving. We're eating better than any of the neighbors."

"If you call cold shrimp three times a day eating," Camilla had spat. "And I still say it was that rotten Don Pietro that undercut you with the restaurants."

"Get out of here! Don Pietro wouldn't do that. I'm a made guy now. A soldier. We're practically like this," said Carmine, putting two cocktail-sauce-covered fingers together.

"Put your balls in there and it would be the truth."

"When the time comes for me to make my bones," snarled Carmine (Fuggin) Imbruglia, "I hope it's for breaking yours."

The years rolled by. Carmine toiled in wire rooms, ran numbers, served as a wheelman, and whenever Don Carmine had a yen for seafood, he asked for Fuggin.

One day, at the height of the Scubisci-Pubescio wars, when Don Pietro and Don Fiavorante Pubescio of California were at war for the title *capo da tutti capi*, boss of all bosses, Don Pietro summoned Carmine Imbruglia to his scarred walnut table.

Carmine noticed a long gouge along the top where a .38 slug had chewed a furrow that had not been there the week before.

Don Pietro was pouring Asti Spumante into the furrow, trying to get it to match the color of the rest of the wood.

"Fuggin," he said softly, "I have need of you."

"Anything, Don Pietro. Just ask. I will make my bones with any Scubisci family member you name."

"Forget bones. I want cod."

"You want me to clip the Lord?" sputtered Carmine. "I wouldn't know where to find him. Would you settle for a priest?"

"I said cod, not God."

"Who's he? I don't know no west-coast wise guy that goes by the name Cod."

"Cod," said Don Pietro patiently, "is a fish. A tasty fish."

Carmine sighed. "Just tell me where the truck will be."

Don Pietro lifted a rag. "Not a truck. A boat. I want you to steal this fishing smack, whose hold is filled to the brim with fresh cod."

"I don't know nothing about hijacking no boats," said Carmine heatedly.

"You will learn," said Don Pietro, going back to his polishing.

It was actually pretty simple, Carmine found.

He rowed out into the Sound in a stolen rowboat and waited for the smack to happen along. Carmine wondered why it was called a smack. Maybe it was running drugs.

When it finally muttered into view, he rowed in front of it, chortling, "This is a snap. It's gonna be just like the shrimp heist, only smoother. I won't need no wrecker."

There was a minor problem when he waved his snub-nosed revolver and shouted, "This is a stickup!" because the boat for some reason wouldn't stop. It bore down on Carmine's tiny rowboat like a foaming monster.

"Fuggin' brakes must be broke," said Carmine, dropping his revolver and rowing like mad. The fishing smack veered off and hove to.

"Need a hand?" the captain called. He was swathed in a yellow slicker and floppy hat that made him look like a refugee from a soup commercial.

"I'm lost," Carmine said, planting a foot on the dropped revolver so it wouldn't be seen.

"Come aboard."

This meant that Carmine had to row to the fishing boat, which caused him to mutter, "Who fuggin' died and made you admiral?" under his breath.

A brine-soaked rope was lowered. Carmine kept sliding down. Finally he tied it around his waist and said, "Just fuggin' haul me up, okay?"

The fishing-smack crew obliged. When Carmine got to the deck, he pulled his revolver out from under his shirttail and stuck it in the captain's startled, element-seamed face.

"This is a heist, admiral," he announced.

"I'm a captain."

"Fine. I hereby appoint myself admiral of this tub. Everybody make like Popeye the fuggin' Sailor Man and jump into the rowboat. This is my tub now."

Since fishermen usually carry no weapons, the crew did as they were told.

Carmine left them bobbing in his wake. He spun the heavy wheel toward land, grinning from ear to ear.

He lost the grin about the time Far Rockaway came into view and his foot couldn't find the brake.

"*Mannaggia la cornata!*" he screamed, remembering a favorite saying of his father's. He was hazy on the meaning, but it seemed to fit the occasion.

The fishing smack piled into a dock, and both colliding objects splintered and groaned terribly.

But not as much as Carmine Imbruglia. He jumped into the water, hoping that like Ivory soap, he would naturally float. When he didn't, he threshed and struggled until he felt the cold silty sea bottom. It was only three feet down.

"Fuggin' sumbidges," Carmine complained as he trudged toward shore. "They musta took the brake pedal with them."

There remained the problem of the cargo.

It took all the rest of that day, and half the night. But Carmine was able to get most of the glassy-eyed cod out of the hold and to shore. A rented U-Haul got it home, where he lined the fish up in his cool basement on endless sheets of waxed paper. This time he left the furnace off.

The next morning he hosed the fishy corpses down to get the sand and muck out of their gills, and after selecting the best specimens for himself, hastily peddled them to every area restaurant he could find. Carmine made a cool seven hundred dollars and change.

Only then did he truck the rest to Don Pietro.

"This is all?" asked Don Peitro, peering into the back of the U-Haul.

"I already took my cut," Carmine explained. "So it wouldn't spoil like last time."

"Next time, you do not do this," Don Pietro warned.

"Next time," said Carmine, "I hope it's a boat they keep up. Would you believe it? Fuggin' thing had no brakes."

Carmine Imbruglia rushed home that day. He had finally made a good payday. He felt good. He felt flush. He squandered an entire dime on the evening *Post*.

Thc headline, when he read it, made him want to throw up: "FOOD POISONING OUTBREAK IN AREA RESTAURANTS. Tainted Fish Blamed."

Eyes popping, Carmine read the lead paragraph. Then he did throw up. Into the wadded-up copy of the *Post*.

He never did finish the paper. Or go home.

Carmine hastily changed trains and doubled back.

They were carrying Don Pietro out of his office on a stretcher when he pounded up Mott Street, panting and sweating.

"What happened?" Carmine asked, hunkering down behind two little old ladies in black scarves on the outskirts of the gathering crowd.

"Poor Don Pietro. They say it is food poisoning."

"I'm dead," Carmine croaked, white-faced.

One of the old women clucked sympathetically. "Did you eat the bad fish too?"

"I'm thinkin' about it."

Don Pietro was rushed to Mount Sinai Hospital, deep in a coma. Weeks passed. Then months. Carmine had lammed for Tampa, since Florida was open territory. He survived by playing the ponies.

After almost a year, he squandered a slug and called his wife from a pay phone at Hialeah.

"Am I still hot?" he asked, low-voiced.

"The don says you can come back. All is forgiven," she told him.

"How much are they paying you to lie to me, Camilla?"

"Nothing. I had you declared dead and cashed in your insurance. I don't need your money or you."

"My own wife, setting me up. I don't fuggin' believe it."

"Then don't. Don Pietro is still in a coma. Don Fiavorante is in charge now. He says he owes you big."

"The truth?"

"The truth, so help me God, Carmine."

"Warm up the bed, baby," Carmine said happily. "Pappa's comin' home."

"Warm your own bed. If you're moving back, I'm moving out of town. And taking the kids with me."

"I ain't payin' child support if you do," Carmine warned.

"Then don't."

Carmine paused. "How much did the insurance company pay you, anyway?" he asked suspiciously.

"One hundred and forty thousand. And after fifteen years married to you, let me tell you, I earned every red cent."

"Goddamm it! I want my fuggin' cut!"

"Not a chance. Good-bye!"

The line clicked in his ear as Carmine Imbruglia heard the roar of the racetrack crowd as the fifth race ended.

Carmine grabbed a passing bettor.

"How'd Bronze Savage do, pal?"

"Broke her legs."

"I hope that fuggin' nag ends up as glue," Carmine muttered.

"That's no way to talk about an unfortunate animal."

"I was referring to my fuggin' wife, thank you," grumbled Carmine Imbruglia. "This is what I get for marrying a broad from Jersey. I should have listened to my sainted mother, may she rest in peace."

Little Italy had changed since Carmine Imbruglia had skipped town. It had shrunk. Chinatown had practically swallowed it whole. Still, the street smells were the same. The fresh baked bread, the sauces, and the pastries that hung sweet and heavy in the warm air enveloped him like a fragrant fog of welcome.

"Ahh, heaven," said Carmine Imbruglia. He felt his life poised before a turn for the better. At age fifty-seven he was about to embark on a fresh start. Maybe even make *capo regime* one day.

Carmine walked into the Neighorhood Improvement Association. Two unfamiliar men came out to greet him.

"How're yous guys doin'?" he asked guardedly.

"Who're you?" one growled.

"Don't yous guys know me? I'm Cadillac."

"Cadillac?" they said, tensing. One fingered his sport-coat buttons close to the bulge of his shoulder holster.

"Carmine Imbruglia."

One of the goons called over his shoulder, "Hey, boss, Fuggin's here!"

Carmine's expression collapsed like a brick wall before a wrecking ball. He forced a smile onto his brutish face as the rounded brown shape that was Don Fiavorante Pubescio stepped out of the familiar black walnut alcove wearing a white shirt open to his bronzed sternum and revealing gleaming fat ropes of gold chains.

"Fuggin!" cried Don Fiavorante. "It is so good to see you!"

Carmine allowed himself to be gathered up into a fatherly bear hug, patting the big soft man on the back as his cheeks accepted the capo's dry lips and he returned the gesture of respect in turn.

"Come, come, sit with me. How has Florida been?"

"Hot."

"Not as hot as Brownsville, am I not correct, Fuggin? I am given to understand that it is to you I owe my good fortune."

As they sat, the waiter poured some kind of sweet-scented tea into a cup before Don Fiavorante. The service was repeated for Carmine.

Carmine Imbruglia could not help but wrinkle his nose at it all. Don Fiavorante looked as California as a cheap Hollywood producer. Carmine had expected as much. But tea?

"Drink up," said Don Fiavorante. "It is good. My personal physician, he insists that I drink tea. This is ginseng."

"Chink tea?"

"Ginseng," said Don Fiavorante politely. He was a polite man. Unctuousness exuded from his bronzed skin like suntan lotion. He was unfailingly genteel.

"Maybe you have been wondering about Don Pietro," he inquired.

"Sometimes," Carmine admitted. In fact, he had nightmares about him. They all involved Carmine being stuffed with cod and consigned to a watery grave.

"Don Pietro resides at Mount Sinai, not living, not dying. He is a how you say . . . ?"

"A vegetable," a bodyguard growled.

"Such a crude word," said Don Fiavorante. "He is a *melone*. A melon. I do not know what kind." The don allowed a wan smile to wreathe his healthy features. "He eats through a tube, and drinks through the same tube. He excretes through another tube. He has more tubes coming out of him than Frankenstein the monster. And from what? Eating a piece of fish."

Don Fiavorante smiled like an ivory-toothed Buddha. He leaned closer, his dark eyes glittering.

"You ever bring me a piece of fish, my friend, I will bring the fish a piece of you. *Capisce?*"

"Never, Don Fiavorante," promised Carmine solemnly, touching his heart.

"From today, you are with me."

"I am with you."

"I am protecting you. You are now a *sottocapo* under me."

"*Sottocapo?*" blurted Carmine Imbruglia. "Me?"

"Starting now. While you have been away, we have had many troubles. Here in New York. In Chicago. Up in Providence and Boston. It is Rico here and Rico there."

"Those damn Puerto Ricans!" snarled Carmine Imbruglia. "I knew they would get too big for their breeches one day."

Don Fiavorante reared back his head and laughed good-naturedly, his teeth as polished and perfect as piano keys.

When he had control of himself, he sobered.

"Up in New England, we have troubles. Patriarca senior is dead. Junior is in Danbury. We have no one we can trust up there. All is disarray. I am making you my underboss in New England. You will pick up the pieces. You will put them back together. You will make Boston hum again."

"Boston? I just got back to fuggin' Brooklyn! I don't know from Boston. Where is this Boston, anyways?"

"It is in Massachusetts," explained Don Fiavorante.

Don Carmine's eyes narrowed craftily.

"Isn't that the place where that Greek who ran for President comes from?" Don Carmine asked slowly.

"The very same."

"The one who kept talkin' about the Massachusetts Miracle?"

Don Fiavorante nodded patiently.

"It is an honor," said Carmine, who had voted for the Greek governor who had promised to share the wealth and prosperity he had created in his home state with the entire country.

"It will be work. I hope you are a worker."

Don Carmine Imbruglia, aka Fuggin, took Don Fiavorante's hand in his and kissed it once in gratitude.

"This is too good to be true," he said, tears starting from his eyes. He was going to be rich. He was going to be a kingpin. At last. And he would make his fortune in the fabulously prosperous wealthy place called Massachusetts.

8

"The Mafia?" said Harold W. Smith in surprise. "Are you absolutely certain, Remo?"

"I couldn't swear to it in court, no, but everything I saw had all the earmarks of the outfit."

"Why would IDC be in business with the underworld?"

"Why don't you ask IDC?"

The line hummed. That meant that Harold Smith was thinking. Remo leaned an arm against the stainless-steel acoustical shield of the pay phone. His face, showing in the polished steel, was reflected as if in a crazy house mirror. The warped effect was not enough to hide the fact that there was a lump in the center of Remo's forehead as big as a walnut. Remo touched it. It felt firm, but with a trace of rubberiness. He hoped it wasn't a tumor. He had had the thing ever since returning from the Gulf. He knew something strange had happened to him there. He didn't know what. It was like there was a blank spot in his memory. But somehow he had gotten the lump—whatever the hell it was—during that blank period.

Presently Harold Smith asked a question.

"You say all you saw was a personal computer?"

"That's right. Like yours, except it had an IDC plate on it."

"And you destroyed it?"

"I think the technical term is 'shitcanning,'" Remo said dryly.

"Whatever. And you have no idea what this may be about?"

"IDC did give me a book, but I barely glanced at it. It was written in some dialect of English I never saw before."

"A software manual."

"If you say so," Remo said, fingering the lump on his forehead absently. "I left that with the goon squad."

"Do you recall the program title?" asked Smith.

"It began with an L and ended with two capital I's. Or maybe they were the Roman numeral two, I couldn't tell. When I saw that, I knew the rest of the book was hopeless."

"Two I's as in Ascii?"

"Spell it."

"A-s-c-i-i,"

"Yeah, like that, only it began with an L."

"That makes no sense. Ascii is a technical term for a plain-text file."

"I don't understand plain-text file," Remo admitted, "and it sounds almost like English."

Remo detected the sounds of keystrokes coming over the wire. Then Smith said, "Remo, according to my data base, the Boston Mafia is in disarray. I do not even have a record of a capo currently in charge."

"His name is Fuggin," Remo said dryly.

"Spell that."

"Your guess is as good as mine," Remo said.

More keystrokes. Then Smith said, "I have no name remotely like that in my files. It's inconceivable that the Mafia would allow an unknown person to assume leadership of their New England operation."

"That's the name I got."

"Remo," said Smith, "can you find your way back to this place?"

"I think so. It's near the airport."

"Attempt to penetrate the place tonight. Recover the computer. Alert me once you have possession. And above all, leave no trace of your penetration."

"Gotcha. By the way, I may need your help."

"In what way?"

"In placating Chiun. IDC hustled me to the airport so fast I couldn't get word to him. The line was tied up. His soap operas, I figure."

"Actually, Chiun and I were consulting," Smith said vaguely.

"Really? Care to fill me in?"

"You'll be briefed once you have executed your mission."

"You're a pal. But do me a favor. Tell Chiun I tried."

"I will communicate your concerns to the Master of Sinanju."

"Let's hope he's still talking to me when I get back," Remo said, hanging up the phone.

Remo scouted for a taxicab. He spotted one that was painted a strange robin's-egg blue and maroon and flagged it down.

The cabby asked, "Where to, pal?"

"What do you call the Italian part of town?" Remo asked.

"The North End."

"Take me to the North End."

The cab whisked Remo to the most congested stretch of traffic he had ever had the misfortune to experience. Cars raced in and out of lanes as if at the Daytona 500.

Traffic settled down to a crawl once they entered a long tunnel whose white titles were gray from years of engine exhaust.

"What do you call this thing?" Remo asked after almost being sideswiped by a patrol car.

" 'The Sumner Tunnel' seems to be everyone's favorite. Although 'this fucking bottleneck' comes a close second."

"I'll go with option two. What are the odds of us surviving it?" Remo asked, feeling his brain go dead from carbon monoxide fumes.

"Poor."

"I tip better for honest. Your tip just doubled. Consider that an incentive to drive safely."

Eventually the cab emerged into sunlight and fresh air. It whipped out of the traffic flow like a pinball caroming off the side of a pinball machine. The force of it should have thrown Remo into the right-hand door, but he centered his balance, righting himself like a compass needle pointing toward the north pole.

"That felt like three G's," Remo said.

"If you don't grab that turn like a brass ring," the cabby explained, "it's hell backtracking. The artery is much worse. Not that the streets are any prize.

"How is that possible?"

"They were laid out by cows."

"I see what you mean," Remo said once they were cruising down the streets of the North End. It looked like a slice of old Italy, with high brick tenements festooned with wrought-iron fire escapes and wet wash waving on clotheslines between the narrow streets. Despite the cool weather, high windows were open and fat housewives and cigar smoking old men leaned out to watch the parade of humanity below. Outside clocks told time in Roman numerals. Green-white-and-red Italian flags waved proudly.

The side streets were narrow and crooked, and impossible to navigate by car. Double-parking seemed to be the law of the land.

"Any spot in particular?" asked the driver.

Remo noticed a Chinese restaurant on a corner and said, "Right there."

After paying the driver off, Remo pretended to start into the Chinese restaurant, then slipped around the corner.

He walked the narrow streets, trying to orient himself. He couldn't recall the name of the street the building had been on. He knew better than to ask pedestrians, knew better than to attract attention in a close-knit neighborhood such as this one.

Salem Street, off the main drag, Hanover, looked vaguely promising. It was a dark alley of dirty brick buldings that suggested they had been there forever. The soot looked eternal. The streetlamps were an ornate black iron. It was very Old World.

Remo started down it.

Even when he realized he had found the building, Remo kept on going. It was a storefont with its lower windows curtained off; the dingy glass above said "SALEM STREET SOCIAL CLUB."

Across the street a burly man sat on a wooden straight-back chair, his shirtsleeves rolled up and a package of Marlboros tucked into the left roll. A lookout.

Remo continued on as if he were a lost tourist and rounded the next corner. Here he might have been negotiating a forgotten section of town. There was a barber shop whose fixtures were so ancient they reminded him of his first haircut, a million years ago in Newark. The nuns of Saint Theresa's orphanage had taken his entire class there one Saturday. Remo could still smell the spicy odor of the hair tonic the barber had used to plaster down his wet hair, as if it were yesterday.

A lifetime ago.

Remo doubled back to Hanover Street and the Chinese restaurant, where he ordered a bowl of fluffy white rice and a glass of water. The rice was tasty, even if it was a domestic Rexoro. The water tasted like it had been hauled out of Boston harbor in a rusty pail.

He ignored the water and nursed the rice, chewing every mouthful to a starchy liquid mass before swallowing, as he waited for darkness to come.

When Remo stepped back out into the street, Hanover Street was ablaze with neon and the narrow sidwalks were choked with every type of person from priests to hookers.

It was still early, so Remo sauntered up and down twisting sidestreets and alleyways that might have been built by a coven of nineteenth-century witches. The ornate streetlamps simulated gaslights and shed a feeble light that suited Remo's nocturnal prowlings perfectly.

After the sun had set, Remo found a high black brick wall one street over from Salem and, looking both ways to be certain there were no lookouts, went up it with spidery silence.

The bricks were irregular enough to make his ascent as easy as climbing a stepladder. Remo quickly gained the roof and crossed the gravel to the opposite end.

Inland, beyond an elevated green artery, the lights of Boston blazed. The North End lay all around him, a shadowy clot of land along the waterfront that had been cut off from the city proper by the artery.

Not far behind him was the spire of Old North Church. To the north, along the coast, the angular spider's web of *Old Ironsides* wavered in the ocean breezes. The Bunker Hill monument stabbed at the stars.

Remo found himself looking down Salem Street. The social club was diagonally across the street, three buildings south. Below, the lookout still rocked back in his creaking wooden chair.

He showed signs of nodding off, which meant that he was probably just taking the air. There were no lights coming from the storefront itself.

Leaning over, Remo released a droplet of saliva onto the lookout's thick black hair.

The man was more alert than he looked. He reacted

instantly, putting his hand up and cursing in Italian when it came away wet.

"Fuckin' pigeons," he snarled as he dragged the chair indoors. A door slammed.

Above, Remo grinned. He worked his way up the street by the roofs. They were so closely packed he didn't have to jump.

When he was directly across from the storefront, he stepped back several paces and sprinted for the parapet's edge.

The street flashed under him like a dark canyon. Remo's Italian loafers made almost no sound as they made contact with the opposite building. He checked his own momentum with a twist of his upper body.

Looking around the roof, Remo discovered a trapdoor. He laid both hands on it and closed his eyes.

The weak electrical current of an ordinary burgler alarm made his sensitive fingertips tingle ever so slightly. Wired. Remo left it alone.

He walked the parapet, looking for the inevitable fire escape. He had not yet seen a building that lacked one. These were firetraps, probably built at the turn of the century—if not before—and never upgraded.

This one clung to the back of the building like exposed iron ribs. Remo's eyes, trained to pick up ambient light and magnify it, detected the faint gleam of moonlight on wires wrapped in shiny black electrical tape. Probably an electric eye or some other alarm system.

Remo decided not to fool with it. He worked his way around to one side and just went over the parapet, finding finger- and toeholds that brought him to a closed window.

It was far enough above the alley below and beneath the roof not to be wired. Just in case, Reme straddled it and examined the casement molding for any signs of wire or aluminum stripping.

Finding none, he attacked the dirt-streaked glass over the simple latch closure with one fingernail. He scored a semicircle of glass, withdrew his finger, and tapped the glass under the curve.

The semicircle cracked free, except along the base, where dried wood putty held it in place. Remo reached two fingers into the gap and extracted the glass like pulling a stubborn tooth.

He pocketed the glass and then pushed the lever open.

That was actually the easy part, he discovered.

The window had been painted shut. It was better than any lock or alarm.

To anyone else, that is.

Remo set himself, and applied controlled pressure to the edges of the lower sash. The tiny cracking and groaning told him when to move on. It took some time, but he got the sash loose enough to move.

The sash had to be eased up slowly or the dry wood would squeal and snarl. He applied upward pressure.

When Remo had an opening he could use, he lowered himself until his head was level with the sill. He slid in like a silent python coiling through a hole on a tree.

Inside, it smelled of dust and must. Remo moved through the gloom on cat feet, found a door, and eased it open.

His ears detected sounds. A steam radiator hissing. The dull roar of an electric furnace far below, probably in the basement. A mouse or rat scuttled among some papers on this floor.

There were no indications of human life. No sleeping heartbeats, no wheezing of lungs, gurgle of bowels, and other human-habitation noises.

Remo padded down two flights of stairs until he reached the first floor. The food smells were heavy here. Garlic predominated. They made Remo slightly nauseous. He no longer ate meat—his digestive tract could no longer tolerate meat, thanks to the refining of his metabolism by Sinanju—and the scent repelled him.

When Remo oriented himself with the alley, he knew which door was the one he wanted. He stepped off the bottom stair and floated toward it.

He had no warning. None of his senses picked up anything. But suddenly an alarm buzzer snarled at him.

Remo moved fast. He hit the door with the flat of his hand, pushing it off its hinges and lock. He caught it before it crashed to the floor and set it against a wall.

In the darkness, his eyes raked the gloom.

"Where the hell is it?" he muttered.

Remo found the wastebasket in a corner. He grabbed it up. Empty.

He whirled. The buzzer continued buzzing. Another had joined it. That meant a second alarm in this room. He didn't know what had tripped it, but there was no time to worry about it.

Remo swept the room. The card table was empty. He decided to check the trash barrels outside. He went to the exit door and kicked it open. A hasp and padlock sprang apart with a bluish spark. Moonlight slanted in like an ethereal curtain.

Remo heard them coming up the alley before he stepped out into it. He slid off to one side and let them come.

There were two. Their fast-pumping hearts told him that.

"See anything?" one hissed.

"No. Just the door."

"You go first."

"Screw you. You go first."

"Okay, we'll both go. Get on the other side of the door."

A shadow crossed the spray of moonbeams at the door. Remo spotted the other one setting himself at the side of the open door. He had a revolver up in one hand. The other came up, making one finger, then two. Remo figured three was the signal.

He was right.

Shouting, they plunged in. One turned on a flash.

And while they were blinking into the backglow of the flashlight, Remo slipped out the door behind them and went up the brick wall like a teardrop in retreat.

He got down on the gravel of the roof and lay flat, figuring to wait them out.

It was a good plan. But he got no cooperation. Other men arrived. A black Cadillac turned into the alley and all four doors opened at once.

Remo waited for the excitement to settle down. When someone started to push on the roof trap, Remo rolled to his feet and glided to the parapet.

He made the leap to the opposite side of Salem Street from a standing start, rolled when he hit, and lay flat as he listened to the humming sounds of the Boston night.

The trap banged open. Remo caught a glimpse of the pale

fan of a flashlight poking about the other roof. A voice called down, "It's clean."

Another voice called up hollowly, "Okay, come down."

After a few minutes, Remo felt it safe to slip along the rooftops. He climbed down at the dark end of the street, and moving with eerie stealth, worked his way unseen from the North End.

9

Harold Smith was saying, "At a guess, you encountered a motion-sensitive alarm. They are quite common, capable of detecting minute changes in the air pressure of the secure environment being monitored. If disturbed by so much as a housefly, the alarm is triggered."

"The Mafia is getting more sophisticated in everything except choice of real estate." Remo frowned. He had found a pay phone in the shadow of Faneuil Hall, which smelled like a fish-processing plant. Traffic hummed on the nearby central artery. "Why don't I stick around and try again tonight?"

"No. They will be prepared for you."

"No one is prepared for me," Remo said. "This time I'll just—"

"Return for debriefing, Remo. This is a serious problem. As yet, we have only the skeletal outline of its nature. Before we blunder in any further, I would like to know what we're dealing with."

"The Mafia. What's so complicated about that?"

"Remo," Harold Smith said steadily, "if the Mafia is attempting to infiltrate IDC, the consequences would be catastrophic. All over this country, organized crime is on the run. More and more, those persons are taking refuge in legitimate or semilegitimate business enterprises. But if they are insinuating themselves into IDC, they will have virtually compromised American business as we know it, from the boardrooms to Wall Street. This cannot be allowed."

"So? I go in and crack skulls. Warn them off. The Mafia will understand that. It's their language."

"No. This calls for surgery."

"Speaking of surgery, this lump on my forehead is starting to worry me. It won't go away. In fact, I'd swear it's growing."

"Perhaps it is time we take care of that too," said Smith crisply. "While we consider a fresh plan of attack."

"What about that computer? We can't just leave it."

"You mentioned earlier that the voice coming from the other room asked for a Japanese technician."

"Yeah? So?"

"Perhaps Chiun will be able to accomplish what you could not."

Remo laughed once shortly. "Smitty, there is only one problem with that little scheme."

"And what is that?"

"Convincing Chiun to pass as Japanese long enough to pull it off. It's a complete impossibility."

"Return to Folcroft, Remo," said Smith sharply.

"Can I come in the front door this time?"

"As long as you do it before daybreak. I will be here."

"On my way," said Remo, hanging up the pay phone and looking around for a taxi.

The taxis of Boston seemed to have gone into hibernation, so Remo decided to walk to the airport, which was not far away. He did not look forward to facing Chiun. It was funny how quickly he had fallen back into his old habit of taking the Master of Sinanju for granted. For over three months, Chiun had been believed dead and Remo had been like a lost child without him.

Remo decided to throw himself on Chiun's mercy. What was the worst he could do?

At Folcroft Sanitarium, Harold Smith replaced the blue contact telephone and turned his leather chair around to face the Master of Sinanju.

"He is on his way back," said Smith.

Chiun regarded Harold Smith with brittle hazel eyes.

"What must be done must be done," he intoned.

"Are you certain he will not be harmed by the operation?"

The Master of Sinanju shrugged his thin shoulders. "He is Remo. He is unpredictable. Who can say how he will react?"

"Then you agree this is the only way?"

"You are the emperor. Remo is your tool. It is your privilege to shape your tool as you see fit."

"I am pleased you see it that way." Smith reached for the intercom. "It is time to alert the surgeon."

Chiun intercepted Smith's hand with his own.

"Before this is done, allow me to present you with several sketches I have made, the better to guide the skilled hands of the physician as he goes about his important work."

From one sleeve of his kimono Chiun withdrew a sheaf of parchments rolled tightly together. With a flourish, he presented them to Harold Smith.

Smith spread them open on the desk. After a quick examination, he looked up.

"I hardly think Remo would be happy with any of these faces," Smith said with dry disapproval.

Chiun shrugged. "Remo is determined to be unhappy, whatever comes. What matter the degree of his unhappiness?"

"I would prefer a more Caucasian look. For operational reasons, of course," Smith added quickly.

Chiun snatched up the parchment drawings.

"Racist!" he spat.

"I do want you to monitor the operation, Master Chiun," said Harold Smith hastily, adjusting the knot in his tie. "To ensure that all goes smoothly."

"Perhaps the surgeon of plastic will see the wisdom of my selections."

"I somehow doubt it," said Smith, clearing his throat.

"It is possible."

"He will be under strict instructions to resculpture Remo's features, not change them utterly. But I am concerned with the lump on Remo's forehead."

Chiun's eyes narrowed. "It is the eye of Shiva. Now closed. Remo does not suspect it for what it is."

"Does Remo have any idea of his recent personality . . . uh . . . change?"

"None. His mind is a blank. It is always a blank, of course, but this time the blankness is total. He remembers his days of slavery to the goddess Kali, but prefers not to speak of this."

Harold Smith regarded the wispy figure of the Master of Sinanju. He hesitated to probe further. When he had taken on the awesome responsibility of CURE, he took on with it the operational obligation to obliterate the organization and all traces of it—including all personnel—should CURE ever be compromised.

When, years ago, he had framed Remo Williams for a murder he had not committed, it had been to create an untraceable and expendable enforcement arm. Remo had been placed in Chiun's hands, to be taught the rudiments of Sinanju, to create the perfect assassin. A man who no longer existed.

It was a perfect plan. As conceived. Chiun would return to his village after training Remo—a critical link in the CURE chain forever severed. Chiun had been eighty then, twenty years ago. With his eventual death, there would be one fewer brain housing the knowledge of CURE, which was limited to Smith, Remo, and the incumbent President.

But an unexpected thing had happened. Chiun had grown to care for Remo. The teacher had become a part of CURE. Not because Smith had wanted it that way, but because there was no way to prevent it. Chiun had insisted that training a white man in the fundamentals of Sinanju was a fifteen-year commitment. Minimum.

Thus Smith had acquired two enforcement arms, paid for by an annual shipment of gold to the desolate village of Sinanju, on the coast of forbidding North Korea.

The bond between Remo and Chiun had been something Smith had not always understood. There had been a prophecy in the annals of the House of Sinanju, a legend that foretold of a Master who would one day train a white man, the dead night tiger, who would be the avatar to Shiva, known to the followers of Hinduism as the God of Destruction.

Chiun believed Remo was this foretold Sinanju Destroyer. Smith had never accepted any of it.

But recent events had proved to Smith that Remo was more than Remo now. More, perhaps, than even Sinanju. It was clear that he was subject to personality shifts. Shifts he never seemed to remember.

Smith no more believed in Shiva the Destroyer than he did in the Jolly Green Giant, but something was bubbling deep within Remo's psyche. Something that threatened to one day break free and overwhelm him.

Such a prospect threatened not only CURE but also the world. Smith had seen the awesome power of the unleashed

Remo for himself. There would be no controlling him should the Remo aspect of his personality ever be totally submerged.

Smith had to know. Even if the truth meant shutting down CURE, terminating Remo. And incidentally swallowing a cyanide pill that would also extinguish his own life.

"Do you foresee this event recurring?" Smith asked the Master of Sinanju carefully.

"Before the Great Lord Shiva surrendered Remo's body, he told me—"

Smith's gray eyes made circles of surprise. "He *spoke* to you?"

"Yes. And he said that the hour would one day come that he would claim Remo as his throne. But that hour was far off, he also said."

"Er, how far?"

"Shiva did not say."

Smith's prim mouth tightened. The Master of Sinanju caught the thinning reflex.

"I know what you are thinking, Emperor," said Chiun.

"You do?"

Chiun nodded. "You are thinking that this spirit which Remo harbors may threaten your realm."

"In a manner of speaking," Smith admitted. He was not comfortable with Chiun's repeated references to his emperorship, but Masters of Sinanju had served as royal assassins going back to the days of the pharaohs. Since Chiun served America through Smith, Smith must therefore be addressed as an emperor.

"And you wonder if you should not extinguish Remo in order to prevent this calamity from coming to pass," Chiun continued.

"My responsibilities—" Smith began.

Chiun raised a wise finger. "Then know this. Shiva grows within Remo. In the past, he has been roused only when Remo's existence was threatened. Should you attempt to harm my son, Shiva will return to protect his own. It is better that you stay your hand, otherwise you will precipitate the very calamity you seek to avoid."

"I see," Smith said slowly. "But what about you, Master Chiun? Remo is as much as a son to you. He is the heir to the House of Sinanju. Does Shiva not threaten the line?"

Chiun bowed his head in the dimness of Smith's Spartan office.

"He does. But I am an old man who has been blessed with the greatest pupil any Master of Sinanju ever had. Yet I am also cursed to know that in my accomplishment I have sown the seeds that doom all I hold dear. But what can I do? I am an old man. You are my emperor. And Remo is Remo. But Lord Shiva is more powerful that us all."

And Harold Smith, who had personally seen the Master of Sinanju tear through a small army like a buzz saw, felt a thrill of supernatural fear course down his spine.

10

Remo Williams sent his rented car into a copse of poplars several hundred yards short of the gates of Folcroft Sanitarium. He made his way to the closed gate on foot.

There were two stone lions atop the gate. They seemed to stare down at him like sentinels excavated from some half-forgotten civilization.

Grinning, Remo simply leapt sixteen feet into the air and landed atop the right-hand lion.

He paused and seemed to float to the ground on the other side.

There was a security guard at a lobby desk, his face buried in a newspaper. Remo slipped in and, staying out of the guard's peripheral range, his movements contained so that he made no attention-getting motions, made his way to the elevator and the second floor.

Remo walked into Harold Smith's office unannounced.

Harold W. Smith looked up from his computer, a startled expression on his face. Reflexively he stabbed a stud hidden under the oak rim. The desktop terminal retreated into his desk well like a shy plastic skull.

"Remo, you startled me," Smith said, flustered.

"Sorry," Remo said, looking around. He sensed another presence.

He pulled the door back and peered behind it. He saw only a blot of shadow. Empty.

"Is Chiun here?" Remo asked suspiciously.

"He is in the building," Smith said evasively. "He expressed an interest in monitoring the operation."

"Okay," Remo said, stepping in. "But before we get to it, let's establish some ground rules."

"I am listening."

"I'm going under the knife. But only to get rid of this freaking lump, whatever it is."

"That is the purpose of the procedure," Smith said.

"*Not* to have my face lifted."

Smith said nothing.

"You're a man of your word, Smith. So before we get to it, I need you to raise your right hand and swear on a stack of computer printouts that the doctor isn't going to get fancy with my face."

Smith swallowed.

"Is that a guilty look I see?" Remo asked suddenly.

"No, I, er, was just wondering if I had a Bible in the office."

Remo frowned. "Bible?"

"You *do* want me to swear an oath, do you not?"

Concern made Remo's cruel mouth quirk up. "Yeah. But—"

"It is properly done with a Bible."

"We could skip the Bible part," Remo started to say.

"Without it, there would be no true oath."

"Okay, then we hunt up a Bible," Remo said with sudden impatience. "Let's just get this over with, okay?"

"Perhaps," said Smith, reaching into a desk drawer, "perhaps I might have one in my desk."

The odd strained tone that had come into Harold W. Smith's lemony voice was enough to tip off Remo that something was not quite right.

He started for the desk, his features darkening.

"What's with you, Smith?" Remo demanded, once he reached Smith's side. "You're acting more Henny Penny than usual."

Smith's mouth opened to protest. And froze.

Remo heard no sound. He sensed nothing out of the ordinary. He had a momentary impression of the unfamiliar, but that was all.

It was just beginning to register on Remo that the strangeness was the cool breeze coming in through the unreplaced plate-glass window when a long-nailed hand the color of old ivory reached out of the impenetrable night to take him by the back of the neck.

Fingers like the bones of a skeletal hand squeezed inexorably.

The last thought that went through Remo's startled helpless mind was: Nice move, Remo. You fell for an old one!

The Master of Sinanju slipped over the windowsill, trailing the skirt of his black kimono. He regarded his pupil with an austere countenance.

"He is ready," he intoned.

"Thank you, Master Chiun," said Smith, looking down. "It would have been awkward had I been forced to promise Remo immunity from the plastic surgeon's scalpel."

Chiun bent down and gathered up Remo's sleeping form like that of an overgrown child. He started for the open door. "Come. It will be awkward enough when Remo awakens with a new face."

Dr. Rance Axeworthy was tired of waiting.

He was the finest knife man in Beverly Hills. It was bad enough that he had been compelled to fly all the way across the country to perform a simple face lift. Normally his patients came to him.

It was bad enough that he was told by the man who ran the institution—the lemon-voiced Smith—that he would not be allowed to consult with his patient before performing the operation. That was unheard-of, if not unethical. As the plastic surgeon to the stars, he was used to ignoring professional ethics.

But to be kept waiting in the operating amphitheater was unconscionable. He had been gowned and washed forever.

Even if he was being paid triple his typically exorbitant fee.

Dr. Axeworthy understood that the patient was a candidate for the witness-protection program. It was intriguing. He had never before worked on a crime figure—unless one counted the odd drug dealer. Not a crime figure in his sphere of activity. Drug dealers were simply entrepreneurs forced to operate on society's fringes because of the stupid laws of this unprogressive nation.

So Dr. Axeworthy had come. But that didn't mean he would wait around all night. He needed a hit of crank.

When the operating-room doors opened, Dr. Axeworthy looked up from his copy of *Variety*.

Under his bushy black eyebrows, his jet eyes widened.

"What on earth!" he exclaimed.

There were three of them. A gray-faced man in an equally gray suit, some sort of costumed Asian person, and a prone figure that had to be the patient.

The patient lay on a wheeled gurney.

"Are you people sterile?" he demanded angrily, instantly asserting dominion over the operating room.

"Hold your tongue, plastic physician," squeaked the tiny Asian. "You are here to perform a service, not ask personal questions."

Dr. Axeworthy blinked. He started to say something else, but professional interest in his patient diverted his attention.

The old Oriental shook off his long colorful sleeves and took up the patient as if he were hollow. The patient was deposited on the stainless-steel operating table with studied gentleness.

Axeworthy's professional instincts took over.

"Hmmm. Good pronounced cheekbones. Strong nose. I like the chin."

"Can you fix the eyes?" asked the Asian man worriedly.

"In what way?" said Axeworthy, lifting each eyelid in turn, noting the irises were dark brown, almost black. The whites were unusually clear and devoid of visible veining.

"In this way," said the Asian, slapping away the doctor's hand and using his fingers to draw the outer corners of the patient's eyes more tightly.

"You want me to make him Chinese?" asked Dr. Axeworthy, lifting his own eyebrows.

"I would sooner you give him the nose of a pig," spat the Asian.

"Then what?"

"I am Korean. So should this man be Korean."

Frowning, Dr. Axeworthy compared the patient's eyes to those of the tiny Asian. They were hazel, an unusual eye coloration in Asians.

"It can be done," he said after a long silence.

"But it won't be," said the man in gray. Axeworthy instantly recognized the voice. It was the lemony Dr. Smith.

"Smith?"

Smith nodded. "This must be done immediately," he said brittlely. "I do not care about the particulars. But I want him unrecognizable. And Caucasian. Is that understood?"

"Absolutely," said Dr. Axeworthy, for the first time noticing the odd lump on the patient's forehead. "Is this a tumor?"

"Yes," said Smith.

"No," said the Asian.

Axeworthy looked at the pair quizzically.

"It must be removed as well," Smith added.

Axeworthy felt the odd protuberance carefully. "It appears fibroid. Probably precancerous. At least, one trusts so. Oncology is not my field."

"The patient has been rendered insensate by nonchemical means," Smith said coldly. "I am assured that he will remain in this state for the duration of the operation. Any use of anesthetic is strictly forbidden."

Dr. Rance Axeworthy nodded. "Allergic. I understand."

"If you fail, you will be punished severely," warned the Asian man.

Dr. Axeworthy drew himself up stiffly. "I resent that! What do you think I am? A butcher?"

"No," said Smith hastily. "You are the finest plastic surgeon in the country, if not the world."

Dr. Axeworthy assumed a pained expression. "Please. I am a cosmetic surgeon. 'Plastic' sounds so . . . tacky."

"That is why you have been summoned here," Smith continued. "And that is why you are being paid handsomely for your services. If you require me for any reason, I will be in my office."

Dr. Axeworthy looked down at the tiny Oriental, who stood resolute on the other side of the operating table.

"And you?"

"I will assist."

"You are a doctor?"

"No. But I will guide you to correctness."

"I work only with colleagues of my own choosing," Dr. Axeworthy said firmly.

Smith paused at the door. "Chiun administered the anesthetic. He will be responsible for the patient's continued state of unconsciousness."

"Acupuncture? asked Dr. Axeworthy, suddenly understanding.

"Perhaps," said the old Oriental, looking away.

Dr. Axeworthy whispered, "I've used it myself, you know. My patients love being on the cutting edge of exotic procedures."

"Please keep me informed," said Smith, closing the doors after him.

After Smith had gone, Dr. Axeworthy took up a blue surgical marking pen and began marking the patient's face, an X over the lump on the forehead and other lines to indicate preliminary incisions.

"We will start with the nose," said the tiny Oriental.

"Have you anything particular in mind?"

His hazel eyes darting to the closed double doors through which Harold Smith had disappeared, the old Asian withdrew a rolled tube of parchment from one colorful sleeve.

"I have made several designs," he confided, "all of which are usable. We have only to select the most suitable one."

"If you don't mind," said Dr. Axeworthy, "my fee is being paid by Dr. Smith. I will follow his wishes."

The old Oriental drew closer. He tugged on Dr. Axeworthy's white gown conspiratorially.

"Name your price. I will double what Smith has promised you."

"Sorry."

"What I have in mind calls for subtlety. No one will ever know. . . ."

11

Carmine (Fuggin) Imbruglia first arrived in Boston with a spring in his step, a smile on his face, and an ancient brass key clamped in one beefy hand.

A car was waiting to meet him outside the Rumpp Shuttle terminal. It was a Cadillac. As black as caviar. A present from Don Fiavorante.

There was a cop hovering by the Cadillac, looking unhappy.

"Is this your vehicle, sir?" he asked.

"What of it, Irish?" The guy looked Irish. Carmine hated Irish cops. They were all drunk with power.

"It shouldn't be here. This is a bus stop."

"So I'm a fuggin' scofflaw. Sue me."

Silently the cop carefully wrote out a ticket and slipped it under a windshield wiper. He started away.

Carmine wadded it up and tossed it past the Irish cop's shoulder and into a green wire trash basket.

"I laugh at parkin' tickets, copper. Back in Brooklyn, I usta wallpaper my john with these things. And when I ran out of wall, I'd tape 'em together and hang 'em up on a hook by the commode. Get the picture?"

The cop kept walking.

"I'm gonna rule this town," Carmine said as he settled into the back of the Caddy.

"First thing we're gonna do," he told his driver during the ride in, "is muscle in on the construction. I hear this town is positively booming."

"Not no more."

"Whatdya mean?"

"There's no construction."

"What is it—the fuggin' off season? Like huntin'? They only build when the weather's nice?"

The driver shrugged his side-of-beef shoulders. "They just stopped building."

"When the fug did this calamity happen?"

"After the last governor lost the presidential election."

"The Greek? Okay, so there's no construction. It'll come back after the shock wears off. So can we get in on the ponies? Set up a nice horse parlor?"

"No horses up here. Only trotters. And they stopped runnin' the trotters a couple of years back when they closed Suffolk Downs."

"No horses? What kinda burg is this?"

"The dogs are still runnin', though. Over at Wonderland."

"Dogs! Who the hell plays the dogs?"

"Up here," said the driver, "all the guys that used to play the ponies."

"You can't fix a dog race. No jockeys. What about the sports book? I hear this is a big, big sports town."

"Well, the Red Sox are in the cellar, where they've been for the last hundred years, the Celtics are losers, the Patriots are threatening to leave the state, but the Bruins are playin' good."

"I never heard of these Broons. What are they—jai alai?"

"They're hockey."

"I never head of a hockey book in my entire life. What about shylocking?" asked a suddenly subdued Carmine Imbruglia. "Surely that ain't dead."

"You can shylock all you want up here. Lots of guys need the dough."

"Great. It's settled. We shylock."

"Of course, with unemployment bein' what it is, collectin' is gonna be another matter entirely."

"Don't you worry. I know how to collect," said Carmine Imbruglia. "By the way, what's your name, pal?"

"Bruno. Bruno Boyardi. They call me 'Chef.' "

"Chef, huh? Can you cook?"

"That's how I been supportin' myself until I got the word you were takin' over."

"Hey, that's pretty funny," chortled Carmine Imbruglia. "I like a guy with a sensa humor."

Behind the wheel, Bruno (The Chef) Boyardi sat with a

stony expression. He hoped there was money in shylocking. He hated restaurant work. It made his hair greasy.

They had emerged from a long tunnel that seemed to be perfumed with carbon monoxide. Carmine looked around. The storefronts were surprisingly bare. Many were empty.

"How's the restaurant trade doin'?" he wondered aloud. "Can we get in on that? Do a little shakedown on the side?"

"What little there's left of it is sucked dry."

Carmine leaned over the front seat. "What you mean, 'what little there's left of it'? This is fuggin' Massachusetts, land of fuggin' Miracles."

"Not no more, it ain't," said Chef Boyardi.

Carmine watched the endless blocks of vacant storefronts pass by his window. Two in three had windows that were papered in faded newsprint and hung with "CLOSED" or "FOR LEASE" signs.

"What happened to this town. An earthquake?"

"No one's sure," said Bruno the Chef. "Ever since the Greek lost the election, this whole territory has gone to hell. It was like a balloon that had been pumped up too much and exploded."

Carmine made shooing motions with both hands. "It'll come back. It'll come back. Don't you worry. I'm kingpin of this town and I'm tellin' you it'll come back."

Carmine Imbruglia's first sight of the North End brought the broad smile back to his face. It was a slice of Little Italy. Even the pungent aromas were identical.

"Say, this is more like it," he said happily.

The Salem Street Social Club was more to his liking too.

Carmine strode up to the front door, and after inserting the ancient brass key in the lock, turned it.

He stepped in. His heart swelled. It was just like the old Neighborhood Improvement Association. Only it was his, and his alone.

The back room was simply furnished. There were a card table and a great black four-burner stove with a double oven. The kind they had in restaurants.

Carmine Imbruglia's pig eyes fell on the computer terminal that sat square in the middle of the card table.

"What the fug is that thing doin' there?" he wanted to know.

"It's a computer, boss."

"I know it's a fuggin' computer. I asked what the fug is it doin' here, not what its species was."

"It's a present from Don Fiavorante. Here's the instruction book."

Don Carmine accepted the blue leather notebook. He squinted at the cover, which had stamped in silver the strange word "LANSCII."

"Is this Pilgrim, or what?" he muttered.

"I think it's computerese."

"Computerese? What does Don Fiavorante think we're runnin' up here, fuggin' IDC? Get rid of it."

"Can't. Don Fiavorante's orders."

Don Carmine tossed the book back onto the table. "Ah, I'll worry about it later. Go hustle me some lunch."

"What'll you have?"

"Pizza. A nice hot pizza. Everything on it."

"Squid rings too?"

Carmine turned like a tugboat coming around. "Squid rings? Whoever heard of squid rings on pizza? Hell, if that's how they do it in Boston, pile 'em on. I'll try anything once. Some vino. And some cannoli. Fresh ones. Don't let 'em give you day-old."

"Don't worry. I'm going to the restaurant where I work nights."

"After you get the food, give 'em your notice. Nobody moonlights anymore. This ain't the fuggin' merchant marine I'm runnin' here."

When the food came, Don Carmine Imbruglia took one look at the pizza and went white with rage.

"What the fug is this? Where's the tomato sauce? And the cheese? Don't they have cows up here? Look at that crust. This fuggin' pie is all crust."

"That's how they do pizzas up here. Taste it. You might like it."

Carmine tore off the point of one dripping slice with his teeth. He spat it out again.

"Tastes like cardboard!" he said between explosions of dry crust.

"Sorry. Have some vino," said Bruno the Chef, pouring.

Carmine waved him away. "I can always drink later. I'm

hungry." He lifted a cannoli to his mouth. He bit down. The brittle shell cracked apart. He tasted the sickly green filling.

And promptly spat it on the linoleum floor.

"What'd they fill these things with—used toothpaste?"

"This is Boston, boss. It's not like New York. They do things a little different up here."

"They don't do them good at all! Get rid of this junk and get me some real food."

"What kind?"

Don Carmine jerked a thumb at the heavy black stove.

"You're the fuggin' chef. Fuggin' surprise me."

Over a puffy calzone bursting with pinkish-gray tentacles salvaged from the pizza, Don Carmine began to feel better about Boston.

"So where are my soldiers?" he asked, shoving a rubbery tendril of squid into his mouth with a greasy thumb.

"I'm it."

Carmine's apish jaw dropped. The tentacle slithered back onto the plate. "Where's the rest of my fuggin' crew?" he demanded hotly.

"Dead or in jail. Rico."

"Them fuggin' Puerto Ricans are everywhere. Hey, what am I worried about? I can make guys now. I'm a fuggin' don. I'm absolute boss of Boston. I need soldiers, I'll just make 'em."

"I know some guys. Vinnie the Maggot. Bugs. Toe Biter—"

Carmine's face assumed a doubtful expression. "With names like those, make sure they got all their shots before you bring 'em around," he said. "Got that?"

At that moment the phone rang.

As Don Carmine resumed his meal, Chef Boyardi went to answer the phone.

"This squid tastes a little gamy," Don Carmine muttered. "You sure they didn't stick you with octopus?"

"I asked for squid."

"Tastes like fuggin' octopus."

"Yeah?" Bruno (The Chef) Boyardi said into the telephone. "Yeah, he is. Boss, it's for you." The Chef clapped a hand over the ancient black Bakelite mouthpiece. "It's Don Fiavorante."

Carmine grabbed the phone.

"Hello?" he said through a mouthful of tentacular matter.

"Don Carmine. How is my friend this day?" came Don Fiavorante's smooth-as-suntan-oil voice.

"It's great up here," Carmine lied. "Really wonderful."

"You have seen the computer?"

"Yeah, yeah. Nice. Appreciate it. Always wanted one of my own."

"Good, good. You will need it to keep track of your rent payments."

Carmine stopped chewing. "Rent?"

"Rent is due Friday. Every Friday you must pay me twenty thousand dollars for the privilege of running Boston."

Don Carmine gulped. "I may need a few weeks to get on the ball here—"

"Every Friday. The next Friday is two days from now."

"But I don't got that kind of money. I just got here!"

"If you cannot pay me twenty thousand dollars on this first Friday," said Don Fiavorante, "I will understand."

"That's good, because I barely blew into town."

"However, if you cannot pay your first week's rent, then you must pay me forty thousand on the following Friday."

"Forty!"

"Plus, of course, your second week's rent of twenty thousand dollars."

"But that's sixty thousand bucks!" exploded Don Carmine Imbruglia. He wiped spittle off the mouthpiece with his sleeve.

"And if you cannot pay on the second Friday, that, too, I will understand. So on the following Friday after that, your combined rent will be, for the first two Fridays, eighty thousand dollars. Plus of course the third-Friday rent."

Don Carmine felt the room spinning. He had never seen that kind of money in his entire life. "What if I can't pay on the third Friday?" he wailed.

"This is not done, and I know you will not fail to repay the trust I have placed in you, Don Carmine, my good friend, to whom I owe my current high estate."

Carmine swallowed a tentacle tip that his tongue discovered wedged between two loose molars.

"I will do as you say, Don Fiavorante," he gulped.

"I know that you will, Don Carmine. I know that you will. Now, all you need to get started you will find in the blue book called 'LANSCII.' "

"That name sounds kind of familiar," Carmine muttered vaguely.

"It should. You have any trouble with the system, you just call the number inside the cover. Ask for Tony."

"Tony. Got that."

"Tony is a friend of mine. He will help you."

"Any friend of yours is a friend of mine too. You know that."

"You are a good boy, Don Carmine," said Don Fiavorante. "I know you will not let me down. The future of this thing of ours is in your hands."

The line went dead.

Don Carmine Imbruglia hung up. Woodenly he walked over to his unfinished meal. With a sweep of his arms he cleared it from the table.

"You don't like my calzone?" asked Bruno (the Chef) Boyardi.

"It tastes like fuggin' octopus," snarled Carmine Imbruglia, dragging the computer terminal over to the place where his plate had been. "I got no time to eat anyway. I just hit town and I'm already twenty G's in the fuggin' hole."

He squinted at his brutish reflection in the terminal screen.

"Oh, mother of God," he said hoarsely.

"What? What?"

"I don't see any channel changer on this thing. I think we got a defective computer. Where did Don Fiavorante get this pile of junk, anyway?"

"Maybe the changer fell off when it fell off the truck."

12

Dr. Rance Axeworthy made the unpleasant discovery less than an hour into the operation.

"This man has had plastic surgery before," he muttered, discovering the telltale scars behind the ears.

"Many times," said the tiny Oriental.

"Then I shouldn't be doing this. Repeating the procedure can have a catastrophic effect on the plastic tissues. Odd that there is so little scarring."

"He heals well."

Dr. Axeworthy paused. He attempted to calculate the risks of facial scarring. High. The chance of a malpractice suit. Low. This was too irregular an arrangement for anyone to sue. Then he recalled the exact sum of his fee.

"I was going to bring out the cheeks," he said thoughtfully, "but I see that this has been done. I will instead fill out the face somewhat. Resculpture the ears. Ears are a telltale identifying mark."

"I am more concerned with the eyes," said the old Oriental.

"I have my orders," Dr. Axeworthy said stiffly.

"A slight tightening of the corners would not be noticed," the tiny man said hopefully.

"I'm going to have to do something to effect an overall change," said Dr. Axeworthy, as if he had not heard.

He stared at the strong face in repose. He could not believe that he was operating without qualified assistance. Still, the fee more than made up for that slight inconvenience.

The patient's earlier history created enormous problems. This required more time. And because there was no time, he remarked, "I'm going to remove the tumor while I think this through."

He injected a strong nerve block into the lump, to further ensure no regrettable complications, such as the patient waking up in hysterics. Tracing the blue ink marking, he made a simple X with the scalpel, bringing forth surprisingly little blood. Using a Metzenbaum scissors, he laid the four triangular flaps of skin aside.

What he saw made him gasp and nearly drop the scalpel.

"Good Lord!"

The old Oriental leaned in to peer at the exposed anomaly.

"Ah, the orb of Shiva," he breathed.

"My God. That can't be a tumor. Can it?"

"It is not."

"It looks almost like . . . an organ."

Using a blunt probe, Dr. Axeworthy touched the thing.

It was soft, like a human eye. Only it was as black as a gelatinous marble. There was no retina or iris. No white at all. No sign of veining. It could not be an eye, he told himself. It looked more like a great black fish egg.

Still, Dr. Axeworthy held his breath as he painstakingly extracted the black orblike thing from its raw pink cavity, looking for the telltale grayish eye-controlling rictus muscles he would have to sever if his worst fears were true.

They were not. Once the thing was out, the clean flat bone of the forehead showed underneath. There was no socket.

Dr. Axeworthy laid the black orb on a stainless-steel tray, dripping with bright red blood.

Carefully he sutured the expert X in the patient's forehead, keeping his worried eyes averted from the extracted orb. He could not bear to look at it, and because of his unprofessional timidity, he failed to notice that the orb had begun to glow a faint violet color.

Dawn had turned Long Island Sound into a quaking lake of burning red and orange by the time Dr. Axeworthy had laid down his bloody scalpel and had begun bandaging the patient's new face.

"It is done?" asked the old Oriental curiously.

"I did the best that I could."

"The eyes must be just so."

"I can't guarantee the eyes," Dr. Axeworthy said testily. "But I did reduce the nose."

The old Oriental watched the last pale winding of gauze swallow the freshly washed tip of the patient's nose and said darkly, "It is still of freakish size."

"Anything more extreme and he would not look normal," remarked Dr. Axeworthy, cutting off the gauze spool and anchoring the trailing end under the chin with a tiny clamp. He stepped back.

"When he wakes up, he will be in excruciating pain."

"He will transcend it. For he is my son."

Dr. Axeworthy's virile eyebrows lifted. "That explains your eagerness to bring out your side of the family."

"His ugliness had been a source of deep pain to me," the old Oriental said sadly. "It sent his mother to an early grave." He brushed at one eye.

"I see. Please inform Dr. Smith—if that is his true name—that the procedure has been completed."

The old Oriental padded from the operating room with the easy silence of a ghost.

After he had departed, Dr. Axeworthy gathered up his instruments. His eyes went to the black thing. He blinked at it.

Was it imagination, or was the orb glowing like a black light bulb? He reached for it curiously. . . .

Dr. Harold W. Smith was supervising the workmen as they were completing the installation of the new office window when the Master of Sinanju entered the office.

Smith lifted a hand to silence the words about to emerge from the old Korean's papery lips.

His eyes on the workmen, Chiun floated up to Smith, who bent his head sideways to catch the whispered words.

"It is done."

"Good," whispered Smith.

"Do I eliminate the doctor?"

"No!" hissed Smith.

"This was always done before," Chiun pointed out.

"Not here."

One of the workmen looked over from the window. "We're about done here."

"Excellent." Smith cleared his throat. "You may leave now."

"Funny thing," one of the workmen called over. "I've been installing windows for a lot of years. This is the first time I ever had to put a trick one in."

"This is a private hospital," Smith told him, thinking quickly. "Boaters have been caught training binoculars on the windows facing the shore. Since extremely delicate patient interviews are conducted in this room, we are concerned about lip readers gleaning highly intimate details about our patients."

"Guess you can't be too careful, huh?"

Chiun tugged at Smith's gray sleeve. Smith leaned over slightly.

"He suspects," hissed the Master of Sinanju. "Shall I dispatch him and his confederate here and now, or shall we await a more profitable opportunity, when no blame will be attached to us?"

"No!" said Smith from behind a thin hand.

"This has been done before," Chiun suggested.

"They can be traced to this office," Smith said huskily.

Chiun frowned like an unhappy mummy.

After the window installers had departed, Smith turned to the Master of Sinanju and said, "I must speak with Dr. Axeworthy."

"I do not trust him," said Chiun darkly. "I suspect him of not following your wise instructions to the letter."

"Why don't you accompany me, then?"

Chiun's hazel eyes narrowed. A light of understanding shone in their ageless depths. He understood now. Wise Emperor Harold suspected the window persons of being in league with the treacherous physician and did not wish to tip his hand.

As they took the elevator to the operating room, he thought with a contained expression that he might not have to pay the dishonest physician his promised tribute after all.

Dr. Axeworhy whirled nervously when they entered the operating room.

"Dr. Smith. Look at this. My God!"

"What is it?" Smith said, hurrying over to the operating table. "Has the patient been injured?"

Axeworthy pointed with an unsteady index finger. "This is the source of the swelling on the patient's forehead."

Smith looked where Dr. Axeworthy pointed. His gray eyes widened at the sight of the viscous black orb that was surrounded by a faint purplish halo on the stainless-steel instrument table.

"What on earth?" Smith blurted.

"I've never seen anything like it," Dr. Axeworthy said excitedly. "I've never heard of anything like it." He turned, his eyes fever-bright. "Smith, you must allow me to take possession of this organ or nodule or whatever it is."

"Why do you wish that?" asked Smith in an austere voice.

Dr. Axeworthy could not tear his eyes from the glowing object. "This thing may make medical history. I think it may be some form of vestigial organ. An organ of some new kind, perhaps. Look at it glow. It's been out of the patient for nearly three hours!"

"I am afraid I cannot allow this."

Dr. Axeworthy drew himself up stubbornly.

"And I am afraid I must insist."

"Really?" Smith's tone sank several degrees.

"I hesitate to say this, but this entire procedure has been unorthodox. I have no qualms about going to the authorities with the entire sordid story, such as I understand it."

"What do you suspect this of being?" Smith asked in a chilly voice.

"I have no idea. A criminal enterprise of some tawdry sort. I imagine Folcroft is a suitable place in which to remake notorious criminals. I am only sorry that I have been made a party to this."

"If you had these suspicions, why did you proceed with the operation?" Smith demanded.

Dr. Axeworthy hesitated. He was obviously thinking, Smith saw. The surgeon cleared his throat and said, "I was playing along. Yes, I was being a good citizen and gathering evidence so I could testify in court. Had I not performed the surgery, there would be no crime, nothing to report to the police."

Harold Smith and the Master of Sinanju exhanged glances.

"You want the . . . ah . . . organ. Is that it?" said Smith.

"And my fee, naturally. I am willing to exchange the organ for my silence."

Smith nodded to the Master of Sinanju and said, "Kill him."

The Master of Sinanju started forward, his hands coming out of his sleeves like talons.

Dr. Axeworthy almost laughed. But there was a coldness of purpose in Harold Smith's eye and a strange confidence in the advancing Oriental's strides.

Reflexively he jumped back a pace, snatching up the black orb. He was careful to cup it loosely in his half-closed fist. If it were an eye, it would be hollow and filled with fluid. He did not wish to injure the orb's organic integrity. *The New England Journal of Medicine* would demand proof or they would refuse to publish his findings.

With his other hand he placed the point of a scalpel to the unknown patient's throat, saying, "One more step and I will slit him from ear to ear!"

The old Oriental stopped in his tracks.

"Have a care," he said in a cold voice. "You know not what you threaten."

"Some cheap hood. What of it?"

Dr. Axeworthy had no sooner touched the scalpel point to the patient's throat than his hand suddenly felt cold. It was the hand that cupped the orb.

He brought it up. His fingers were uncurling like a pale sunflower opening. He was not making them uncurl. He was certain of that. They were uncurling on their own. He had nothing to do with it. And he could not stop it because his hand was suddenly numb, as if from a local anesthetic.

The orb was slowly revealed. Dr. Axeworthy found himself staring into the glowing purple-black orb.

Even though it was as featureless as a licorice drop, he experienced the eerie sensation that the eye was scrutinizing him.

Dr. Axeworthy brought the orb to his face. He didn't want to. He had no control now over his own arm. His other hand joined the first to lift the orb closer to his own widening eyes.

He screamed then.

Chiun, Reigning Master of Sinanju, beheld the look of terror on the face of the physician. It was washed in a violet radiance. He held his ground, sensing danger.

In his ear came Harold Smith's harsh voice.

"Master Chiun, what is happening?"

Before Chiun could venture an answer, the physician's upraised cupped hands began to glow from within. Through his purplish skin his finger bones shone white.

"Help . . . meee. . . ." The physcian's voice was tiny, almost squeezed down to inaudibility. "Help . . . meeeee!"

Without any warning, his hands began to melt into a lavender vapor. The vapor wafted and flowed into the physician's mouth and flaring nostrils like a viper seeking sustenence.

Chiun swept backward, pulling his emperor from the room.

"What is happening?" Smith repeated, his face stark as marble.

"It is the orb of Shiva," Chiun hissed. "It is doing the only thing it can do. Destroying."

The double doors gave before them. Chiun pushed Smith into the safety of the corridor. He turned and leaned his weight against the double doors, one hand on each.

After several seconds the Master of Sinanju put his surprised face to the round window of one door. His eyes narrowed at the sight that was transpring within the operating room.

Rooted like a lightning-lashed tree, Dr. Rance Axeworthy watched the stumps of his wrists as they melted away. He was screaming. At least his mouth was screaming and his chest heaved air in and out. But no sound was emerging from his straining lungs.

His forearms melted into gaseous exhalations, eating down to the elbows. Then the biceps went, until the last of his arms were a violet mist swirling around him.

The decay did not stop there, Chiun saw.

It continued until his head, a cloud of purple smoke, simply floated off his shoulders. The inexorable process worked its way down his chest to his waist, consuming Dr. Rance Axeworthy's torso until his legs stood apart and disarticulated.

They wobbled, tipping over. One went left. The other right. They swiftly lost all substance and then there was only a purple fog rolling along the white tile floor.

In that mist, the orb of Shiva rolled.

Smith, hearing nothing, put his patrician nose to the window of the other door.

"Where is Dr. Axeworthy?" he croaked.

"He is the mist," intoned Chiun, his eyes cold slits.

"Impossible!"

"You saw it begin with your very eyes," Chiun said. "I have seen it end. And I say that mist is the doctor."

Angrily Dr. Smith pushed his way back into the room.

Slowly he approached the operating table, where Remo lay oblivious.

His feet disturbed the mist, sending little clouds and twists and vortices eddying silently away. There was no scent, no odor at all.

In the center of the floor, the black orb glowed violet.

"What is it?" Smith asked.

Chiun approached. "The thing I have told you of. It is the third eye of Shiva. According to legend, it had the power to destroy all it beheld with its awful fury."

Smith swallowed. "Are we safe?"

Chiun's eyes narrowed to dark gleams of concern. "We are never safe from Shiva. But it did not harm the physician until he dared to threaten Remo. It should be left alone."

"We cannot just leave it there. It is too dangerous."

"I will not touch it. Nor will I allow you to do so," Chiun said firmly.

Smith pursed his lips silently. His haggard face was very pale now. His eyes had a haunted, sunken look about them.

Then, as they watched, the orb of Shiva began to collapse like a melting ice cube. It lost shape, fell in on itself, and was soon a moist black puddle resembling hot tar.

Then it just evaporated in place, becoming nothing, leaving no trace, and offering no explanation for its actions.

Harold Smith cleared his throat noisily.

"I cannot account for what I have just witnessed," he said softly.

"There is no need to," said Chiun, going to his pupil's side and examining his facial bandages for spots of blood or loose windings. "But in having Remo liberated from Shiva's third eye, we may have saved him from a premature incarnation."

Smith tore his stricken eyes from the spot on the floor where the orb of Shiva had vanished.

"Remo will be out of commission for some time," he said,

forcing his voice to remain steady. "I must count on you to accomplish his mission."

Chiun bowed formally. "If it can be accomplished by Sinanju, O Emperor, I will acomplish it for you."

"Do I have your word on this?" Smith asked.

"No sacrifice is too great to fulfill your wishes."

"Then here is what you must do. . . ."

It was fortunate that Folcroft Sanitarium housed among its patients several insane persons, because the scream of pure anguish the Master of Sinanju emitted was passed off as an inmate awakening from a particularly horrific nightmare.

13

Antony Tollini could not avoid it any longer.

All morning long, the phone messages had been piling up.

"Mr. Tollini, the Boston client said the last customer-service person had been unable to fix the problem."

"Call him back. Tell him we're sending another."

"Mr. Tollini, the Boston client says that the last person you sent not only refused to fix their system but also threw it into the trash."

"My God. Tell them I sincerely, sincerely apologize. He's a new employee. They sometimes make mistakes."

"Mr. Tollini, the Boston client says they want a Jap."

"A what?"

"A Jap. He actually said 'a fuggin' Jap,' but I think he means a Japanese technician."

"Are you sure?" Tony Tollini demanded. "Are you positive?"

"The client said something about their being good in what he called computertry."

"Do we have any Japanese applicants on file?"

"Applications are not filed by race or ethnicity. But the Boston client insists that he have a new customer service engineer today. He's very insistent."

"What were his exact words?" asked Tony Tollini from the safety of his office. He was communicating by intercom.

The secretary could be heard swallowing.

"He said, 'Don't make me look like a jerk or I'll have your fuggin' nuts.' Unquote."

"My God," moaned Tony Tollini, clutching his head. "Listen, you go through those résumés. Pull out any Japanese,

Chinese, Vietnamese names you can find. Have them all on my desk within the hour."

"Yes, Mr. Tollini."

"And send in Miss Wilkerson."

"Yes, sir."

Tony Tollini sank behind his desk in his office at the very end of the corridor of the southern wing of IDC world headquarters, burying his face in his upraised hands.

"I'm having a migraine," he moaned. "As if my life wasn't already falling apart. I'm having a colossal migraine."

There was a knock on the door. Tony jerked his head up, drawn face whitening.

"Who?"

"It's Wendy."

"Are you alone?"

"Yes."

"Are you sure?"

"Yes!"

"No one has a gun to your head, do they?"

"Stop it! Don't talk like that. You're scaring me half to death."

"Come in, then," Tony Tollini said resignedly. "I'm already dead."

The woman who walked in was in her early thirties and wore her hair piled high in a breathtaking reddish-gold upsweep. She wore Lady Brooks gray, with a touch of black and white. Her eyes were green and her arching eyebrows were almost regal.

She shut the door behind her, saying, "What's wrong? As if I can't guess."

"The last CE guy went berserk," Tony Tollini said miserably. "He broke the PC."

Wendy Wilkerson sank into a chair, saying, "Oh, God."

"They want a Jap. Today."

"Excuse me?"

"A Japanese service engineer. And they want him now."

"This can't go on, Tony. If the board finds out, do you know what will happen to you?"

Tony Tollini's head came up like a startled giraffe's. "Me? You mean us. This was *your* idea."

"It was a joke! How many times do I have to tell you? I never meant you to take it seriously."

"Well, the joke's on us. We have to do something fast. I can't hold them off much longer. I have to send out a real customer-service engineer."

"Are you crazy? If another one doesn't come back, we'll have the FBI, never mind the board, on our backs. I don't know about you, but I'm beginning to think there are worse fates than to be exiled to an office at the end of the south wing."

"Name one."

"Discovered stuffed in the trunk of a Buick, for one."

"I'll take it," said Tony Tollini, trying to get the childproof cap off a bottle of aspirin. After grunting and groaning without success, he simply bit the thing off with a savage jerk of his head.

He swallowed four pills. Dry.

"I'm going down to customer service. You'd better come."

"Why me? I'm only director of product placement."

"I need the moral support. And we're in this together, like it or not."

They walked down the corridor and turned into a more brightly lit corner of IDC world headquarters.

"I sure miss having seventy-five-watt bulbs in my work area," Wendy Wilkerson said forlornly.

"I heard in Atlanta they have to make do with forty-watters."

Wendy Wilkerson hugged herself tightly and shivered.

"It's a cold cruel world out there."

"In here too."

They went through the door marked "CUSTOMER SERVICE."

Amid a profusion of spaghetti wire and computer equipment in various states of disrepair, lab workers in white smocks and medical-style caps were conducting diagnostic tests.

"Attention, everybody," said Tony Tollini, lifting his hand to get their attention. "I have an important announcement."

Heads turned. Surgical gauze masks were pulled away from puzzled mouths.

"I need a volunteer," said Tony.

Everyone froze. Fingers in the act of removing surgical caps stopped as if paralyzed. A single gasp could be heard.

"Our Boston client needs us. Needs us desperately."

A man corkscrewed to the floor in a dead faint. A woman wearing horn-rimmed glasses ducked under a workbench and shivered like a toad under a sheltering rock during a hard rain.

"Please," Tony said. "This is important. I need help here."

"You go, then," a voice snarled.

"Who said that?" Tony Tollini demanded, head swiveling angrily. "Who spoke?"

No one volunteered. The surgical masks completely disguised lip movement.

"I tell you what," Tony said suddenly. "We'll draw straws."

"Are you in the pool?" a pinch-faced technician demanded.

"I'm VP of systems outreach," Tony Tollini said fiercely. "And I am ordering you all to draw straws."

No one had any straws, so Tony Tollini snipped a length of blue wiring into equal lengths and one slightly shorter one.

He turned to Wendy Wilkerson, saying, "Wendy, you do the honors."

Nervously Wendy Wilkerson gathered up the bits of bright blue wire and arranged them in her fist so that they stuck up to equal height. She held out a trembling fist. There were tears in her eyes.

Timidly the technicians in the room clustered around Tony Tollini and Wendy Wilkerson. No one made a move for the bright blue bits of wire which gleamed copper at their tips.

"Come, now," Tony Tollini urged. "Don't freeze up. IDC men do not shirk before a challenge. Remember, the odds are better for those who draw first."

A trembling hand reached out. It withdrew a bit of wire. No one was quite certain if it was long enough, so they held their breath.

"Let's go," Tony urged. "Slackers face shorter odds."

Another hand reached out. Another short bit of wiring came to light. The two bits were compared side by side. They matched.

Whoops of joy came from the two who had drawn the wires. They reverberated throughout the room. The remaining technicians looked sick. One began to retch. Another threw up. A third said, "My God! This is a clean room. He threw up in a clean room."

"Enough." Tony pointed to the man who had spoken. "You, you're next."

Before the next straw-drawer could move, the doors behind them flew apart and a loud, squeaky voice announced, "I seek the one known as Antony Tollini."

All eyes turned to the source of that loud voice.

It was an old man, impossibly ancient, his eyes cold as agates. He was an Asian in native costume.

Antony Tollini stepped forward and said, "I am Antony Tollini."

The tiny man bowed deeply. "And I am Chiun."

"Chiun?"

He lifted an imperious finger. "Chiun the Great."

"Great what?"

"Great computer genius, of course."

Tony Tollini's jaw dropped. "You?"

"I am pleased that you have heard of my renown."

"Excuse me," Tony said stiffly, "but I'm familar with the world's leading experts in the field, and I've never heard of you."

"That is because I did not wish you to," said the old Oriental called Chiun flatly. "But this has changed. I now seek employment in your tribe."

"Tribe?"

"Yes. This is a corporation, is it not?"

"Yes."

"I understand corporations are very tribal. I, myself, once owned my own corporation."

"Would I know the name?"

"It was called Nostrum, Ink."

Tony gasped. "Nostrum! The Wall Street venture capital company? I read about you in *Forbes*. But I didn't know you were in information services."

"My mighty hand is everywhere," said Chiun.

"Are you by any chance . . . Japanese?" asked Tony Tollini suddenly.

The face of Chiun wrinkled with distaste, like a prune shriveling in stop-motion.

"Some have called me so," he said in a grudging voice.

"What was that?"

"It is one rumor," Chiun said through tiny set teeth.

"Are you or are you not?" Tony Tollini pressed.

The answer was a single word, low, tight, and sibilant, like a cobra cursing.

"Yes."

Tony Tollini's tight features broke out in a pleased smile. "You," he said brightly, "are hired."

The old Oriental bowed smartly. "Of course," he said. "I am Chiun. Believed by some to be Japanese," he added bitterly.

"Can you leave right now?"

"Once we have made arrangements for my salary," Chiun said quickly.

"We'll give you three thousand per week and a three-hundred-dollar-per-diem for expenses," Tony said instantly.

"I will require one-half of my niggardly fee in advance," Chiun said stiffly.

"Advance? IDC doesn't do advances. You'll see your first check in two weeks."

"I will see half my fee now or I will seek employment elsewhere," Chiun said sternly.

"Let's take up a collection!" a technician shouted.

"Yes, let's!" cried another.

Wallets were opened and coins extracted from pockets. Like votaries before an implacable idol, the IDC employees laid the money before the sandaled feet of the Great Chiun, the Japanese genius.

The Master of Sinanju cast a cold eye down at the heaping pile of bills, coins, and gold cards lying at his feet.

"This will not suffice," he said.

Groans came from the huddled technicians. A solid gold money clip sailed into the pile pinching a lone dollar bill.

"Take it. It's my bus fare home."

Chiun shook his aged head. "That is better, but you lack twelve dollars to satisfying my modest demands."

Tony Tollini nudged Wendy Wilkerson in the ribs.

"Get it out of petty cash," he hissed. "Fast. And have a car brought around. I think our problems are solved."

"You can't send him," Wendy shot back.

"Why not?"

"Look at him. He's such a sweet old man."

"He's also a genius. And it's either him or one of the staff. Unless *you'd* like to volunteer?"

"I'll be right back," said Wendy Wilkerson, hurrying from the room. Her heels clicked away like nails being driven into a coffin.

14

The Master of Sinanju rode to the airport in silence, the book called "LANSCII" on his lap. He deigned not to glance over it. Such things were for whites, who understood machines—one of the few things whites were good for.

At the airport Harold Smith was loitering in a waiting area, craning his neck to see past a baggage X-ray machine, pretending to be searching for an arriving passenger.

The Master of Sinanju paused and placed the blue notebook on a standing sand-filled ashtray. He moved away.

Smith moved quickly to the ashtray. He bent to relace one of his gray oxford shoes. When he straightened up, the blue notebook was under one arm.

He exited the terminal and hurried to his dilapidated station wagon, which was parked nearby.

The Master of Sinanju endured the flight to the city called Boston despite the hectoring of the galley servant who insisted that he ride in the front of the plane, where everyone knew death sat should the plane fly into the side of a mountain, as frequently happened.

"I will ride over the wing," he told her.

"But, sir, your ticket says first class," the stewardess pointed out. "You are entitled to our best service."

"And the best service you can render me is to allow me to sit over the wing so that if it should fall off, I will know this."

"I've never head of a wing actually dropping off in flight."

"Then it is bound to happen," Chiun snapped, "for every other calamity imaginable has already befallen these pitiful metal birds you whites command."

At that example of invincible logic, the stewardess relented, and a coach passenger was delighted to discover upon boarding that the flight was overbooked, but instead of being bumped, he would be permitted to sit in first class.

The wing did not fall off, although the Master of Sinanju did notice that it wobbled alarmingly upon takeoff.

He spent the flight confiding to an elderly woman that he was the victim of a foul slander.

"What slander?" the woman gasped.

"That I am Japanese," Chiun admitted in a pained voice.

"You poor dear Chinaman. How awful."

After that the Master of Sinanju pointedly refused to listen to the details of the ignorant woman's hysterectomy, going so far as to insert his fingers into his ears by way of hint.

At the Boston airport there was a Roman servant awaiting him.

"You the Jap computer guy?" he asked.

"I am Chiun. I am not called the Jap."

"Name's Bruno. The boss is waitin', and boy is he steamed."

"I am very interested in meeting this steamed boss of yours," said Chiun, walking beside the servant. "Is he also a Roman?"

"The boss is Italian, like me. Proud of it, too."

"Pride is very Roman. It is good to be proud of your heritage," Chiun sniffed. "Even if you have sunk into mediocrity."

"Is that an insult?"

"And ignorance," added Chiun, whose ancestors had worked for the Roman emperors when the sons of Rome had not been debased by the pagan cult called Christianity. If only the lions had been more plentiful . . .

The corner of Boston called the North End made the Master of Sinanju think of parts of the outer world he had visited when he was very young, in the beginning part of this century. It did not make him feel nostalgic, however. Nothing in the modern world was to be admired. Although the Ottoman Empire had its good points.

He was taken to the side door of an ugly brick structure, where the cracked glass face of a computer stared back like the shattered eye of a Cyclops. Three swarthy Romans stood around it like glowering votaries.

"This is the troublesome machine?" asked Chiun.

"What does it look like?" said Bruno. He laughed. "This here's the Jap," he told the security guards.

His voice dripping disdain, the Master of Sinanju said, "I will proceed to fix this. But first I must know what has befallen it."

Bruno shrugged. "It's simple. It broke."

"Explain."

"First the boss was having trouble with it. It wasn't doin' what he told it to. So he gave it a good whack."

"And?"

"It went blooie."

Chiun nodded safely. "Ah, blooie. Yes, I have seen blooie before. A common scourge of machines. It is possible to fix this."

"Then the last guy IDC sent, when he couldn't fix the disk, broke the whole machine. His name was Remo, too. Can you imagine a guy named Remo doin' that?"

"I cannot imagine one named Remo not doing that," said Chiun, advancing upon the machine.

His hazel eyes narrowed at the strange oracle the whites called a computer. Emperor Smith had explained certain things about these machines to him. His eyes went to the black panel which concealed the all-important hard discus.

He inserted two long fingernails into a vent and pulled sharply.

The black panel popped off, exposing naked machinery.

"Ah-hah!" cried Chiun. "Behold! No wonder this machine stubbornly refused to do its master's bidding."

Bruno crouched to see better. "Yeah? What is it?"

Chiun reached in and extracted a thick-edged black disk.

"This," he said. "It is the wrong record for this brand of machine."

"It is?" Bruno asked, dumbfounded.

"This is designed for a seventy-eight-rpm computer. You have the thirty-three-and-one-third kind."

Chiun held the shiny black hard disk up to the light triumphantly.

"Do they work that way?" asked Bruno doubtfully.

"It is a professional secret," said Chiun conspiratorially. "I am only revealing this to you because you have been abused by Remo the Terrible."

"What do we do?" asked Bruno, straightening up.

"I must secure the proper record."

"You don't have one with you?"

"Alas, no. I was misinformed by my employer as to the true nature of the problem. I must return to Idiocy right away."

"You mean IDC."

"I mean what I mean. For I am Chiun, world's greatest repairer of computers such as this."

"I'd better check with the boss."

The Master of Sinanju nodded. "I must treat with your master. So this is good."

Bruno went to a door and knocked once.

"What?" a raspy voice growled.

"The Jap figured out what's wrong with the box."

"Is it fuggin' fixed?"

"No. He's gotta take a part back. Says we got a seventy-eight when we shoulda had a thirty-three and a third. Like on a record player."

"That don't mean nothin' to me."

"It's like records. You know."

The door opened.

"Is that right?" asked Carmine Imbruglia, for the first time hearing something about computers that made sense.

"You the Jap?" he demanded, staring at the Master of Sinanju.

"I am Chiun," said Chiun frostily. He raised the hard discus. "And this is the source of all your vexing problems." Chiun looked more closely at the one known as the boss. "You are a moneylender?" he asked.

"What's it to you?"

"You remind me of a moneylender. Such as lived in Roman days."

"You need a loan? I can front you a few bucks. Six for five."

"No, I need only a conveyance from whence I came."

"What's that in American?" asked Carmine suspiciously.

"I must return to my employer, who will replace this faulty record."

"That ain't the hard disk, is it?"

"No."

"That's good, because I ain't lettin' the hard disk outta my sight," said Carmine firmly. "I told them that before. It stays here."

"You are very wise," said Chiun blandly.

"Just to be safe, I want you to show me the hard disk, okay?"

"Why?"

"I'm from Brookyn, right? I don't know nothing from computers. You show me and I'll let you go get the right record."

"Very well," said the Master of Sinanju. He peered into the open aperture, saying, "It is that silver object there."

Don Carmine Imbruglia blinked into the aperture like a gorilla into a hole in a tree.

"That little silver dingus?" he asked, surprise in his raspy voice.

"The very same."

Don Carmine squinted his piggish eyes. His brutish face scrunched up like a fist.

"So *that's* what it looks like. All this trouble over that little thing. It looks like a little washer. Who knew?"

"It is the way with these machines," said Chiun firmly.

Carmine straightened.

"Okay, you done good. About time, too. Bruno, you take this little Jap genius back to the airport. Give him anything he wants. Then you stay there until he gets back. You understand?"

"Got it, boss."

"When this is over," said Don Carmine to the Master of Sinanju, "I wanna talk to you about maybe doin' a little work for me on the side. Savvy?"

"On what side?" asked Chiun curiously.

"On *my* side."

The Master of Sinanju bowed.

"When I return," he said, "we will have much to discuss, you and I."

15

The supersecret organization, CURE, ran by computer.

In the basement of Folcroft Sanitarium, behind a sealed wall, a bank of mainframes hummed like a grandmother doing her knitting.

For the three decades Dr. Harold W. Smith had overseen the organization, those data banks had grown and grown, absorbing and retaining vast files on every American, every business entity, and every conceivable fact that might be of use to Dr. Smith in his tireless effort to hold in check the forces that threatened to rend America apart.

Smith loved his computers. Although he had seen action during World War II as an OSS operative and later in the CIA, in his declining years Smith preferred the quiet order of his office and its simple terminal that could access virtually any computer on the continent.

Today he had his system up and running, its tentacles reaching out through the phone lines to the mainframe at IDC world headquarters, only a few miles away from Rye, New York.

The blue LANSCII notebook lay propped up beside it.

Smith was conducting a surreptitious search through the IDC data banks for the LANSCII program. The IDC system had succumbed to a brute-force password testing program like a sand castle swept aside by a surf.

He had been doing this for over an hour. Although it should have taken no more than ten minutes to isolate LANSCII if it were there, he kept at it.

"It must be on file. LANSCII is an IDC program," he muttered to himself.

But it seemed not to be.

When at last he was forced to admit defeat, Smith logged off IDC and picked up the blue notebook. He looked at the cover again.

He knew that LAN was a computer term meaning "local area network." A fancy name for a PC. Assuming it was identical to the end letters of Ascii, the double I would mean "information interchange." Ascii actually stood for Association Standards Committee for Information Interchange.

But this strange configuration had him stumped. Except that it sounded hauntingly familiar. But Smith as yet could not place it in his memory.

"What could the SC stand for?" he muttered.

Cool fall sunlight streamed through the replacement window behind Smith's hunched form. He frowned.

A buzzer buzzed.

"Yes, Mrs. Mikulka?" Smith said absently.

"Dr. Gerling asked me to tell you the new patient remains in stable condition."

Smith looked at his watch. "Thank you. Inform Dr. Gerling I will expect the next update at precisely three-oh-five."

"Yes, Dr. Smith."

Smith went back to the blue notebook. His knowledge of computer systems, in the days when CURE was new, had been as good as anyone's. Superior to most. Over the intervening decades, Smith had kept up with the fabulous developments in the field. But in recent years he had been forced to concede that technology had outpaced his ability to keep abreast of it.

Still, he was able to understand most of the LANSCII program. It was a combination spreadsheet and inventory accounting program. A variation on existing software.

True, some of the rubrics and subsets were odd. But computer terminology had a tendency to be either overly technical or playful to a degree Smith found asinine.

What on earth, he wondered, was meant by VIG? Or LAYOFF? The former appeared to be an employee tracking component, but it was not connected with the configuration surrounding the LAYOFF rubric, which appeared to be some sort of insurance program along the lines of futures trading.

A moment later his secretary buzzed him again.

"Yes?" Smith said, this time a trifle testily.

"Mr. Great is here to see you."

"Who?"

"He says his first name is Chiun. You know, *that* man."

"I see," said Smith. The Master of Sinanju had been a frequent visitor to Folcroft, and Smith had allowed his secretary to believe that Chiun was a former patient subject to delusions. It covered virtually every outburst the old Korean might make. "Send him in," Smith said crisply.

The door flew open. Chiun came billowing in like a blue-and-silver cloud—the colors of his kimono. He waved a hard disk in the air triumphantly.

"Behold, Emperor! The very prize you seek!"

"You extracted the disk," Smith said, his face falling into long drawn lines of regret.

"Of course," Chiun said proudly. "Was there any doubt?"

"But," sputtered Smith, rising from behind his shabby desk, "hard disks are not supposed to be removed like a common CD. They require delicate handling. A clean-room environment. The data have no doubt been destroyed."

"Why do you say that?" asked Chiun, taken aback by the sheer ingratitude of his employer.

"It's too complicated to explain," said Smith with a sigh. "But suffice it to say that dust and debris on the surface of the disk, no matter how minute and seemingly inconsequential, would obliterate the very magnetic particles that store the data."

Chiun wrinkled his tiny nose at the incomprehensible babbling of his emperor. He raised the disk into the air on the tip of one long-fingered nail. With the other hand he set it to spinning. Faster and faster, he spun the disk.

Then with a touch of the same finger, he brought it to an abrupt halt.

"It is now clean," he said tightly.

Smith blinked. He knew it was hopeless, but he also knew the power of the Master of Sinanju. He came out from behind his desk with his long face quivering with suppressed hope.

"It is worth a try," he said, taking the disk between two fingers.

As Chiun watched, Smith opened a port in his terminal. It was one of two capable of accepting auxiliary hard disks. He inserted the new disk into the drive, closed the port, and engaged the disk.

The drive whined warningly.

"Not a good sign," Smith murmured.

"I endured great personal hardship to recover that object," Chiun pointed out. "Canards and abuses were heaped upon my poor head like cold raindrops." The tone of his voice told Smith that the Master of Sinaju was miffed.

Greenish symbols appeared on the screen. They looked like a combination of English and Chinese. Garbage.

"I am sure you did," Smith said, moderating the drive's speed. The whine lessened, the symbols on the screen shifting in and out of readability.

"I allowed myself to be known as a Japanese," Chiun said, drawing near.

"As I explained to you earlier, you were undercover. In disguise. No one will know it was you."

"I was forced to identify myself to ignorant persons as Chiun, former chief of Nostrum, Ink, the mighty corporation of which everyone has heard."

"That was quick thinking. I am very pleased."

"And so I am branded in some eyes," Chiun continued, "a lowly and avaricious Japanese instead of a graceful Korean. My ancestors would weep tears of bile if they knew of this."

Smith said nothing. He was absorbed in his manipulation of the mysterious disk. Letters were resolving themselves.

"How does Remo fare?" asked Chiun, changing the subject. As always, the white was unreachable when communing with his machine.

"He is fine. Just fine," said Smith, his pinched face almost the color of the glowing screen. A sickly phosphor green.

When he had the whine muted, Smith tapped several keys. He got a sign-on screen. It read:

LANSCII

Smith would have grinned, had smiling been in his nature. The screen winked out, was replaced by another image. This one read:

LOCAL AREA NETWORK
SICILIAN CRIME
INFORMATION INTERCHANGE

Dr. Harold W. Smith stared at this with a stupefied expression as the screen was replaced by a user-friendly menu.

Frantically he exited the system and rebooted. Again he got the sign-on. Then the second screen. He stabbed a pause button.

The glowing green letters stared back at him mockingly.

LOCAL AREA NETWORK
SICILIAN CRIME
INFORMATION INTERCHANGE

"Good God," said Harold Smith hoarsely. He disengaged the pause.

"What is it, Emperor?" asked Chiun, coming around to Smith's side of the desk to see what had so amazed his emperor. If it were important enough, it might be something to throw in Smith's face at the next contract negotiation.

Smith did not reply. He was going through the system. His eyes widened. At one point he input the name VIG.

A screen came up, showing a simple ledger accounting format. It was headed VIGORISH.

"Vig? Vigorish!" said Smith, his lemony voice tinged with disbelief.

"I do not know these words," remarked Chiun with interest.

" 'Vigorish' is a slang term for the interest paid in usurious loans," Smith explained, not taking his eyes from the screen. "Sometimes shortened to 'vig.' "

"Of course. The Roman they call the boss is a money-lender. He offered me five for six."

Smith nodded. "A shylock."

Chiun shrugged. "It is not so bad. Brutus was infamous for demanding sixty-percent interest."

Smith looked up quizzically.

"Brutus?"

"The thug who betrayed Caesar."

"I see." Smith returned to his screen. He paged through the data, squinting harder as he concentrated. He discovered that the LAYOFF program was simply a method of tracking the laying off of high-risk sports bets. An insurance scheme, as he had deduced.

Half-forgotten underworld slang came back to him. He found programs covering running numbers, a method of randomly selecting floating-dice-game locations and what appeared to be an accounting of the daily take on supermarket cash registers. It was an old trick, Smith knew. A manager would be strong-armed and coerced into installing a checkout line unsuspected by the parent chain. All proceeds from the phantom register would go into criminal hands.

All the old, familiar patterns of racketeering were present. Each of them made superefficient by IDC software.

Finally he exited the system and leaned back in his cracked leather chair.

Letting out a sigh of unhappiness, Smith said, "What we have here is a software system specifically configured to serve the needs of the Mafia."

"Ah, yes, the Black Hand," said Chiun. "I know of them. Bandits and thieves without any shred of honor."

"They have not gone by that name in a long, long time."

"But their ways have not changed," said Chiun, wondering if that remark were an aspersion cast upon his great age. Whites were notoriously disrespectful of age. Even old whites such as Smith.

"Now they have," said Smith tightly. "This computer system could be the first step to bringing the Mafia into the next century."

"Then I say we dispatch them swiftly," Chiun said quickly. "Eliminate them in this century so they do not live to enjoy the next."

Smith shook his head. "No, not that way. If this catches on, it could spread to the Yakuza and the Colombian drug lords. There is no telling where it might stop."

"A few select assassinations could have a desired effect on the rest," Chiun pointed out.

"Master Chiun," Smith said suddenly, "did you notice any other equipment adjacent to the terminal you extracted the disk from?"

"No. There were only the plastic oracle and the hard discus."

"Disk."

"The Romans would call it a discus, just as would the Greeks."

"This is only the tip of the iceberg," mused Smith. "It is important to learn why and how the Boston Mafia was able to coerce IDC into pioneering software specific to their needs."

"I will be pleased to bring the moneylender to you, on his knees and fearing for his life," Chiun offered hopefully.

Smith shook his head. "No, this is best investigated from the IDC end."

"Since I am currently in their employ, although as a Japanese, I am prepared to venture into their toils once more," Chiun said in a wounded but heroic voice.

"No," Smith said firmly. "I believe this is something best handled by Remo."

"Remo?" Chiun squeaked. "Why? What is wrong with my service that you would cast me aside like a cracked rice bowl?"

"Nothing, nothing," Smith hastened to say. "It is just that Remo is—"

"Hopeless, callow, and inept," Chiun spat contemptuously.

"—Caucasian," said Smith.

Chiun made a face. He began pacing the floor, waving his hands in the air. "I am ruined," he cried. "First I am forced to pass for Japanese. Now my very Koreanness is cast aside as if unimportant. Where will the ignominies end?"

Smith stood up. "Listen to me, Master of Sinanju. You were just sent to Boston by IDC, ostensibly to repair the Boston Mafia's system. You stole the hard disk. Eventually this will be discovered."

Chiun whirled. "I can return the disk," he cried. "No one will suspect. They do not know it is missing." He struck a proud pose. "Unlike me, they know nothing of computers."

"No. This disk contains all the financial data for the day-to-day running of the Mafia. Their loans, their gambling, everything. For the moment, they are paralyzed."

"A perfect opportunity to strike a mortal blow."

"Not yet," said Smith. "Listen carefully. When Remo's face has healed, he will be unrecognizable to the staff at IDC. I will send him back into the firm, where he can get to the bottom of this. It is the perfect solution."

"And what of my services?"

"Your services, I am sure, will be invaluable—as our campaign takes shape."

"Campaign? We are going to war?"

Smith nodded grimly.

"Against the Mafia."

16

Tony Tollini shivered at his desk, his stark white shirt soaked in sweat despite the temperature-controlled environment.

At the end of the business day—five o'clock—he tiptoed out from behind his desk and opened the office door a crack.

Out in the anteroom, his secretary was putting on her gray rabbit-fur overcoat.

"No calls?" he asked fearfully.

"None, Mr. Tollini."

Tony Tollini's face lost its wound-like-a-mainspring tightness. He almost smiled. The would-be smile crawled across his lower face like a grimace.

"Is that all?" the secretary asked.

"Yes, yes. Thank you," said Tony Tollini, thinking that perhaps the ingenious Chiun had saved the day after all.

Once his secretary had disappeared down the hall, Tony knocked on the next office over. It read "WENDY WILKERSON, DIRECTOR OF PRODUCT PLACEMENT."

"Good news," he called through the door.

Wendy opened her door a sliver. One round green eye appeared, as if at a mouse hole.

"What?"

"No calls from Boston," Tony said in a hushed voice.

The door opened wider. So did the eye. "You don't think . . . you can't imagine . . . ?"

"I think he did it," Tony said excitedly. "The little guy pulled it off!"

"Great!" Wendy rolled her green-as-emerald eyes ceilingward with relief.

"Care to join me in a celebratory dinner? I know this fabulous Italian place."

"Pul-leeze. Anything but Italian."

"Chinese?"

"Let me get my coat!" Wendy said quickly.

Out in the parking lot, they strolled along as if all the cares of the world had been lifted from their shoulders.

"I'll follow you, okay?" Wendy said.

"It's just up the highway."

"I know the place. Their fish in a rice basket is scrumptious."

They split off, going to their respective cars.

Tony Tollini was whistling by the time he got to his Miata. He inserted the key in the driver's door, and was reaching for the handle when he felt sudden pressure on his elbows.

"Tollini," a baritone voice growled. "The boss wants to see you."

Tony Tollini froze. He looked to his right. There was a man towering over him with a jutting jaw like a bestubbled iron plow.

He looked left. The man to his left was shorter, but infinitely wider. Tony Tollini could not remember ever seeing a man so wide in his life. He looked like a wall jammed into a sharkskin suit.

"Boss?" Tony croaked, his mustache drooping in defeat. "You mean the CEO of IDC, don't you? Please say that's what you mean. Even if it's not true."

"I mean *our* boss," said the human wall. "And he ain't happy."

Tony Tollini left his keys in the door of his car. He had no choice. Fingers like cold chisels were guiding him by the elbows, somehow managing to simultaneously grind his funny bone in such a way it felt like champagne got in his marrow.

He tried to cry for help. Only he could not. There were cold chisel fingers squeezing his lips into something resembling a chamois bag opening with the drawstring mouth pulled tight.

Tony Tollini was escorted to the open trunk of a black Chrysler Imperial. He took the hint. He even helped pull the lid closed. It was almost a relief. No one would massacre him in the trunk. He hoped.

When Wendy Wilkerson piloted her Volvo out of the IDC parking lot, she looked both ways, thinking that she had missed Tony Tollini. All she saw, however, was a long black Chrysler Imperial slithering into traffic.

Thinking Tony had gone on ahead, she drove north to the Chinese restaurant up the road.

When after twenty minutes Tony Tollini did not show, she became uneasy and sped home, where she ate reheated Chinese and lay awake all night staring at the shadowy ceiling.

Tony Tollini did not sleep that night. He was hauled out of the Imperial's trunk in a shadow-smeared alley and taken to a black walnut alcove where sat Don Fiavorante Pubescio.

"Uncle Fiavorante," Tony sputtered, forcing a weak smile. "Great to see you again. Really great. Really."

His outstretched hand was ignored.

"Sit," said Don Fiavorante.

Tony sat. He didn't know what to do with his hands, so he folded them as if in church. The saints on the walls made it seem appropriate somehow.

Don Fiavorante began speaking, using the hushed, authoritative tones of a priest hearing confession. "I have had a call from my friend Don Carmine. You remember Don Carmine?"

"We've never met, actually," Tony admitted sheepishly.

"I have told you of him. He is the business associate of mine for whom you did a certain thing."

"It wasn't my fault!" Tony said quickly. "The disk crashed. He must have—"

Don Fiavorante raised an immaculately manicured hand for silence.

"Have some tea. It is ginseng," said Don Fiavorante as tea was served by a silent waiter. "Much easier on the stomach than espresso."

"You have sent your people to my friend Carmine. None of them could do anything with this machine of yours. Not one."

"I tried to tell him that we needed to take the system into a clean room, have it checked over by media recovery specialists. But he refused to listen."

"My friend Carmine is funny that way. He does not wish that other people know his business. This is understandable."

Tony Tollini relaxed. "Then I'm not in trouble?"

"But someone has removed his property."

"What?"

"A Japanese gentleman. He came, he saw, and he took. He promised to return with a new part."

"What part?"

"This wily Japanese called it a record. But from what Carmine described to me, it was the hard disk over which there is so much trouble. This was yesterday. Yesterday, and this Japanese gentleman promised to return yesterday. No Japanese gentleman yesterday. No Japanese gentleman today. Don Carmine is very upset. He called me. He asked me, 'Don Fiavorante, my friend, how can I pay you rent when I have no financial records? All is on the stolen disk.' "

Don Fiavorante shrugged as if it were a small matter.

"I told Don Carmine that I would give him, how you say, grace on his rent. He pays me next Friday and I ask only that he pay double."

"Double?" Tony gulped. He took a hit of the ginseng tea.

"That is what my friend Carmine said. He does not like to pay double. He prefers to have his records so he can pay me on time. Without these records, he does not know who owes him and when. It is bad business not to know these things."

"I never saw the guy again!" Tony protested. "I thought he was still up there, doing good work."

Don Fiavorante Pubescio leaned across the black walnut table, which bore a faint scar of an old bullet furrow. "This is what you want me to tell Don Carmine? That you never saw this Japanese again?"

Tears were starting to race down Tony Tollini's pale cheeks.

"No. No. Give me another day. Please, Uncle Fiavorante."

Don Fiavorante eased back in his chair. "I tell you what," he said, pursing his lips. "I think you are not, how you say, complicit in the stealing of this disk. I think this Jap was a crook. So I will make you a proposition."

"Anything," Tony said tearfully.

"Go to Boston. Meet with Carmine, who is a friend of mine. You will work for him, help him get on his feet. You know many things. He needs help." Don Fiavorante tapped his temple. "He is not smart, like us."

"But I have a job. At IDC."

"Where they treat you like a *buffone*. No, you go to Boston. You make Carmine happy. If he is happy, I will be happy. If both of us remain happy, your continued happiness is assured."

"He won't kill me, will he?"

"A very good question. You are very bright to ask that question. I will ask my friend Carmine."

Don Fiavorante snapped his fingers and a telephone was brought to the alcove and set before him. Picking up the shiny receiver, he dialed a number.

"Carmine!" he said, after a brief pause. "How are you? Good, good. Yes, he is here. I have spoken to him. He knows nothing about the unfortunate theft, and I believe him. What can I say? He is my wife's sister's son. I have told him he must work with you now, but he has a question. He wants to know if you intend to, how you say, kill him."

Don Fiavorante listened. Finally he said, "Good, I will tell my nephew."

Tony looked expectantly at his uncle as Don Fiavorante replaced the receiver.

"My friend Carmine, in answer to your question, said, 'I'm gonna fuggin' kill the cogsugger if he don't make it right with me. After that, I'll fuggin' see.' "

"I'll take the job," said Tony Tollini instantly.

Don Fiavorante Pubescio smiled broadly. "I knew you would. Now, go. Carmine is waiting. Give my regards to your mother, such a sweet woman. There are so few like her anymore. *Addio*."

17

Remo Williams woke up with his face on fire.

Not knowing where he was, unable to see, he found his center, in Sinanju believed to be the solar plexus.

The long years of training came into play. Remo got his breathing under control first. Letting the pumping of his lungs serve as a focus point, Remo willed the fear of the unknown to drain from his mind. His adrenals stopped flooding his system. He redirected the blood to his face, the only portion of his anatomy that hurt.

At first, the agony increased. His facial nerves felt like traceries of acid. That told Remo he was injured. Then the pain began to ebb and he concentrated on controlling it.

In a way Remo could not understand, but which was as familiar to him as walking, he sent the pain signals coursing out of his facial nerves and down his neck to his torso, and then, radiating in ever-diminishing waves, to his extremities.

The burning of his face ebbed like fading music. He felt a dull ache in his arms and legs. When his fingertips and toes tingled as if mildly burned, he knew he had his nervous system under control.

Remo lay supine a moment, listening. There were no sounds of consequence. He tried to move.

His arms came up. No bones broken. He brought them to his face. His fingertips hovered over his stiff throbbing features momentarily, as if afraid to touch the wounded flesh.

Remo brought them down.

Touching a rough but soft material, he felt around his face. Bandages!

Then he remembered. Smith's office. The ambush. Oblivion.

Remo bolted to his feet.

"Chiun! Goddamm it, Smith! Where are you?"

Outside, through a door or a wall, a worried voice cried, "Summon Dr. Smith. The patient has wakened."

Feet ran away, making the slippery sounds of soft shoes on polished tile.

Remo assumed he was in Folcroft, somewhere.

Sitting up on the side of his bed, he folded his arms and waited. He was not happy.

When the Master of Sinanju and Harold Smith finally arrived, they were accompanied by a doctor or a nurse. Remo couldn't be certain. His ears registered the unique heartbeats of Chiun and Smith, but the third was unfamiliar.

"How do you feel?" asked a self-assured male voice.

"Like breaking the necks of certain parties," Remo growled.

Harold Smith spoke up. "Would you excuse us, doctor?"

"Of course. I will be outside." The unfamiliar heartbeat went away.

"Remo," Chiun squeaked plaintively, "thank the gods you have survived your ordeal unharmed. When Emperor Smith informed me that he had gone ahead with this horrible thing despite our express wishes, I was stricken as never before."

"Cut the crap, Chiun. I know you were in on it."

"Never!"

"I didn't keel over in Smith's office because I caught a chill from the open window," Remo said bitterly.

"It is possible. One never knows," returned Chiun in a subdued tone.

"Smith, do you have anything to offer to this?" asked Remo tighty.

"The tumor has been successfully removed," said Smith.

"Then why am I tricked out like Claude Raines?" Remo wanted to know.

"Since you were under," Harold Smith explained in a voice that was not comfortable with itself, "we saw the necessity of going ahead with the surgical adjustment of your features."

"I prefer to think of it as an improvement," Chiun sniffed.

Behind his gauze mask, Remo's eyes widened in shock.

"You didn't! Tell me you didn't!"

"The procedure was done according to my express instructions," Smith said levelly.

"But I assisted," added Chiun pointedly.

"Smith, did you stay for the operation?" Remo demanded.

"Actually, no," Smith admitted. "I saw no need."

"Has anybody peered under these mummy wrappings and checked out my face lately?" Remo asked worriedly.

Smith replied, "The truth is, Remo, that you've been out for almost two weeks now. It was a precaution we felt necessary so that your face could heal more quickly."

"In other words," Remo said sourly, "for all you know, I look like Sonny Chiba."

"I hardly think that—"

"Emperor Smith," Chiun said loudly, "if my son has been burdened with the face of a Son of Chiba, I will insist upon a new doctor of plastics. This is not acceptable."

"Oh, no," Remo groaned. "You didn't tell the doctor what to do, did you, Chiun? Tell the truth."

"I . . . advised him," Chiun admitted slowly.

"He was under strict instructions not to do anything unorthodox," Smith insisted.

"I hope you got that in writing in case we have to sue for malpractice."

Smith said nothing.

"You *did* get it in writing, didn't you?" Remo asked.

"Er, the doctor in question has already . . . departed Folcroft."

"Covering our tracks, were we?"

"There were complications."

"To what?"

"To . . . the doctor."

"Why do I get the feeling that you're hiding something here?" Remo said edgily.

"Because we are not," said Chiun. "And your backward white mind predictably insists that we are."

Remo sighed into his bandages, smelling his stale breath. He had a fierce case of morning mouth. "When do the bandages come off?" he asked slowly.

"The attending doctor believes that the healing should have started by now," Smith told him. "The bandages can be changed. Of course, you should not expect complete facial mobility just yet. Even though your healing powers are quite accelerated."

"Okay, I guess we might as well get it over with."

Smith opened the door and called out into the corridor, "Ask Dr. Gerling to come here. The patient is ready."

Chiun piped up, saying, "You will like the new you, Remo."

"So help me, Chiun, if I end up looking like a refugee from a Hong Kong chopsocky movie—"

"It is better than looking like King Kong, as you formerly did," the Master of Sinanju sniffed.

The doctor arrived a minute later and asked genially, "How is the patient?"

"Angry enough to chew nails," Remo said.

"Well, this should not take long."

Remo listened as the doctor rolled some kind of wheeled object—probably a tray of instruments—up to the side of the bed.

"I am bringing a mirror up to your face," the doctor told Remo. "Is that all right with you?"

"Just let's get this over with," Remo said testily.

The doctor began to snip away the gauze, pausing often to unwind the long strips. As successive layers came away, Remo saw two patches of light emerge. He made his pupils compensate for the brightness. If he had not been lied to, it had been a while since they had been subjected to light.

More gauze came away. Finally the last layer was peeled from his eyes and Remo could see them reflected in the mirror.

Dr. Harold Smith and Chiun stood out of range of his vision, somewhere behind him, so they were unable to see Remo's face.

Only a patch of pale skin showed here and there through the gauze. The doctor continued snipping and unwinding busily.

The nose emerged. Then the rounded plane of one cheek. And the point of the jaw.

Finally, as if a key thread had been yanked, the gauze abruptly dropped away and Remo Williams was staring at his naked, dumbfounded face.

The silence in the room was thick.

All at once Remo threw his head back and began laughing uproariously.

"What is it, Remo?" Smith demanded hoarsely.

"He's hysterical," said the doctor.

"I must see this," cried Chiun.

Before anyone could move, Remo turned around, jumping off the bed. He spread his arms like a stage performer, saying, "Behold the new Remo!"

Harold Smith gasped and turned as pale as the walls.

Chiun's tiny mouth made a circle of shock, his eyes narrowing into walnuts of inscrutability.

And although it hurt like hell, Remo Williams grinned from ear to ear, enjoying their horror-struck expressions.

18

The first thing that Antony Tollini did upon being ushered into the glowering presence of Don Carmine Imbruglia was to fall down on his knees and beg for his life.

"Anything you want," he said, his voice twisted with raw emotion. "I'll do it, Don Carmine. Please."

Tony Tollini shut his eyes. He hoped if they shot him, it would be in the head. Quick.

Don Carmine Imbruglia was seated at the Formica-topped table not far from the great black stove on which a tiny saucepan of basil cream sauce bubbled pungently.

"You cost me fuggin' money," he roared.

"I'm sorry," Tony said, squeezing his eyes. A single transparent worm of a tear crawled from one corner and scooted down into the relative safety of his mustache.

" 'Sorry' don't fuggin' pay the piper," pointed out Don Carmine. "I ask for repair guys, I get stiffs. I ask for better repair guys, and I lose wise guys. Then I lose the hard-on disk. Now *I* gotta fuggin' hard-on. And because you're Don Fiavorante's nephew, I can't whack you out, which is a perfectly natural thing to do under the circumstances."

"Thank God."

"But I can bust your balls," added Don Carmine. "Where's that testicle crusher?"

"Out bein' fixed," reported Bruno the Chef. "You broke it on Manny the Fink, remember?"

"That's right. I did." Carmine frowned down on Tony Tollini. "Okay, you can keep your balls. For now. But I gotta have satisfaction."

"What can I do to make it up to you?" Tony pleased.

"I owe Don Fiavorante forty G's. You got forty G's?"

Tony Tollini's black eyes snapped open. "Yes, yes, in my bank account. As a matter of fact, I have almost sixty thousand."

"Okay," said Don Carmine in a mollified voice. "I get all sixty."

"But you said forty!"

"That didn't include the money I can't collect from the dough I put out on the street at twenty percent on account of that fuggin' hard-on disk."

"Can I write you a check?" said Tony.

"After you gimme your watch," said Don Carmine.

Tony blinked. "Why?"

"You're a sharp fuggin' dresser. I figure you got a sharp fuggin' watch I can hock for another grand."

Morosely, Tony Tollini removed his Tissot watch and handed it over.

Don Carmine Imbruglia accepted the proffered tribute. He looked at it with blinking eyes.

"What the fug is this? A fuggin' joke?"

"What?"

"You holding out on me, you yubbie bastid?"

"No, I swear!"

Don Carmine held up the watch for all to see, saying, "Look at this watch! He palmed the fuggin' numbers. I never heard of anything so brazen."

"Numbers?" said Tony blankly.

Don Carmine passed the watch to his lieutenants. It was passed from hand to hand.

"Hey, it's made out of a rock," exclaimed Bruno (The Chef) Boyardi.

"What do you take me for?" snarled Don Carmine Imbruglia. "Stupid? Tryin' to foist a rock off on me?"

"It's a Tissot," Tony explained. "It's supposed to be made from a rock. It cost me almost two hundred dollars."

Don Carmine took the watch back and looked at it again. "You got rooked, smart guy." He tossed the watch back. "Here, I can't do nothing with this. The fences'll laugh me right out of town."

Tony Tollini caught the watch.

"You and I," said Carmine. "We're gonna make some money together."

"How?"

"You're a smart guy. You know computers. Don Fiavorante says you're gonna fix me up with the best computers money can buy. Only they ain't gonna cost me nothing."

"They ain't? I mean, they aren't?"

"Naw. 'Cause you're gonna filch 'em from IDC."

"Oh," said Tony, getting the picture.

Then Don Carmine explained his needs.

"I got runners, see? You understand runners and numbers slips? What can you do about that?"

"We'll bring in faxes," Tony said quickly.

"I don't hire queers. That's out."

"No, I said a fax. It's a telephone that transmits sheets of paper."

Don Carmine looked blank.

"With the writing on it," Tony added.

"They got those now?" said Don Carmine, his beetling brows lifting in surprise.

"I can have this room filled with plain paper copiers, faxes, beepers, dedicated phones, word processors, and PC's equal to all your needs," said Tony Tollini, suddenly on familiar ground. Sales. "What's more, I can get you fault-tolerant systems. They're completely bulletproof. You'll never have a hard disk failure again, Mr. Imbruglia."

"Call me Cadillac. Everybody does."

"Yes, Mr. Cadillac."

"Now you're talkin' my language. Boys, help Tony here set this up."

They helped Tony Tollini off his knees. He made a call to IDC and ordered an open system.

"I want our best stuff," he told customer service. "And program everything to run LANSCII."

Within two days Don Carmine was on line. The Salem Street Social Club was crammed with equipment. He stood blinking at the big black fax that had been placed on a dead burner of the black stove for lack of a better place.

"Looks like a fat phone," he said doubtfully.

"I'll show you how it works," said Tony Tollini eagerly. "There's a restaurant near here that accepts fax orders. Here's the menu."

Frowning, Don Carmine looked over the folded paper menu.

"I'll have the clam chowder," he said.

"Great," said Tony Tollini, who typed a brief letter on the word processor, printing it out and sending it through the fax machine.

Don Carmine watched as the sheet of paper hummed in one slot and came out the other to the accompaniment of startled beeps.

He ripped the sheet free and looked at it.

Turning to Tony Tollini, he said, "It's still fuggin' here. What is it, broke?"

"Just wait."

Minutes later, there came a knock at the front door.

Instantly Pauli (Pink Eye) Scanga and Vinnie (The Maggot) Maggiotto drew automatics as Bruno the Chef answered the door.

"It's okay," he called back. "I got it."

He came back with a paper bag and handed it to Don Carmine.

"What's this?"

"Your eats, boss," said Bruno confidently.

Don Carmine broke open the bag and pulled out a plastic container. He lifted the lid, sniffed experimentally, and looked inside.

"This stuff is all white!" he roared.

Bruno looked.

"It's clam chowder. Ain't it?"

"This stuff looks like fuggin' baby puke. Where's the tomato soup?"

"They don't put tomato soup in clam chowder up here," said Bruno.

"Then what do they put in, fuggin' cream? Send this back. I want clam chowder with tomato sauce in it."

And as an expression of his wrath, Don Carmine picked up a heavy cellular phone and threw it at a nearby computer screen.

The glass cracked, seemingly sucking in the rows of amber columns. Silence followed.

Don Carmine turned to a cringing Tony Tollini. "What happened to bulletproof!" he roared.

Eyes widening, Tony sputtered, "They're not literally bulletproof!"

"What other kind is there!"

"It's just a technical term," Tony bleated. "The system is built of arrayed redundant mirror components. If some break down, the others take over."

"Oh," said Don Carmine slowly. "Now I understand perfectly."

"You do?"

"No wonder these computer things work like they're magic. It's all done with fuggin' mirrors."

His eyes sick, Tony Tollini swallowed his reply.

While Bruno ran the errand, Don Carmine demanded of Tony, "Got any other things you want to show me, genius?"

The phone rang then. The Maggot answered it. He called over to Don Carmine, "It's Don Fiavorante. He wants his money."

"Tell him I got it."

"He wants it now."

Don Carmine frowned. His eyes lit up suddenly. "Ask him if he's gotta fax."

"He's says he does."

"Tell him to hang up. I'll give him his money in no time."

Don Carmine pointed to Tony Tollini. "You, genius. You write that check for forty G's now."

Tony sat down at the Formica table and pulled out his checkbook.

"Make the check out to Fiavorante Pubescio, the crook. Only leave out 'the crook' part, okay?"

Obediently Tony began writing.

When he was done, Don Carmine looked at the check and handed it back, grinning.

"Fax this to Don Fiavorante," he said.

Tony swallowed. "But I can't . . ."

"Why not? Won't checks fax?"

"They will, but . . ."

"No buts. Fax the fugger."

An unhappy look on his face, Tony Tollini trudged over to the fax machine, inserted the check sideways, and dialed the number Pink Eye read off to him.

The check went in. And then it came out again.

Don Carmine plucked it free.

"You know," he said, pocketing the check, "modern technology is fuggin' wonderful."

He was so pleased with his new computerized office that

when Bruno the Chef came back and said, "They say they don't know how to make tomato clam chowder up here," Don Carmine simply shrugged and sâid, "Screw it. We'll go out to eat. Maybe we'll take over one of these joints. Make 'em do chowder right and join the fuggin' human race for a change."

"Why don't I stay here?" said Tony quickly.

Carmine paused, his expression becoming suspicious. "Why you wanna do that?"

"Somebody should stay here to answer the phone," said Tony, who knew that Don Fiavorante was sure to call back about his nonnegotiable check.

"Good thinkin'. You stay by the phone. We'll get you a doggy bag if you promise not to go on the fuggin' rug while we're out," Carmine said, laughing.

When Don Fiavorante did call minutes later, Tony Tollini was profuse in his apologies.

"I'm sorry, Uncle Fiavorante," he explained. "Don Carmine hasn't mastered the modern office system yet. I'll drive the check down tonight, okay?"

"You are a good boy, Tony. I trust you. Why don't you send it Federal Express?" Don Fiavorante's voice sank to an unctuous growl. "But if I don't have my rent money by ten-thirty sharp tomorrow morning, it will not be a good thing, *capisce*?"

"*Capisco*," said Tony Tollini, who called Federal Express the minute he got off the phone with his uncle.

In the weeks that followed Tony Tollini almost forgot he was in league with the Mafia.

Business hummed. Carmine Imbruglia hummed.

From the Salem Street Social Club, the bettor slips came in by fax. Tony logged them onto the PC system. Any incidental paper was destroyed once it had served its purpose or the information was entered into the LANSCII program.

There were a few incidents, to be sure, such as the time an odds list immolated itself while passing through the fax.

"What's with this fuggin' fax?" demanded Don Carmine. "It's trying to sabotage me."

"It's the paper," complained Tony. "I told you, you don't need to use flash paper anymore. It's outdated."

"What if the feds bust in?"

"You just erase the computer records."

Don Carmine squinted at the glowing amber lines on the PC screen.

"How do you erase light?"

"By typing star-asterisk-star. It wipes the hard disk clean."

"Star-asterisk-star," muttered Don Carmine, making a mental note to look up the spelling of asterisk. "Got it. Can I get it back afterward?"

"Maybe. Unlikely."

Carmine shrugged. "What the hell, it's better than twenty-five to thirty in the pen," he said philosophically. "We're making money hand over fist, although we're barely making rent."

"You should think about expanding," said Tony, who, although he was still working off his debt to Don Carmine at thirty-six percent interest, felt a flush of pride in his work.

"Whatchu mean?"

"You need larger quarters. And you should think about incorporating."

"You mean, go legit?"

"Not that exactly. But create a corporate shield around yourself."

Don Carmine waved to his ever-present bodyguards, Pink Eye Scanga and Vinnie the Maggot.

"I got all the shield I need right here. Ain't that right, boys?"

"Whatever you say, boss."

"You know," Carmine said slowly, "I hear there's fast money in heroin up here. Maybe we should get into that."

"I thought the Mafia—"

"Hey! We don't use that word around here," Carmine snapped. "There's no such thing as the Mafia. This is just Our Thing. Got that?"

"Got it," said Tony Tollini. "I thought the, you know, didn't get involved in drug trafficking."

"What joik told you that?"

"My Uncle Fiavorante," said Tony truthfully.

"He was pullin' your fuggin' leg. If there's a dishonest buck in it, we do it. Now, how do we move drugs without it gettin' back to us?"

Tony Tollini considered this business problem seriously. "You could Fedex them, I suppose."

"Fedex? Is that like faxin'?"

"Not exactly. It's slower. Takes a day or two."

Don Carmine nodded sagely. "That makes sense. It's one thing to send paper through the telephone. Sending drugs is harder. We should start with cocaine, though."

"Why is that?" Tony wondered.

"What are you, retarded or somethin'?" Carmine jerked a nubby thumb at Tony Tollini. "Listen to this guy. He's askin' why we should start Fedexin' coke and not smack."

Don Carmine's underlings laughed on cue.

"You dink," said Don Carmine, lifting the fax receiver and holding it up to Tony Tollini's suddenly white face. "Cocaine is powder. Like salt. It's the best thing for sending through the little holes," said Carmine, stabbing at the receiver mouthpiece with a blunt finger.

"That's not how Fedexing works," said Tony woodenly.

Don Carmine looked at the phone receiver.

"You know," he said slowly, "I'm thinkin' maybe we should try Fedexin' salt first. You know, in case we dial a wrong number. It could be embarrassin', not to mention expensive. Coke ain't cheap."

There were no dissenting opinions to this observation. Tony bit his tongue.

The next day, Vinnie the Maggot showed up with a suitcase filled with cocaine in one-ounce plastic bags. The case was opened under Tony Tollini's eager eyes.

"Where did this come from?" Tony wondered.

"Got it off a guy," said the Maggot casually.

"Just like that?"

"Well, I had to shoot him first, of course."

"Oh."

"Okay," said Don Carmine briskly. "I got a customer to send it to. Get to Fedexin'."

Tony Tollini looked at the small lake of pure white coke under his nose.

"Maybe someone should sample it," he suggested eagerly.

"Good idea. We mighta got took. You wanna do the honors?"

"Gladly," said Tony Tollini.

He popped a bag and sifted a small pile of white powder onto the table. Unscrewing his solid silver ball-point pen, he emptied it of its ink reservoir and used the hollow lower end to inhale a line.

"Whew! Great!" said Tony, his eyes acquiring a shine.

"Good stuff?" asked Don Carmine gruffly.

"The best," said Tony, grinning.

"Great. You now owe me three hundred little ones."

The shine went out like a wet match. "Three hundred!"

"Street price. What—you think I'd give you a free hit? Hah, I don't give nothin' free out of the goodness of my own heart. Is that pen silver?"

"Yeah," said Tony unhappily.

Don Carmine snapped his fingers twice. "Give it here. My price just went up. Three hundred and a silver pen. Nice doin' business with you, joik. Now, get the phone number from Pink Eye and Fedex an ounce to the guy what lives there."

"I need the address too."

"Makes sense," said Don Carmine. "You gonna move somethin' heavy like coke you need the address too. It's only reasonable."

Tony picked up the fax receiver.

Don Carmine watched him carefully. If he had to whack out this guy, he would want to know exactly how to Fedex coke.

To Don Carmine's surprise, Tony Tollini simply dialed a number, spoke briefly, and then hung up.

"It's all set," Tony said, turning to Don Carmine.

"Whatchu mean, it's all set? You never moved the coke. It's still fuggin' in the case there!"

"They pick it up."

Don Carmine pushed out a thick lower lip. "Who does?"

"The Fedex people."

"Oh. Oh. This I gotta see. What's their cut?"

"They usually charge about twenty dollars a delivery."

"Fine. It comes outta *your* end."

"Why?"

"On account of you didn't tell me first," Don Carmine snarled. "You wanna spend my money, you tell me first. The double sawbuck comes outta you. Consider it an object lesson. A cheap one."

Less than a half-hour later there came a knock at the door.

"I'll get it," said Bruno the Chef casually.

"Wait a minute, wait a minute," Don Carmine said with hushed urgency. "Everybody wait one fuggin' minute here. I smell a rat."

"What?" asked Bruno, dropping into a crouch.

"Check out the window. Look past the curtain. What d'you see? Tell me what you see."

Bruno stopped dead in his tracks and scrunched down. He looked over the green chintz curtain that blocked off the lower part of the storefront windows.

"I see a van," Bruno said, eyeing the street.

"Right. What's on the side of the van?"

"Words. I can make one out. Says 'Federal.' Wait a minute! 'Federal'!"

"That's just—" Tony Tollini started to say.

"The feds!" hissed Carmine Imbruglia. "You. Maggot. Toss me your piece."

A .38 revolver went sailing into Carmine Imbruglia's meaty hand.

"Cover me. I'll show those feds not to mess with the Kingpin of Boston."

"No, wait," Tony tried to say, waving his hands frantically.

"Shut him up," Carmine barked.

A hand went smack against Tony Tollini's face and he crumpled in a corner.

Carmine Imbruglia stepped up to the door, placed the stubby muzzle of the .38 to the wood panel, and fired twice.

The wood splintered in a long vertical line. Gunsmoke tang overwhelmed the close, garlic-scented air.

Triumphantly Don Carmine Imbruglia threw open the door.

"Get a load of this," he said in disbelief. "He's wearin' a uniform." Don Carmine craned his thick neck up and down the narrow street. "I don't see no backup. Musta come alone. Hey, check this out!"

His bodyguards in tow, Don Carmine Imbruglia ambled over to the white van that was marked "FEDERAL EXPRESS."

"Look at this!" he muttered. "It says 'Federal' plain as day on the side. Some nerve these feds got. They even advertise."

"I never saw nothin' so stupid in all my life," clucked Pauli (Pink Eye) Scanga.

"Hey, what the fug, right? It's the nineties. We use computertry and the feds advertise. It's a whole new fuggin' ballgame."

Everyone had a good laugh, except the Federal Express deliveryman, who moaned and rolled on the sidewalk, clutching his stomach as the blood pumped out of two bullet holes near his navel.

"Drag the sumbitch inside," ordered Don Carmine. "We gotta lam outta here."

When Tony Tollini was revived by the simple expedient of having his head thrust into the cold water of the Salem Street Social Club toilet, he sputtered, "What happened?"

"We gotta lam," said Don Carmine. "I clipped a fed. Soon the whole place will be swarmin' with them."

"That wasn't—"

"Don't tell me. The fuggers got 'Federal' written all over their van. We busted in and found this."

Don Carmine shook a black electronic device in one thick paw. Tony recognized it as a Federal Express package-tracking computer.

"This was the bug he was tryin' to plant," explained Don Carmine. "Some balls, huh? Walked right up to the door to do it, too."

"But—"

Don Carmine suddenly looked up. A smile lit up his brutish face.

"Hey, I just realized somethin'!"

"What is it, boss?" asked Bruno.

"I just made my bones. With a fed, too. Ain't that somethin'?"

"Congratulations, boss," said Pink Eye.

"You done great," added the Maggot.

"I feel like celebratin'. Let's get this junk outta here. We'll find a new place later. Tonight is our night to fuggin' howl."

19

"I cannot fathom it," said Dr. Aldace Gerling as he examined Remo's new face with practiced fingers. "There is minimal scarring, virtually no sign of a recent operation." He turned to Harold Smith. "Yet you gave me to understand that this patient underwent extensive facial reconstruction only two weeks ago."

Harold Smith thought fast. He said, "That was what I understood. Obviously there has been some mistake."

"There has been an abomination," spat Chiun in disgust.

"Oh, I don't know about that," said Remo airily. "I kinda like it."

"Bah!" said Chiun.

Dr. Smith turned to his chief staff physician.

"Dr. Gerling, could you excuse us? Obviously your services are no longer needed."

"As you wish."

Dr. Gerling withdrew from the room. Smith closed the door after him. He faced Remo.

"I do not know what to say," he said, tightening the knot in his tie, which threatened his skinny Adam's apple.

Remo, rubbing his jaw and regarding his new face in the upright mirror, said, "Guess the joke's on you, Smitty."

"This of course cannot be allowed to stand."

Remo's new face hardened. It hurt as the muscles realigned the face, but he didn't care. "Smith, it stands."

The Master of Sinanju drew Harold Smith off to one side. "Emperor, how is this possible?"

"There is only one explanation," Smith said tiredly. "As you know, Remo underwent several of these procedures in the past, each one intended to make him unrecognizable.

Previous to this surgery, and at Remo's insistence, we restored certain of his natural facial contours. Just enough to satisfy him."

"I can hear every word you two are saying," Remo reminded them with no trace of rancor. He was looking at his chin, and liking what he saw.

"Obviously Dr. Axeworthy inadvertently restored the remaining components of the original face," Smith continued. "It makes sense. Remo's facial contours had been reduced over successive surgeries, to their absolute foundation. Dr. Axeworthy must have realized that and gone in the only direction the procedure could go. Building up. He simply restored the final pieces of the true Remo."

"Damn good job of it too," Remo said proudly. "It's the old me. A little more mature maybe, but I can live with that. Maybe I'll start using my old last name too."

"You will not," Smith snapped. "And you know this is a serious matter."

Remo turned to Harold Smith. His face was serious but there was a humorous light in his deep-set dark eyes. He was enjoying Smith's consternation.

"Hey," he pointed out, "you wanted this, not me. You wanted the face that I had wiped out. You got it. And now you got this. It's been twenty years since I walked a beat. I have no family, and all my so-called friends from those days have probably forgotten me. They think I died in the electric chair anyway. I still look younger than I would have if I hadn't been dragooned into the organization. So you're covered and I get to keep my true face." Remo smiled. It was his old smile. "I'd say it worked out."

Smith stood fuming, saying nothing.

The Master of Sinanju, his hands in the sleeves of his pale ivory kimono, drew close to Remo. His aged head tilted one way, then the other, as he examined Remo's face critically.

"Ah," he said.

"Ah, what?" Remo asked suspiciously.

"The doctor did not fail entirely."

Remo blinked. "What do you mean?"

"Nothing," Chiun said innocently, abruptly turning away.

Remo blinked again. Suddenly he turned to the mirror. He looked at his eyes. They were set deep in his skull, above the pronounced cheekbones that had dominated his face since puberty. A familiar face. Good, strong, handsome, without being pretty.

The trouble was, the eyes were in shadow.

Remo pressed his nose to the glass.

It can't be, he was thinking.

He lifted his chin, bringing his eyes into the light. The trouble was, he couldn't look at his own eyes squarely.

Did they look slightly . . . oblique?

"Smith, come here a sec," Remo called.

Smith came up as Remo turned around.

"Look at my eyes," Remo said anxiously. "How do they look?"

"Brown," said Smith, who lacked imagination.

"Forget color. I mean the shape."

"What do you mean?"

"They don't look . . . ?" Remo swallowed, glancing in the direction of Chiun, who was making a show of sniffing a vase of peonies on a bedstand. "They don't look . . . slanty, do they?"

Smith frowned as he peered more closely at Remo's eyes. "Tilt your face up. Now down. Sideways."

"Come on, Smith. Stop fooling around."

"I am sorry, Remo, but your brows are casting shadows. It is difficult to see clearly."

"What's so freaking hard about telling if I have Korean eyes or not!" Remo shouted.

"Can't you tell?" returned Smith.

"No," Remo said, frowning. He called over to the Master of Sinanju. "What about it, Chiun? What did you make that doctor do?"

"Nothing," Chiun said. "He did nothing. He has restored you to your former sad, round-eyed state." The Master of Sinanju sounded unconcerned.

"Are you playing head games with me? Because if you are—"

"The games that have been played are with your face, round-eyed one," said Chiun unconcernedly. He hummed. It was a happy hum. It was the hum of a person who had secured a minor victory in the midst of a defeat.

"I want that plastic surgeon back," Remo said. "I want my eyes rounded off!"

"I am afraid he is dead," Smith said tonelessly.

"What did he die of, anyway?"

"A round eye killed him," said Chiun. "Heh-heh. A round eye killed him."

"Shhh," said Smith suddenly.

"Are you in on this too, Smith?" Remo demanded hotly.

"No!"

"Then what is he talking about?"

"Please, please," Smith said. "I need you both. We have a crisis on our hands."

"What crisis?" Remo wanted to know.

"Have you forgotten the IDC matter, Remo?"

"Oh, right," said Remo, subsiding.

"You were correct, Remo. IDC and the Mafia are in cahoots somehow. After you went under the knife, Chiun rescued the hard disk."

"It was nothing. Any non-round-eyed person could have done it," Chiun said loftily.

"Har-de-har-har," snorted Remo.

"It seems that IDC has created a software specifically designed for Mafia purposes."

Remo shrugged. "So, we take it off the market."

Harold Smith shook his gray head. "Not so simple. We still do not know how this has come to pass. That will be your job, Remo. Penetrate IDC and learn the truth. Then we will take action."

"No problem. I have a new face. I'll just reapply to Tony Tollini. He'll never suspect it's me again."

"Tony Tollini has been missing for the past two weeks," Harold Smith said levelly. "As is a large amount of IDC office equipment, including faxes, dedicated phones, and other high-tech office material."

"Well, we know where to find them."

"No longer," said Smith. "The Salem Street Social Club has been vacated completely. The Boston Mafia has gone underground. We have no leads at present. It's as if it had ceased to operate."

"Maybe they had a power surge and their disk crashed again."

"Criminal activity in Boston has actually increased. We think they're up there. Somewhere. Maybe a lead can be developed at IDC."

"I'll give it a shot," said Remo, again looking at his face.

"These eyes are fine," he said doubtfully, as if trying to convince himself.

"I agree," said Chiun, sniffing a peony as if it were the most beautiful flower in creation.

Which caused Remo's eyes to fly back to the mirror. They were wide and round as they looked back at him. He realized that fright was making them that way. He squeezed his eyelids tight. Suddenly they looked definitely oblique.

Remo spent the next ten minutes trying to work his eyes into a natural shape, neither too round nor too narrow.

His face began to hurt again.

20

Wendy Wilkerson was living in fear.

To be more precise, she was working in fear.

Ever since the disappearance of Vice-President in Charge of Systems Outreach Antony Tollini she had wondered if she would be next. She took the week following Tony Tollini's disappearance off.

No one had complained, which was not surprising. As director of product placement, she was even less important than the VP in charge of systems outreach—a position so new that no one at IDC knew what the person holding the job was supposed to do.

Since no one knew what Tony Tollini was supposed to be doing for Bold Blue, he had not yet been missed either.

After a week and a half, Wendy Wilkerson decided it was safe to return to work. She needed her check.

It was strange, thought Wendy, lunching on a peeled apple and plain yogurt in the relative security of her dimly lit office, how the higher-ups seemed oblivious to the entire mad mess.

She could understand how Tony's absence could go virtually unnoticed, his biweekly salary checks piling up on his secretary's desk. This was the south wing, where upper management never ventured.

But why, after two fruitless police visits, had the absence of the missing programmers and customer-service engineers not been questioned? It was as if as long as the bottom line remained relatively constant, the board of directors didn't care.

Wendy shivered inside her immaculately tailored business suit, wondering if Tony were alive or dead. She was sure he was dead. There was no other explanation for why they hadn't come for her too. Tony was a corporate weasel. He would have handed her up to the Mafia to save his own skin in no time flat.

As she pared a wedge out of a Granny Smith apple, there came a timid knock at her inner office door.

"Yes?" said Wendy.

"Miss Wilkerson, there is a man here who would like to speak with you."

"About what?" Wendy asked, her heart stopping. It was Tony's personal secretary.

"About . . . about Mr. Tollini."

The precise wedge of Granny Smith apple poised on the point of being swallowed, Wendy's mouth was suddenly dry. She tried to swallow the apple, her mind racing.

They were here!

Just as the apple wedge went sliding down her slippery esophagus, Wendy's throat constricted. The apple wedge wandered off-course, producing a sputtering paroxysm of coughing.

Wendy began hacking.

"Miss Wilkerson! Miss Wilkerson! Are you all right in there?" demanded the secretary.

"What's going on?" a hard male voice demanded.

"I think she's choking," cried the secretary, rattling the doorknob, which Wendy had taken the precaution of locking.

The door exploded inward, propelled by a cruel-faced man with dark recessed eyes and wearing an expensive silk suit.

His hard face tight and grim, he came toward Wendy with such ferocity of purpose that she tried to scamper into the safety of the desk well.

A hand got the shoulder of her tailored business outfit and pulled her back into her seat.

Wendy would have pleaded for her life, but she couldn't get anything past her spasming windpipe.

She wondered for a wild minute what would kill her first, the blocked airway or the terrible Mafia executioner who had come to rub her out.

With undeniable strength, the man lifted her up onto the desk and laid her across the blue blotter, upsetting her yogurt. He pulled her head straight back by her red-gold hair while his other hand reached for her midriff.

She closed her eyes, hoping the apple would kill her before

she was violated. After she was dead, he could do anything he wanted. Just please, not before.

The sound was like a gentle slap. But it made Wendy's abdomen convulse so hard she saw stars. All the air spewed out of her lungs.

The apple wedge jumped from her yawning mouth and came down to splatter on her forehead.

"Okay," said the Mafia enforcer. "You can sit up now."

Wendy declined. The fact that she could breathe again only meant she was going to suffer at the mafioso's hands.

"I said, you can get up now."

"Perhaps she needs a drink of water," suggested the secretary helplessly.

"Go get some," said the Mafia enforcer, his voice less harsh now.

Wendy opened her green eyes. The face that looked down at her had the deep-set eyes of a skull. They were flat and dead, with no trace of warmth.

"What are you going to do to me?" she asked.

"Ask you some questions."

Wendy sat up. His voice was direct but nonthreatening. "Who are you?" she asked.

"Call me Remo."

Wendy leaned back again, shutting her eyes. Remo. Her worst fears were true. She shuddered.

A firm hand forced her upward again. Hard-as-punch-press fingers pried one of her eyes open.

"Why are you acting this way?" asked the killer called Remo.

"Because I don't know what else to do," replied Wendy truthfully.

High heels clicked near. "Here's your water."

The one called Remo accepted the water from the secretary and brought it up to Wendy's lips. Wendy took the paper cup in her hands and greedily gobbled down the cold spring water. It had never tasted so good, she decided.

"Will you leave us alone now, please?" said the man who called himself Remo.

"Of course."

"No!" said Wendy.

"Yes," said Remo.

The secretary hesitated. Remo plucked a yellow pencil

from a Lucite holder and jammed it into an electric pencil sharpener. The motor whined. The pencil disappeared into the orifice. Complete.

As he reached for another, Remo said casually, "When I run out of pencils, I might start thinking about using fingers."

The secretary hid her hands behind her back and raced for the door, which she drew quietly closed.

Remo turned to Wendy and said, "Guess no one told her they make the pencil holes too small for fingers." He smiled. No lights of humor lit his flat deadly eyes, Wendy saw.

"Heimlich?" Wendy asked, touching her throat. Her esophagus felt like a balloon that had been stretched too tight.

"Call it what you want. I hear you were tight with Tony Tollini."

"We were in the same boat together, if that's what you mean."

"Same boat?"

Remo eased Wendy off the desk and into her chair. She looked up at him. He looked exactly like she pictured the real Frank Nitti would look. She wondered if he was an enforcer. She decided not to ask. No point in setting him off.

"We're both IDC orphans," she said.

The man's eyebrows drew together in perplexity. He winced as if the act of thinking hurt. Definitely an enforcer, she decided.

"This is the south wing, where they dump us," Wendy added.

The man looked around. "Nice office."

"Sure, if you like sixty-watt bulbs and eating from a brown paper bag instead of the subsidized company cafeteria."

"Tsk-tsk. How terrible. But enough of your problems. I want to know everything there is to know about Tony Tollini."

"He's missing."

"I know."

"The Mafia got him."

"I know that too. But what I don't know is why."

Wendy frowned. "You don't know why?"

"Would I be wasting my breath if I did?" asked the man, shooting his cuffs absently. She noticed his shirt sleeves were too long for his jacket. Typical hood. All he needed was a snap-brim fedora.

"Aren't you from Boston?" she asked.

"Hardly."

"New York, then?"

"I sorta kick around, actually."

Wendy's frown deepened. Maybe he wasn't a typical hood after all.

She decided to take a chance.

"Are you from the board?" she asked.

"No, but I'm getting bored. And I want some answers or I'll try to replace that wedge of apple with another." He hefted the chewed Granny Smith in one hand menacingly.

Normally Wendy Wilkerson would not be frightened by a mere apple, but inasmuch as she had nearly succumbed to a piece of one, she found herself suitably intimidated.

"Why don't I start at the beginning?" she said quickly.

"Go," said the man, taking a ferocious bite from the apple.

Wendy took a deep breath and plunged in. "They transferred me here from accounting. I had misplaced a decimal."

The man stopped chewing. "Aren't they kinda common? Like paper clips."

"In an electronic ledger," Wendy explained. "It meant our bottom line was worse than had been thought. They . . ." She hesitated. Her voice sank to a whisper. "They actually had to terminate some people to cover the shortfall in projected revenue."

"You mean lay off?"

"Shhh! Don't say that word around here!"

"Why not?"

"International Data Corporation never—repeat, never—lays off employees," Wendy explained. "They may terminate for cause, attrit positions, or deploy into the out-of-IDC work force, but we do not lay people off. In so many words."

"If you've been tossed out on the street," asked Remo, "what's the difference?"

"Ask Tony Tollini—if he's still alive."

"Meaning?"

"The week after I got promoted to director of product placement, Tony was promoted to VP of systems outreach."

Wendy Wilkerson looked away as if ashamed. She swallowed hard while trying to compose herself.

"Yeah?" Remo prompted.

"He was promoted because as director of sales he had had to let some staff go. Unfortunately, he used the L word."

"L?"

"Lay," said Wendy, "off." She said it as if enunciating two disconnected words not having any remote coincidence in nature or commerce.

"He used that word in public," she went on, "in a press release. When the board heard about it, they promoted him to the south wing so fast he was still in shock when they were moving his personal effects in."

"Time out. You say he screwed up, but then they promoted him?"

"At IDC," said Wendy, "if you screw up, one of two things happens. You get shipped out of Mamaroneck, never to be heard of again, completely derailed from the fast track. Or they promote you to the south wing, which is like a second chance."

"Other than the weak light, how bad can it be?"

Wendy sighed, giving her red hair a toss. "It's hell. First, they give you a title that has no meaning and no concrete job description. Then they ignore you, all the while expecting you to produce for the firm. If you don't, it's like being buried alive, fast-track-wise."

"But you get paid, right?"

"There's more to life than money, I'll have you know," Wendy said tartly. "I lost my secured parking spot and my secretary. I have no perks. The other wings pretend I don't even exist. And worst of all, I've been director of product placement for almost six months and I have no idea what I should be doing. What is product placement, anyway? Do you know?"

Remo frowned. "Isn't it where they sneak things like billboards and soda cans into movies? Kinda like hidden advertising."

Wendy Wilkerson's green eyes went as wide as if they had detonated. She grabbed Remo's arms in shock.

"You know! I mean, are you sure? Where can I verify this? Oh, my God. In six horrible months you're the first person who has had so much as a clue."

Remo shook off the grasping claws and said, "Let's stick

with the subject. Okay, you've been exiled to the dipshit wing of IDC. Where does the Mafia come into this?"

Wendy Wilkerson folded her arms under her breasts, hugging herself. "Tony was made VP of systems outreach. You should have seen him that first week, with a stack of dictionaries, trying to figure out his job description. Finally he gave up. He decided to make things happen, hoping something would click."

"And?"

"Nothing did. At first. We were having lunch one day in his office, just commiserating. You know?"

"Sure. I commiserate all the time. Keeps me from nodding off."

Wendy nodded understandingly. Remo rolled his eyes.

Wendy went on. "The firm had been taking a beating. They announced a new policy. Market-driven. It was revolutionary. Unprecedented. Before this, IDC created systems and then tailored them to customer needs. But the market was too soft to go on that way. The board decided that the customer should dictate his own needs and IDC should try to fill them. Amazing, huh?"

"Isn't that just another way of saying the customer is always right?" Remo asked.

Wendy blinked. "I hadn't thought of that. Maybe it wasn't so revolutionary, after all."

"Guess not," Remo said dryly.

"Anyway," Wendy continued, "Tony and I were discussing the impact this would have on us. I had been watching the Geraldo show that morning. He had on these horrid people from the witness-protection program. Former hitmen and informers. They all wore silly hats and wigs and fake beards."

"Sounds like every other episode," Remo remarked.

"Geraldo asked one if he wasn't afraid of the Mafia catching up to him one day, and the man laughed, you know. He scoffed at the idea. I still remember what he said. He said, 'The Mafia can't do nothing to me. They're still back in the fifties. They got no computers. They can't run license plates. They can't even file their taxes by electronic mail.' The man was very smug about it."

"You don't mean—"

Wendy's green eyes grew reflective as bicycle flashers. "As a joke, I repeated this to Tony. I said the Mafia is a hundred-billion-dollar-a-year organization. They need computers. They need faxes. They need word processing. It was a joke, you know? I was just trying to break up the monotony of our corporate exile."

"Don't tell me—"

Wendy nodded. "Tony didn't think it was a joke at all. He immediately saw the possibilities. And he had this uncle, whom he barely knew.

"Uncle?"

"Uncle Fiavorante. He was big in California. Now he's in New York, running things down there."

"Not Don Fiavorante Pubescio?" said Remo, jaw dropping.

"I think that's the name."

"Let me get this straight. The Mafia didn't come to IDC. IDC went to the Mafia?"

"Shhh," said Wendy. "Not so loud. The board still doesn't know."

"They don't?"

"They always ignore the south wing until it generates revenue or screws up completely. Tony went to his uncle, got an agreement to participate in a pilot program, and the uncle picked Boston as they first city to try out the program."

"LANSCII?"

"That's right." Wendy frowned in surprise. "How did you know? It's supposed to be a trade secret."

"Word is getting out," Remo said dryly.

"Tony had the programmers come up with a super-user-friendly software. It was kind of a joke. Easier to use than VMS. They named it after Meyer Lansky, the old-time mob financial genius."

Remo snapped his fingers. "I knew I'd heard the name before."

"Everything was going fine until the Boston hard disk crashed. It took all their bookkeeping records. Can you imagine those people? Not making backup copies? What could they have been thinking of?"

"Oh, I don't know," said Remo airily. "Maybe they didn't see it as data."

Wendy frowned. "What else would it be?"

"Evidence."

Slow realization made Wendy Wilkerson's features go slack.

"Oh. That's right. They would see it that way, wouldn't they?

"Up in Boston, you get hard time for possession of backup copies," Remo said.

"No need to get smart. This is serious."

"This is loony tunes," Remo snapped. "Let me see if I can piece the rest together. When the disk crashed, Tollini sent people to fix the disk. Only it wouldn't fix. And they never came back. How did he keep all those missing people from attracting too much attention?"

"He only sent south wing CE's. When they started to balk, he hired fresh faces off the street, and then shredded their résumés and denied they had ever shown up in the first place. What were the police to do? This is IDC."

"Their jobs, for one thing."

"Oh, I know it sounds horrible," Wendy said quickly.

"It is horrible. People have died."

Wendy threw up her hands. "I know. But what could we do? Tony hoped to get it straightened out, and then he was going to take the pilot program to the board. A foothold in a billion-dollar-a-year business enterprise. They would have made him a board member for sure."

"You don't mean to tell me the IDC board would have signed on to servicing the Mafia?" Remo asked.

"Why not? They're an untapped market and we're market-driven. Besides, we have a saying here. IDC can do no wrong. Corporately speaking, of course."

"One last question and I'll leave you to the horrors of sixty-watts bulbs and brown-bagging it."

"You mean you're not going to rub me out?" Wendy said in surprise.

"Maybe next visit," Remo said dryly. "Any idea where this Boston outfit is now?"

"No. And I'd rather not know."

"Spoken like a true corporate tool."

"You probably consider that an insult, right?"

21

Harold Smith sat in stunned silence as Remo Williams finished his account of Wendy Wilkerson's story.

Remo lounged on a long couch by the Folcroft office door, which was closed. Chiun stood off to one side, coolly ignoring his pupil.

"IDC actually approached the Mafia?" Smith blurted when he finally found his tongue.

"That's what she told me," Remo said. "I'd say that's reason enough to shut them down for good."

Smith shook his gray head. "No. Not IDC. They're too big. Besides, this is a clearly rogue operation. The board appears not to be involved."

"From what I heard," Remo said dryly, "the board doesn't exactly go out of its way to police their own backyard."

"We must locate the current Boston Mafia headquarters," Smith decided.

"What's the big deal? You've got your handy computer. Get on it."

"It is not possible, I am afraid. If I had a phone number, I could enter their system. But we have no idea where they are. And believe me, I have been searching. Wherever they are headquartered, it is not an obvious place."

"Okay. Then Chiun and I will go to Boston and start turning the town upside down. We fish out a few wise guys, shake them up, and get them to lead us to the main nest."

Smith fingered his immaculately shaven chin in thought. Behind the transparent lenses of his rimless glasses, his weak gray eyes were reflective.

"If we go in and destroy them, even to the last man, that would not be enough," Smith said.

"Of course it would," snorted Remo.

"Silence, round eyes," snapped Chiun, addressing Remo for the first time. "Of course it would not be enough."

"Oh, yeah?" Remo growled, turning. "Since when are you against solving a problem by laying waste to an enemy?"

"When my emperor gleans a better way," Chiun retorted. "Tell the round eyes, Emperor. Bestow upon him the virtue of your brilliant sunlight."

"Oh, brother," Remo groaned.

Smith said, "From what you tell me, Remo, this is being sanctioned and directed by Don Fiavorante Pubescio, out of New York City. If we simply annihilate the Boston Mafia, Don Fiavorante will move the LANSCII pilot program elsewhere or rebuild in Massachusetts." Smith made a thoughtful face. "No, we must first so discredit the LANSCII system in Pubescio's eyes that he abandons it completely. Then we can swoop down on the Boston mob."

"I vote first a preemptive sweep," said Remo.

"I vote against," said Chiun.

"What's eating you anyway, Chiun?" Remo demanded.

"You never called me."

"Your freaking phone was busy! You were cooking up that plastic-surgery scheme with Smith, remember?"

"You obviously misdialed," sniffed the Master of Sinanju.

"Repeatedly?"

"Deliberately."

"Have it your way, then," Remo said disgustedly. He stood up. "By the way, Smitty, you were right. This flashy suit did the trick. Wendy thought I was a hood."

"The woman was obviously a canny judge of character," Chiun sniffed.

"You know," Remo said, lifting a silk sleeve to the light, "it's been so long since I've worn one of these, I'd forgotten what it feels like. These things are hot."

"Then remove the absurd attire," said Chiun.

"Please do not, Remo," Smith said sharply. "I am sorry, Master Chiun. But Remo's new face—"

"You mean my old face," inserted Remo, winking at Chiun. The Master of Sinanju flounced around in annoyance.

"—means that he is unrecognizable at IDC and in Boston," Smith resumed. "The suit will conceal his large wrists, making identification virtually impossible. He will need that when we begin to break into the inner circle."

"And how are you going to do that?" asked Remo, interested.

"Brilliantly," said Chiun.

"I see our campaign as having three prongs," explained Smith thoughtfully. "Infiltration. Confusion. And destruction."

"I'll take destruction," said Remo.

"Confusion is more appropriate for Remo," Chiun said quickly. "Let me have destruction, O Emperor."

Harold Smith raised a placating hand. "Please, please. We can sow confusion only if we can gain access to the LANSCII system."

"Any ideas?" Remo asked.

"Yes," Smith said. "I believe I do." He looked toward the Master of Sinanju. "And Master Chiun will be our Trojan Horse."

"That I'd like to see," Remo said.

"Of course I will be pleased to do my emperor's bidding," said Chiun, bowing formally. His slitted eyes flicked in Remo's direction. "If for no other reason than to show certain persons the true value of experience and wisdom."

"Here we go," said Remo. " 'I'm not old and everyone else can go on a guilt trip to Mars.' "

"How do you propose that I strike at these Roman thieves?" Chiun asked, straightening.

"By employing their own methods against them."

Remo and Chiun looked to Harold Smith for enlightenment.

"Beginning with extortion," said Smith.

22

Walter Weld Hill, of the Wellesley Hills, sat at the top of a real-estate empire only slightly less shaky than thirty-seven soggy Styrofoam cups stacked one on top of the other.

For Walter Weld Hill had bought into the Massachusetts Miracle. True, he was an old-line Republican, and the previous governor had been a glowering troll of a Democrat, but business was business. And who could argue with roaring success?

As the Massachusetts state economy exploded like a hydrogen bomb detonating greed, money, and expansion in equal measures, driven by soaring real-estate values, runaway fiscal irresponsibility, and an economy fueled by the futuristic computer buildings that sprouted along Route 128 like radiation-bloated spores, Walter Weld Hill had plunged in with all twenty fingers and toes.

Hill Associates put up office parks, skyscrapers, and condos wherever there was a bare patch of dirt. Not that the lack of a patch ever got in their way. Perfectly sound skyscrapers were imploded to rubble in the middle of Boston's sprawling downtown, to be replaced with new structures whose chief advantage was that they were twice as tall and rented for five times the square footage of their predecessors.

Hill Associates had almost single-handedly plugged the gaps in the Boston skyline throughout the 1980's.

Now, early in the 1990's, Hill Associates teetered on the edge of bankruptcy in a state where employment was in double digits, the computer industry had gone west, and revenues had dried up like a tangerine in the Gobi.

From his office high in the Wachusett Building, not far from South Station, Walter Weld Hill, whose ancestors had come to the land of opportunity on the ship directly behind the *Mayflower*, watched, day by day, week by week, as the family fortune was sucked into the economic black hole that was the Commonwealth of Massachusetts.

Hill was going over bankruptcy papers when his secretary buzzed him.

"Yes?" he said tightly. It galled him to resort to the cheap dodge of bankruptcy. It was so . . . common.

"Mr. Marderosian on line two."

"Is it important?" asked Walter Weld Hill, who, while he had rebuilt Boston, did not sully his manicured hands with day-to-day building management. That was why he hired people like Marderosian to run Mattapoisett Managing. The Hills built. They did not manage. Other people managed.

"He says that it is."

"Very well," said Walter Weld Hill, depressing the line-two button as he picked up the receiver.

"Mr. Hill, we seem to have a problem."

"Tell me about it," Hill said aridly, pinching the bridge of his nose. It helped relieve his sinus headaches, which were growing more bothersome by the week.

"I drove by the Manet Building this morning," he said, his voice odd.

"Which is that one?" asked Hill, who seldom bothered keeping a mental inventory of his properties when times were good, and could not care less now that they were not.

"The new one. Down in Ouincy."

"Oh, yes," said Hill, wincing. It was coming back to him. There had been a stretch of salt marsh along the Quincy side of the Neponset River, overlooking Boston. For a decade other builders had erected office buildings there that filled up within a week of the ribbon cutting. He had developed the last remaining plot at the tail end of the boom. But only after the other buildings had not sunk into the marshy soil, as he expected they might.

Now, three years after the ribbon cutting, not a single office suite had been rented and Hill Associates was paying a monthly maintenance fee in excess of forty thousand dollars.

Hill's voice lifted. "I don't suppose it has burnt to the ground, by chance?"

"No, Mr. Hill. But it's occupied."

Walter Weld Hill's bloodless fingers came away from his long nose. His blueblood-shot eyes narrowed in confusion. "Occupied. When did this happen?"

"It never happened. We haven't shown the place to a potential lessee in over a year. But when I cruised by, there were lights on, people coming and going. Parking slots filled. From what I understand, this has been going on for over a week."

"Squatters?" blurted Walter Weld Hill, to whom nothing that happened north of Rhode Island and south of New Hampshire was a surprise anymore.

"I don't know how else to explain it."

"You confronted them, of course."

"I was rebuffed, Mr. Hill. In fact, I was forcibly ejected."

"But you manage Manet!"

"That fact did not seem to carry any weight with the security staff of LCN."

"Never heard of them."

"Neither have I. New England Telephone doesn't have a listing for them either. I checked."

"This is absurd. Have you been drinking, Marderosian? One cannot conduct business without telephones. Not even in this third-world joke of a state."

"But that's the point, Mr. Hill. NET claims they have no phone lines to the building, but I memorized a number on the reception-desk phone. It works. And they have all utilities—water, sewer, et cetera, but there is no record of any connections being made by the utility companies."

"How," asked Walter Weld Hill, "is this possible?"

"By bribery, I would assume."

"And who," went on Hill, "would have the money to bribe someone in this state?"

"LCN does, I guess."

"Give me that number," said Walter Weld Hill crisply.

When he had the number transcribed on a rag-paper notepad, Walter Weld Hill hung up and dialed the number directly. A low male voice aswered on the first ring.

"LCN. We make money the old-fashioned way."

Walter Weld Hill blinked. He had heard that catch phrase before. At the moment, he could not place it, however.

"Please connect me with your most rarefied executive," he said firmly. "This is Mr. Hill of Hill Associates calling."

"Do you want our pharmaceuticals division, entertainment, loans, fencing, or waste disposal?"

"What on earth sort of firm are you running over there?"

"A successful one," said the strange voice. It sounded bored.

"I see. And who is in charge?"

"We don't use names, buddy. Company policy."

"Very well, since you seem determined to make my life difficult, please inform whoever is in charge of your rather diversified enterprise that the owner of the complex you are currently illegally inhabiting is about to call his law firm, Greenglass, Korngold, and Bluestone."

There was a pause. "Just a sec. I'll connect you with the CM."

"That is GM, you ninny." Walter Weld Hill smiled dryly as he listened to a procession of beeps and boops as the call was rerouted through the building that officially had no working telephone system. Mentioning his law firm invariably produced the desired result.

A moment later a gruff, raspy voice demanded, "Yeah. Whatcha want?"

"Er, I asked to speak with the individual in charge of LCN."

"That's me talkin'. What's this about lawyers?"

"You are occupying my building."

"This crummy joint?"

"It is a superior structure," Walter Weld Hill said stiffly.

"If you ask me, it looks like it was made outta old sunglasses," the gruff voice snorted. "You ever see these windows? Dark. I never seen windows so dark. It's miracle we can see outta them. The only reason I took it was because it was empty and I didn't have time to evict anyone."

"Thank you for your opinion," Hill said aridly. "Whom do I have the pleasure of addressing?"

"Call me Cadillac. Everybody does."

"Quaint name. Well, Mr. Cadillac, I am afraid you have really stepped in it. Illegal occupation of a commercial dwelling is a felony in this state."

"No kiddin'?" The voice sounded surprised, like an intelligent ape discovering that a banana was peelable. "I got arrested for a felony once. They charged me with riot. I was only playin' Johnny on the Pony with a couple of guys who owed somebody a few bucks. On account of all the broken bones, the cops called it riot. Isn't that a riot?"

"I am not amused."

"Don't be. I wasn't makin' no jokes. So what's on your mind?"

"Since we seem so free with my building, I believe you owe me, in the very least, rent money."

"Rent! For this crummy place? I got news for you, bud. This place had no lights, no phones, and no water. I hadda hook 'em up myself. And believe me, it cost plenty. I figure you owe me for getting your joint together so good."

"Why don't we have my lawyers discuss the particulars with your lawyers, my good man?" suggested Walter Weld Hill.

"Lawyers? I ain't got no lawyers."

"Why am I not surprised?" said Walter Weld Hill with a dry-as-toast sigh.

"I guess we can't do business, can we? I mean, who are your lawyers gonna talk to if I ain't got lawyers of my own? My mailman?"

"Why don't I simply visit the premises with my lawyers?"

"How many you got?"

"I believe the firm of Greenglass, Korngold, and Bluestone is staffed by nearly a dozen trial attorneys and other functionaries."

"Greenglass, Korngold, and Bluestone!" exploded the gruff voice. "They sound like fuggin' jewelers. You sure they're lawyers?"

"They happen to be the most eminent in the state," Hill said sourly, thinking: This man is a positive vulgarian.

"Okay, tell you what. I can see you're serious about this. Get your lawyers. Bring 'em over. All of them. Every last one. I'll get my people together and we'll do a sit-down. How's that sound?"

"Tiresome," said Walter Weld Hill, who had never before encountered a business person who did not turn to jelly at the names of Greenglass, Korngold, and Bluestone, Attorneys-at-Law. It appeared he would have to go through with it. In person.

"I shall be over within the hour," he promised.

"Great. I can hardly wait. Just ask for Cadillac. I'm the CM."

"I believe that is GM."

"Not here, it ain't."

As Walter Weld Hill hung up, he pinched the bridge of his nose once more. This was such a comedown for the man who introduced the Palladian Arch to Boston.

Walter Weld Hill's white Lincoln arrived a fashionable seven minutes after the assorted vehicles of Greenglass, Korngold, and Bluestone had pulled into the parking area of the Manet Building, situated in the crook of a tentacular tributary of the Neponset River.

Sol Greenglass, senior partner, bustled up, his hand-tooled leather briefcase passing from hand to hand excitedly.

"We're ready, Mr. Hill," said Sol Greenglass, who, because he was not a Brahmin, was not allowed to invoke Walter Weld Hill's Christian name.

"Very well," said Walter Weld Hill, shading his eyes as he looked up at the gleaming silvery-blue mirrored-glass face of the Manet Building. He frowned. "Does this remind you of sunglasses?"

Sol Greenglass looked up. "A little. So what?"

Walter Weld Hill frowned like an undertaker. "Nothing. We had best get about this."

The other lawyers formed a train behind Walter Weld Hill as he strode toward the aluminum-framed foyer entrance.

Two paces behind, Sol Greenglass was almost literally rubbing his hands together with anticipation.

"When they see us sail in like this, en masse, they're going to positively plotz," he chortled. "I love it when they plotz."

"Yes," said Walter Weld Hill vaguely. He had no idea what "plotz" meant. It was one of those vulgar Jewish words. He took pains to remain unacquainted with them, just as he scrupulously excluded the forces of Greenglass, Korngold, and Bluestone from his social circle.

They passed into a rather garish lobby. At a curved desk a male security guard had his face buried in a racing paper. He pointedly ignored them.

The directory looked like the menu in a seedy diner, white plastic letters mounted on a tacky aquamarine board. Some of the letters were actually askew.

Walter Weld Hill read down the department listings.

There were no names. But between "Consiglieri" and "Debt Collection"—odd listings, those—was an odder listing: "Boss."

"How droll," said Walter Weld Hill, noting that the "Boss" held sway on the fifth floor.

They crowded into the spacious elevator together. It was filled with Muzak of a kind Walter Weld Hill, for all his varied social experience, had never encountered.

"My word. It sounds like opera."

"I think it's *The Barber of Seville,*" said Sid Korngold.

"Eh?"

"Rossini," supplied Abe Bluestone.

"At least their taste is not entirely bankrupt," muttered Walter Weld Hill, wincing at his own use of a particularly painful word.

The elevator stopped, dinged, and let them off on the fifth floor.

Briefcases swinging, jaws jutting forward, the law office of Greenglass, Korngold, and Bluestone marched in lockstep behind their client as they negotiated the stainless-steel maze of corridors.

"What is that odd odor?" asked Hill, his long nose wrinkling and sniffing.

The collective noses of Greenglass, Korngold, and Bluestone began sniffing the air too. Finally a junior lawyer ventured an opinion.

"Pot," he said.

"What is that in English?" Hill asked Sol Greenglass.

"Marijuana."

"My Lord! Isn't that illegal?"

"Last I heard."

They discovered that the odor was coming from behind a section marked "PHARMACEUTICALS."

"How odd," murmured Walter Weld Hill. "One would think that physicians would not indulge in such distasteful medications. Remind me to report LCN to the AMA."

"Yes, Mr. Hill."

They passed to the end of a long white corridor from which emanated an even more disagreeable odor.

"What is that pungent smell?" asked Hill.

"Garlic."

"Ugh," said Hill, holding his nostrils closed with finger and thumb. "Detestable."

Walter Weld Hill was still holding his nostrils against the offending ethnic odor when they came to a black door at the end of a long corridor, before which two large men stood guard.

At first Walter Weld Hill mistook them for LCN lawyers because they wore pinstripes. On second glance he noticed that the stripes were rather broad even for the lax standards of the day.

And the men jammed into the suits looked rather on the order of dockworkers, Hill thought.

Sol Greenglass stepped up to one of the sentries.

"I am Mr. Greenglass of Greenglass, Korngold, and Bluestone, representing Mr. Walter Weld Hill," he announced.

One of the men stepped aside to reveal the block letters "CRIME MINISTER" on the blank white door. The other opened the door and stuck his head inside.

"Boss. Company. I think it's the lawyers."

"Great," boomed a gruff voice. "Wonderful. I love lawyers. Show 'em in. Show 'em right in."

The brute at the door signaled with the point of his jaw for them to enter.

Walter Weld Hill allowed the senior partners to precede him. It would make his own entrance all the more impressive. And he wished to get this ordeal over with as soon as possible. In all the generations of Hills, he had never heard of this happening before. Squatters in this day and age. What was the world coming to?

When Walter Weld Hill finally crossed the threshold, he found himself in a long conference room.

There were some odd appointments, such as the rather Catholic portraits on the walls, and over in one corner, a large black stove that belonged in the back of a low-class restaurant. On one wall was a sign that said:

WE MAKE MONEY THE OLD-FASHIONED WAY

WE STEAL IT

"That's not correct," muttered Walter Weld Hill, his eyes going to the man rising at the far end of the table, just under the sign. He wore a sharkskin suit over a black shirt. His tie was white. A hopeless combination. Obviously unsophisticated.

"Come in, come in," said the man, gesturing broadly. "I'm Cadillac. Welcome to La Cosa Nostra, Incorporated."

Dead silence followed that statement. Every member

of Greenglass, Korngold, and Bluestone froze in mid-action.

The man in the sharkskin suit began chortling. "What?" he said. "You think I'm serious? It's a joke. I was just kiddin'. Honest. Just a little joke to break the tension. Don't be so serious all the time. It's bad for the digestion."

No one laughed, but everyone resumed normal breathing.

Sol Greenglass slammed his leather briefcase onto the conference table, saying, "Mr. Cadillac, I have here a summons to appear before the honorable Judge John Joseph Markham of Dedham Superior Court."

"Hold your horses," said the man in the sharkskin suit. "Which one of yous is Hill?"

"I am Walter Weld Hill," said Walter Weld Hill disdainfully.

The man bustled out from behind the conference table. "Glad to meetcha," he said, taking Hill's right hand and levering it like a water pump. "These your lawyers?"

"Of course," said Hill, attempting to disengage.

"Great. I never saw so many lawyers before in my life. They look like Jews. Are they Jews?"

"I believe they are. What of it?"

"Hey, I didn't mean nothin' by that. A lawyer is a lawyer, right? And Jews make great lawyers. They understand business. Know what I mean? That's good when you're having a sit-down."

"I imagine their contribution will be profound. Are you now ready to comply with my wishes?"

The short brute of a man scrunched up his face, leaving a single eye to peep from the fleshy knot. "You gonna try to evict me?"

"No, I am absolutely going to evict you, you squatter."

"Hey, I just happen to stand five-eleven. I'm not squat. Who you callin' squat? I resent that remark."

The man was flouncing around the room like a dancing bear, throwing up his blunt-fingered hands and gesticulating with every word. He reminded Walter Weld Hill of the maître d' at Polcari's, an acceptable restaurant of the ethnic sort.

"Resent it all you want," he returned coldly, "but you are vacating these premises."

"Hey, don't use that language on me. I'm from fuggin'

Brooklyn. You think I don't now what them words mean? You think I don't know what all these lawyers mean?"

"I am sure that you do," retorted Walter Weld Hill. He snapped his fingers. "Sol, the summons."

Sol Greenglass whipped out the legal document and presented it to the man who called himself Cadillac.

"This is a summons to appear—"

"Yeah, yeah. Well, thank you very much," said the man called Cadilliac impatiently, stuffing the summons into his suit coat. He beckoned toward Sol Greenglass. "You, come with me."

"What?"

"Here," said Cadillac, "lemme help you."

Sol Greenglass found himself being led out into the open side of the room. "The rest of yous, come on. I'm gonna show you all a little trick."

"We are not interested in your tricks," said Walter Weld Hill in his sternest voice.

"You'll be interested in this. You, stand there. The rest of yous form a line. Yeah, like that."

Under the prodding and pushing of the boss of LCN, the entire legal staff of Greenglass, Korngold, and Bluestone was made to stand along one side of the long conference table. At the far end, Walter Weld Hill stood frowning. What was the man up to? he wondered.

"Okay, okay, okay," said Cadillac. "Now, I want every one of yous to turn and face me. Humor me, okay? I like bein' humored."

Reluctantly, grumbling, the lawyers turned.

Cadillac clapped his hands together. "Yeah. That's good. Hill, you still back there?"

Walter Weld Hill had turned as well. He stuck his head out from the twenty-deep phalanx of lawyers. "What is it?" he asked tightly.

"I told you I'm from Brooklyn, right?"

"Repeatedly."

"Down in Brooklyn, we got a riddle that covers situations like this."

"I doubt that."

The man called Cadillac reached down under the end of the conference table. He did not take his tiny eyes off Hill.

"It goes like this," said the man, withdrawing a forty-five-caliber machine gun so old it sported a drum magazine. With both hands he shouldered the weapon level to the exposed chest of the first man in line, the junior litigator, Weederman.

Walter Weld Hill's heart skipped a beat. Then he realized he was protected by no fewer than the bodies of twelve of the finest litigators this side of Worcester.

"I am not afraid of you," he said primly.

"I ain't told you the riddle yet."

"If you must."

Cadillac beamed a smile as broad as his namesake. "It goes, 'How many lawyers does it take to stop a bullet?' " And then Cadillac cocked the old weapon.

At the sound of the charging bolt being pulled back, the sturdy phalanx that was Greenglass, Korngold, and Bluestone gave out a collective gasp and broke for every exit. They stumbled over one another in their mad rush to leave the room, in some cases stepping out of their own expensive shoes.

Suddenly Walter Weld Hill found himself staring down the maw of the Thompson submachine gun, his chest protected by nothing more substantial than his double-breasted suit.

He swallowed.

And as he swallowed, the man who called himself Cadillac growled, "The correct answer is, 'None.' 'Cause when the guns come out, the lawyers get lost. Any questions?"

"Actually, I must be going," said Walter Weld Hill, his knees shaking. "I have an appointment with bankruptcy court in less than an hour."

"Bankruptcy court? Gee. That's too fuggin' bad."

"Isn't it, though?" said Walter Weld Hill, walking backward to the open door behind him. He continued walking backward until he rounded a corner and the machine gun was no longer in view. Then he twisted around and ran for the elevator, vowing that if he survived the coming financial debacle, he would move Hill Associates lock, stock, and barrel to a more hospitable business environment.

Romania came immediately to mind.

23

"And then I said, 'The correct fuggin' answer is none.' That's when I pulled the fuggin' tommy and stuck it in the first lawyer's kisser. You shoulda seen 'em scramble. You would have thought they was cockroaches when the lights come on."

Raucous laughter filled the corporate boardroom of LCN in Quincy, Massachusetts. The Maggot snorted. Pink Eye tittered through his sharp nose.

Don Carmine Imbruglia waved for silence and continued his story.

"That's when the stiff who owned this joint mumbles that he's late for bankruptcy court and, get this, he exits the joint backwards! Like if he turns around he's gonna pee his pants. His own joint, and he walks out of it backwards!"

The laughter returned. Don Carmine joined in it. His squat body shook with merriment until tears squeezed from his squinched-shut eyes.

It settled down only when Bruno the Chef ambled in carrying several bags of takeout food in his big paws.

"Chow's in, boss," he said good-naturedly.

"Great," said Don Carmine, rubbing his hands together. "I'm so starved I could eat an Irishman, washed or not."

Everyone laughed. Don Carmine watched as Bruno the Chef brought out the food. As it was served to him on china taken from a cupboard, Don Carmine's expression settled into the familiar lines of befuddlement it assumed when confronted with New England cuisine.

"Did I order this?"

"It's supposed to be seafood marinara. I asked for seafood marinara. With linguine."

"This ain't fuggin' linguine. It looks like egg noodles."

"Maybe it'll taste all right with the marinara sauce on it."

Don Carmine attempted a forkful. He spit it back into the plate. "*Ptoo!* You call this marinara sauce? There's no garlic. Only onions." He pawed through the remaining bags, extracting a cellophane package of sliced bread.

"This fuggin' looks like Wonder Bread," he complained. "I don't believe this. I can get better Italian bread down at the Cathay Pacific. This state in unbelievable. The chinks bake better bread than the wops."

"Want me to take it back, boss?" asked Bruno the Chef.

"Later. Right now I wanna decent fuggin' meal. Go cook me somethin'."

"Sure. What's your pleasure?"

"Clam chowder. Manhattan clam chowder. The red stuff. Fresh clams, too. And if I so much as chip a single tooth on a piece of shell, you're gonna hear about it."

"No sweat, boss," said Bruno the Chef, leaving the room to seek fresh clams.

As he was going out, Vinnie (The Maggot) Maggiotto was coming in, clutching a grayish, slick sheet of paper.

"I'm the fuggin' Kingpin of Boston and I can't get a decent meal," Don Carmine was saying. "What happened to the respect we once got? I was fuggin' born too fuggin' late, I guess." He spied the Maggot and asked, "What's that?"

"Fax from Don Fiavorante."

"Give it here," said Don Carmine. He fingered the slick paper unhappily. "You'd think a classy guy like Don Fiavorante would spring for better paper to write on," he muttered. "Stuff's always waxy."

"Maybe it gets that way coming through the phone," postulated the Maggot as Don Carmine read through the note carefully, moving his lips with every syllable.

"Listen to this," Don Carmine said suddenly. "Don Fiavorante wants to know how come our sports book is doing so well. Wait'll I tell him, huh?"

"You bet, boss," said the Maggot, producing a notepad and pencil.

Don Carmine scribbled a hasty note and said, "Fuggin' fax that."

Obediently the Maggot walked over to a nearby fax machine and started to feed the sheet into the slot.

"Wait a minute!" Don Carmine roared. "What the fug are you doin'?"

The Maggot turned. "Like you said, boss."

"Like I said, my fuggin' ass. That's a business secret. You don't fax it open like that. The wire could get crossed and someone might hear what's written on it or something."

"Sorry, boss," said the Maggot, withdrawing the sheet sheepishly.

Don Carmine snatched it away. "You gotta watch yourself every step with this technology stuff. You guys have no conception how this works. No conception."

Don Carmine carefully folded the sheet into thirds and produced an envelope. He placed the folded note inside, sealing it with a tongue that belonged on a size-fourteen brogan, and handed it back to the waiting Maggot.

"There. Now you can fax it."

While the Maggot was studiously feeding the envelope into the fax machine, Don Carmine Imbruglia picked up the evening *Patriot Ledger* and turned to the sports page.

As Carmine's eyes settled on the race results, they narrowed reflexively. Then they expanded like blackened kernels of surprised popcorn.

"What the fug is this!" he howled.

"What is it, boss?" wondered the Maggot.

"Get Tony, that weasel. Haul his butt over to the Bartilucci yards. I'm gonna make him rue the fuggin' day he ever met me."

"Gotcha, boss," said the Maggot.

Tony Tollini lived for the day when he had worked off his debt to Carmine Imbruglia.

The trouble was, that day looked further and further distant.

No matter how hard he worked, helping build LCN into a moneymaking operation, his own vig kept going up. At first it was because Don Carmine kept remembering new losses that had been logged on the stolen hard disk. Then it was for rent in the condo in which Don Carmine and his men had installed themselves.

It was the Windbreak condominium complex, on Quincy Shore Drive, barely a stone's throw from LCN headquarters. It had been deserted when they had all moved in. There were no other tenants. Tony had the impression that Don Carmine was not exactly paying rent to the owners, yet he insisted on adding a thousand dollars a week to Tony's mounting debt. And food. Don Carmine had it sent over every week. More than Tony could eat, much of it spoiled or out of code. That was four hundred a week.

"I'm never going to get out from under," moaned Tony Tollini one day as he was walking along Wollaston Beach. "I'm never going to see Mamaroneck again." Even the dimming memory of the IDC south wing made him nostalgic for his old life. He would cheerfully eat mashed-potato sandwiches from the comfort of his old desk if only he could somehow be transported back there, free of debt, free of LCN, and most of all, free of the knowledge that if he attempted to run for it, he would have not only Don Carmine after him but also his own Uncle Fiavorante.

Hands in his pockets, Tony Tollini trudged back to his condo apartment.

He got as far as the Dunkin Donut shop on the corner of Quincy Shore Drive and East Squantum Street when a long black Cadillac rolled up onto the sidewalk to cut him off.

Doors were flung open. Tony's hands came out of his pockets in surprise. Familiar chisellike fingers grabbed his elbows and threw him into the waiting trunk. The lid slammed down and the car backed off the sidewalk, jouncing, to rejoin the hum of traffic moving toward the Neponset River Bridge and Boston.

In the darkness of the trunk Tony Tollini could only moan two words over and over again: "What now?"

The first thing that Tony Tollini saw when he was hauled out of the trunk was a rusty white sign affixed to a chain-link fence. It said "BARTILUCCI CONSTRUCTION COMPANY."

They walked him around to the back of a long shedlike building of rust-scabbed corrugated sheet steel.

Don Carmine Imbruglia was waiting for him. He sat up in the cab of a piece of construction equipment that Tony had never seen before. It resembled a backhoe, except that instead of a plow, a kind of articulated steel limb ending in a blunt square chisel hung in front of the cab like a praying-mantis foreleg.

"What did I do?" asked Tony, eyes widening into half-dollars.

"Lay him out for me," ordered Don Carmine harshly.

They laid Tony Tollini on the cold concrete amid rusty

discarded gears and other machinery parts, which bit into his back and spine. His face looked up into the dimming sky, which was the color of burnished cobalt. A single star peeped out like a cold accusing eye.

Machinery whined and the articulated limb jerked and jiggled until the blunt hard chisel was poised over Tony Tollini's sweating face like a single spider's fang.

Don Carmine's raspy voice called over, "Hey, Tollini. You ever heard the expression 'nibbled to death by fuggin' baby ducks'?"

Tony Tollini didn't trust his voice. He nodded furiously.

"This baby here's a nibbler. They use 'em to bust up concrete. You know how hard concrete is?"

Tony kept nodding.

"You wanna bust up concrete," Don Carmine went on, "you need brute force. This baby has it. Watch."

Machinery toiled and the nibbler's blunt implement jerked leftward. It dropped, almost touching Tony's left ear. The Maggot was holding down Tony's head so he could not move.

Then a stuttering noise like a super jackhammer filled Tony Tollini's left ear. The hard ground under his head vibrated. The lone star in the cobalt sky above vibrated too.

When the noise stopped, Tony's left ear rang.

Don Carmine Imbruglia's voice penetrated the ringing like a sword slicing through a brass gong.

"You been holding out on me, Tollini!"

"No, honest. You have all my money. What more do you want?"

"I ain't talkin' money. I'm talkin' the hard-on disk."

"Which one?"

"The one the Jap stole, what do you think? You told me you hired him right off the fuggin' street. Never saw him before. Right?"

"It's the truth, I swear!"

The nibbler jerked up. It moved right, like a mechanical claw in a grab-the-prize carnival concession.

"I'm from Brooklyn, right?" Don Carmine was screaming. "I don't know my fuggin' ass from yesterday's paper."

"You do! You do! I know you do!"

The nibbler slashed to the right.

Tony screamed and tried to avert his face.

The hard nibbler point only brushed the tip of his nose, but it felt like the cartilage had been yanked off.

The point dropped. It started hammering again, this time in Tony Tollini's right ear. He was crying now, loud and without shame. He was asking for his mother.

When the sound stopped and Tony could hear a resonant ringing in both eardrums, Don Carmine was saying, "Tell me about the guy Remo. You hire him off the street too?"

"It's true!" Tony swore, blubbering. "On my mother. It's true."

"Then how come he breaks my computer and three of my best guys end up dead? That's a fuggin' coincidence, right?"

"I don't know."

"So how come the Jap is trying to con me into buyin' my own hard-on disk back?"

"I don't know what you're talking about!"

The nibbler jumped up. It moved leftward again. Tony tracked it with his eyes. The concrete on either side of his head was shattered. The only place left for it to go was his head, which suddenly felt as fragile as an eggshell.

When the point was poised over Tony's mouth, he shut it. The nibbler's engine started up. He could smell the diesel-exhaust stink.

The nibbler point retreated a few inches until it was over Tony's sternum.

Then it dropped.

The weight was like the Washington Monument on Tony Tollini's fragile chest. He couldn't breathe. But he could yell.

"I didn't do nothing! Ask Uncle Fiavorante. I didn't do nothing. On my mother, Don Carmine."

"You watch what you say about your mother, weasel," Don Carmine warned. "She is Don Fiavorante's sister. I won't have you defamin' the sister of Don Fiavorante with your fuggin' cogsugger lies."

"Please. Don't kill me."

"Show him the ad, somebody," ordered Don Carmine.

A newpaper was thrust into Tony Tollini's field of vision. He blinked the blurry tears from his beady frightened eyes and scanned the crumpled page.

Smack in the middle of the racing results was a black-bordered notice. It read:

LANSCII DISK FOUND

WILL RETURN FOR PROPER REWARD
CALL CHIUN 555-522-9452

"Chiun was the name the Jap gave," Don Carmine growled. He glared at Tony. "*Your* Jap."

"He's not my Jap," Tony moaned.

"You sent him."

"I hired him off the street, Don Carmine. Please don't nibble me to death like a baby duck."

"I own you, Tollini. If I wanna nibble you into the ground, I can. And you know why. Because I'm the fuggin' Kingpin of Boston, that's why. Now, tell me where the hard-on disk is."

"I don't know. I swear to God!"

"Okay, if that's the way you want it," said Don Carmine, jerking levers. The nibbler sank an eighth of an inch, but it made Tony Tollini's tortured sternum creak like a loose shutter in the wind.

"Had enough?"

"I swear," Tony sobbed.

The nibbler dropped again.

Now Tony could not breathe because his cracking ribs were compressing his lungs. His heart felt like it was about to burst.

He clicked his heels together and thought: There's no place like home. There's no place like home.

Abruptly the nibbler lifted. The pressure went away. When Tony opened his eyes, he could inhale again. He filled his lungs greedily.

A shadow crossed his face. He looked up. Don Carmine's brutish face was looking down at him. "Scared you, didn't I?" he said.

"Yes. Don't shoot me."

"I ain't gonna fuggin' shoot you." Don Carmine made motions with his paws. "Let him up, boys. Let him up."

Tony Tollini's head, wrists, and ankles were released, and he was hauled to his feet.

"What are you going to do to me?" he asked, his voice cracking.

"Nothin'. You're tellin' the truth. You gotta be. A weasel like you ain't man enough to be stand-up in the face of a nibbler." He swept his hands around to indicate the rusting construction yard with its idle equipment and piles of metal. "How'd you like my latest acquisition?"

"You bought a construction company?" asked Tony, prying a rusty gear off the back of his dirty Izod shirt.

"Naw. I just stuck a gun in the owner's face and he said it was mine. That's what I love about this state. Nothin's worth nothin' no more. So people don't put up a fuss when you take it away from them. I figure when things bounce back, I'll be in the driver's seat."

Tony found a hearty arm around his shoulders. He looked. It was Don Carmine's arm.

"I like you, Tony. Did I ever tell you I liked you?"

"No."

"You're sharp. You got brains. You also got what we call intesticle fortitude." He shook a lecturing finger in Tony's miserable face. "This is a good thing to have."

They were walking toward the Cadillac now. Bruno the Chef opened the rear door. Carmine stepped in. Tony meekly walked around to the trunk and waited for the lid to be opened.

"G'wan," said Don Carmine. "Get in here. From now on, you ride up front with me."

Tony slid into the back seat. The others got in. The Cadillac pulled out of the construction yard.

"Something's up," said Don Carmine as they hummed south along Route One. Tony saw sights he had never seen before. A miniature golf course guarded by a twenty-foot-tall orange plastic dinosaur, strip joints with fruit names like the Golden Banana, the Green Apple, and the Pink Peach. Chinese restaurants sprouted along the roadside like deformed mock-bamboo mushrooms.

"What do you mean, boss?" asked the Chef.

"Something about this doesn't add up. Think about it."

Everyone thought. Even Tony Tollini, although thinking wasn't in his job description.

"Anything, any of yous?" asked Don Carmine.

"Nope."

"Naw."

"I ain't got a thing," admitted the Maggot.

"Hah. That's why yous are all soldiers and I'm the kingpin. Listen up," said Don Carmine, ticking off points on his left hand with a stubby forefinger. "Tony hires this Remo character off the street. He breaks the box and whacks out Frank, Luigi, and Guido. Bing bang boom. Just like that. Dead. All three of 'em."

"Yeah?"

"What was the last thing I said before they dragged this Remo away?"

Everyone thought. The Maggot ventured an opinion.

"Scroom?"

"No, not scroom. I said, 'Get me a Jap.' Right?"

"Yeah. So?"

"You dummies. I say 'Get me a Jap' in front of this mook, Remo. He lams. I say 'Get me a Jap' to Tony here. And what happens?"

"He sends up a Jap."

"Right."

"So?" Pink Eye pointed out in a reasonable voice. "You're the Kingpin of Boston. Of course he sends up a Jap. Who wouldn't?"

"But follow my thinkin'. He wasn't any old Jap. He's a fuggin' thief. He robs me blind. Now he wants to sell me back my hard-on disk. What does that tell you?"

"Japs are crooks?"

"No. This is something new. There's someone on to us. You, Tony. This Remo. Why'd you send him?"

"I thought he would work out."

"You were wrong," Don Carmine snapped. "Why else?"

"Because he wrote that he would be the answer to my problems on his résumé."

"Ba boom," crowed Don Carmine Imbruglia. "There it is. This guy's a plant. They were both plants. You were conned, Tony my friend."

"I didn't mean to be."

"It's okay. You're new at this. Someone's trying to muscle in on our operation. Okay, it happens. Now we know. They don't know that we know, but we know. That gives us the edge."

"So what are we gonna do, boss?"

"So far we're okay. They may be cops. We don't know. They may be feds. We don't know that. They may be the fuggin' KGB. We don't know that either. They don't know where we are on account of I shot that Fedex guy accidentally on purpose and we hadda relocate."

"It was a good thing we did, huh, boss?" said Bruno. "Otherwise they could find us anytime they want to."

"Damn right. It was a fate accompli. It was destiny. So now we're gonna buy back our hard-on disk and then we're gonna grab this Jap thief and whoever's with him. We're gonna grab him and we're gonna sweat him. Then we know. Once we know, we kill everybody." Don Carmine made a broad dismissive gesture. "End of fuggin' problem."

"You don't think it's that Japanese Mafia, do you?" Pink Eye wondered.

"How many times I gotta tell you? There's no Mafia. We don't use that word in my outfit."

"Not even a Japanese Mafia?"

"Okay, there's a Japanese Mafia. Everybody knows that. But no Italians. The Japs just purloined the word from us. Sure, this could be them." He snapped his fingers impatiently. "What do they call themselves? It's some Jap name. Kazoo or something."

"Yeah, Kazoo," said the Maggot, nodding. "I heard of the Kazoo. They cut their own fingers off when they screw up."

"And that's what we're gonna do to them when I get my hands on them," said Don Carmine Imbruglia fiercely. "I ain't afraid of no Kazoo. We're gonna give these robbers a call right after we eat."

"Oh, shit, boss," said the Chef.

"What?"

"I think I forgot to turn off the stove."

24

One of the many phones arrayed around the office of Dr. Harold W. Smith began ringing at precisely 7:43 P.M.

Smith looked up from his computer. Remo looked around the room.

"Which one is it?" Remo wondered, trying to isolate the ringing.

It was the Master of Sinanju whose sharp ears picked out the correct telephone. He pointed. "That one." His smile was tight but pleased as Remo and Smith simultaneously lunged for the correct telephone.

Smith happened to be closer. He snatched up the receiver. "Yes?"

He listened intently as Remo hovered at his elbow.

"Yes, I have your item. The price for its return is seventy-five thousand dollars. Take it or leave it."

Remo edged closer as Smith placed a hand over his free ear. "I am pleased we agree on its worth," he said brittlely. "Now, where do you wish to make the exchange?"

Smith frowned as he leaned into the earpiece.

"Yes. That is no problem. Midnight it shall be."

Smith hung up. "They want to take delivery at the Bartilucci Construction Company in Saugus, Massachusetts," he explained as he looked at a small black box attached to the base of the telephone. Every phone in the room was equipped with a similar box.

When he returned to his computer and input the telephone number the box had captured, Harold Smith pressd the Send key. He waited.

While the system hummed busily, Remo said, "That's it? All these freaking phones for a two-minute conversation?"

"Not exactly. I placed identical ads in every Massachusetts newspaper. A different phone number in each ad, a different phone for each number. It was a long shot. The Mafia prefers to conduct their phone business via pay-phone booths. But it should give us a geographical locale."

Smith waited for the automatic search localizer to read out the telephone number captured by the black box—really a NYNEX Caller Identification box—and identify the locale.

"Ahh," he said. "A Massachusetts area code."

"Some breakthrough," Remo said sourly.

"The next three digits indicate the city of Quincy," Smith went on. "The northern section. Let us see if the final four digits represent a pay-phone location."

Smith frowned. "Odd. It's not a pay-phone. We may be able to trace this to a residence."

As Harold Smith's fingers flew, Remo glanced over to the Master of Sinanju. He was surreptitiously examining Remo's eyes. Remo put a hand over them and looked away. Chiun pretended to look out the two-way window.

"This is odd. This is very strange," Smith was saying.

"What is?" Remo asked, approaching Smith's terminal, his eyes curious.

"According to the phone-company data files, the number that answered the ad is not a working number."

"Is that possible?"

"If they are using pirated telephone connections, it is. It has been done before."

"So it's a dead end?"

Smith logged off. He brought up a wire-frame state map of Massachusetts and input the names "Quincy" and "Saugus."

"Hmmm. They are not remotely near one another at all. That may mean Quincy is a private residence." He looked up. "We will deal with this later. Master Chiun, I would like for you to meet these people at the place they named and give them back their hard disk."

"What of the seventy-five thousand dollars mentioned?" asked the Master of Sinanju.

"Of course, collect it if you can."

"There is no 'can' when Sinanju collects a debt," Chiun said loftily. "There is only 'must.' "

"You will of course return the money to me."

"Minus my finder's fee, of course," suggested the Master of Sinanju, his eyes twinkling.

Smith sighed. "Is ten percent acceptable?"

"Yes," said Chiun slowly. "I will allow you to retain ten percent. But only because you are my emperor. Otherwise it would be five."

Both Harold W. Smith and the Master of Sinanju glowered at Remo as he broke into gales of laughter.

Clearing his throat, Harold Smith returned to his computer. He had to finish maintaining the LANSCII hard disk before it was delivered to Saugus.

25

It was supposed to be a simple errand, thought Nicolo "Nicky Kix" Stivaletta. Meet the Jap. Hand the Jap the payoff. Take the hard-on disk. Then whack out the Jap where he stood.

"Simple. In and out. Bing bang boom. And home in time for *Hunter*," as he told Vinnie (The Maggot) Maggiotto, who had earned his nickname because he'd once been arrested for the heinous crime of dumpster diving. The Maggot's hairless bullet of a head contributed to its longevity.

"What if the Jap ain't alone?" the Maggot wondered.

"Then you got somebody to clip too," said Nicky Kix, who had come by his street name because of his habit of kicking in the ribs and skulls of people after he had brought them down with a sawed-off shotgun.

"Okay, I got somebody to clip too," said the Maggot, who had often boasted to his fellow Deer Island inmates that he had clipped as many guys as he had fingers. In fact, the Maggot had never clipped anything. Including his nails. The Maggot was not renowned for his grooming skills.

The headlights of their Dodge raced ahead of them as they came off the Saugus exit of Route One, north of Boston. They threw the chain-link fence of the Bartilucci Construction Company into sharp relief as the car slid through the open gate.

"Okay," said Nicky Kix. "It's show time."

They got out.

"See anything?" Nicky asked uneasily.

"Nothing. Maybe he ain't showed yet. Maybe he ain't gonna show," the Maggot added, silently hoping he would not have to clip anyone.

Then a low, stern voice seemed to surround them.

"I am here, messengers of the dreaded boss."

"Where? Where is he?"

A figure detached itself from the shadow of the long storage building.

He stepped into the headlight beams, clad in a kimono of dull black silk, his eyes narrowing to slits, his hands unseen in the tunnels of his joined sleeves.

"Put your hands where I can see them," warned Nicky Kix, amazed that the old Jap wasn't blinded by the lights.

"Show me your ransom first," returned the old Jap.

"Okay," said Nicky. "Have it your way." He pulled a thick manila envelope from inside his jacket, fat with greenbacks.

He held them up to the lights so the edges of two twenties were visible. "All seventy-five grand," he added, keeping a straight face. There was actually less than fifty dollars in the envelope sandwiching a dollar-size sheaf of cut newsprint.

"Very well," said the Jap, bringing his hands into view.

One hand—the left—was clutching a black plastic box.

"That's it," breathed the Maggot.

"I know that's it," hissed Nicky. "Now shaddup and let me do all the talkin'. Okay," he said, lifting his voice. "Let's swap."

The Jap advanced. As he loomed larger and larger in the light, seeming to make no sound as he moved toward them, Nicky Kix lifted the envelope with one hand and reached out with the other to accept the all-important disk.

"When I've got the disk," he hissed to the Maggot, "you shoot him. In the stomach, not the head."

"I thought the head was better," the Maggot breathed back, beads of dirty sweat popping up on his shiny forehead.

Nicky Kix was speaking through clenched teeth so it would look as if he were smiling.

"It is," he said. "If you wanna clip a guy right off. I just want him down so I can kick the shit out of him while he's squirming and bleeding."

"Okay," said the Maggot, swallowing hard.

The old Jap was now less that five feet away. Then four. Three.

He stopped with less than two feet separating him from the outstretched money envelope. The hard disk came up into the moonlight. Nicky Kix laid blunt fingers on it as long-nailed fingers simultaneously snatched away the envelope.

To cover for what was about to happen, Nicky Kix said, "You don't need to count it. It's all there."

"You are Romans," said the old Jap. "I need to count it."

And to Nicky Kix's astonishment, the old Jap blatantly ignored underworld etiquette and riffled through the money.

"Now!" he hissed to the Maggot. "He's gonna catch on. Now!"

"But," said the Maggot, his eyes fear-sick, "I forgot to bring a gun."

That was all Nicky Kix needed to hear. He went for his own weapon.

It was a silenced .22 Beretta. He brought it out of a worn shoulder holster. He was going to put one in the old Jap's stomach and then kick him around the yard as Don Carmine had sanctioned.

Nicky Kix made the gun level with his belt, putting the barrel in line with the old Jap's stomach. As he began to caress the trigger, the old Jap's head came up angrily, his dark eyes flashing. He had discovered the newsprint. Too late now, you old riceball, Nicky thought savagely.

Nicky Kix pulled the trigger.

The resulting scream of terror was bloodcurdling.

A wolfish grin started to warp Nicky Kix's face. Until he realized that the scream had come not from in front of him, but to his immediate right. He looked right.

Vinnie (The Maggot) Maggiotto was doubled over on his feet, clutching his paunchy stomach. He was squirming and stamping his feet and making incomplete footprints in the blood that was dribbling down his pant legs to the ground. Then he fell over and began to kick and writhe like his hairless namesake.

Nicky Kix looked down. He saw that his .22 was pointed in a different direction than his brain had thought it was. A long-nailed hand had redirected it with such suddenness that Nicky never felt his own hand move.

Nicky Kix took a quick step backward, the .22 sliding from the light redirecting touch of the old Jap. He brought the muzzle back in line. And fired.

The old Jap twisted on one foot, the other suddenly stamping down in a different place.

Nicky knew he had missed only because his wayward bullet had struck a silvery spark at a fencepost behind the wily old Jap. He tried again.

The old Jap was quicker. He spun, feinted, and ducked.

Nicky thought he had followed every wily move. He was sure he had a solid bead when he drew back on the trigger. He felt the recoil, heard the dry pop of the cartridge separating, and was rewarded with the sound and spark of a slug ricocheting off the idle nibbler machine.

"You have what you want, cheater," intoned the old man. "Go now and I will let you live."

"Screw you," said Nicky, going for a lucky third shot.

He never got a chance to fire again.

From behind the nibbler a tall lean shape plunged.

Nicky Kix didn't stick around to figure out who this new guy was. He might be packing. And Nicky remembered that his job was first and foremost to get the hard-on disk to Don Carmine.

He jumped for the open door of his idling Dodge. Without closing it, he sent the car screeching into reverse, out the gate, and around and into traffic.

He floored the gas pedal, remembering to close the driver's side door only after he was on Route One.

Back at the Bartilucci Construction Company, Remo Williams watched the Dodge back out of the yard as if chased by a junkyard dog.

"Are you okay, Little Father?" he asked anxiously.

"Why do you ask?" said Chiun, stepping up to the squirming figure of the Maggot.

"I heard shots."

"They became excited," said Chiun, resting a sandal on the twisting head of the Maggot. "And are you not forgetting your duty? You must follow that one."

"I will, I will," Remo said impatiently. "I just wanted to be sure you were all right."

"Of course I am all right," said Chiun harshly, bringing down his foot. The Maggot made a cracking sound with his head and a kind of lamb's bleat with his last breath. A yellowish-red squirt of combined blood and brains jumped from each ear. "I am the Reigning Master of Sinanju. Not some doddering ancient."

"Okay, okay, I just wanted to be sure." Remo started off. He turned suddenly. "You'll be okay until I get back?"

"Be off, callow youth!"

Reluctance in every movement, Remo melted into the darkness.

Out on the street, Remo shook off his lack of resolve. He ran up onto the curving on-ramp and into the humming night traffic of Route One. He knew the fleeing car had to be going south, so he ran south.

Legs pumping, he seemed to float along the breakdown lane. Cars whizzed by, their headlights warming the back of his neck, practically his only exposed piece of skin.

Remo was wearing his silk suit and it was hampering every movement. Still, as he settled into a rhythm, he began to pick up speed. Soon the cars were no longer whizzing by. Remo was zipping past them. His eyes were peeled for the Dodge. He would recognize it from its plate.

A mile clicked by. Remo's hair was flying back, the wind in his face. His new face. No, strike that, he thought. His old face. His first face. He was feeling good. He was running at optimum speed and it was just a matter of trailing the thug's car to its destination.

Except for the Boston traffic, it would have worked.

Remo had gone less than three miles when he realized the occasional speeders and lane cutters were not the exception but the rule.

"They're maniacs up here," Remo growled as he was forced to enter the thick of traffic when a Porsche barreled up the breakdown lane as if it were marked off for his personal convenience.

"Screw this," Remo decided. Three cars behind the Dodge, he picked a flat-roofed yellow-and-silver MBTA bus and maneuvered behind it.

His breathing lowered to keep out noxious exhaust fumes, Remo matched the bus's lumbering speed, only a few inches behind the rear bumper.

When he knew the timing was right, he jumped.

Except for the fact that this was a highway, he might have been a kid back in Newark hitching a ride to the back of a trundling bus. Except Remo didn't stay on the bumper. He went right up the back to the roof.

Up there he stood braced on both feet, like a surfer negotiating the swells. The bus ran smoothly, and Remo had a good view of the Dodge. He grinned. This was going to be a piece of cake.

And because he was standing up in full view, he saw the Dodge take the Melrose exit simply by cutting in front of two lanes of traffic.

Over a dozen cars slammed on their brakes at the same time. Including the bus Remo was straddling.

Amid a cacophony of crumpling fenders and shattering safety glass, Remo was thrown off the bus roof as if pitched from a bucking bronco.

Normally he could have compensated for the centrifugal force of the bus's sudden change in direction. The shifting flow of air on his bare arms and his body would have triggered body reflexes before Remo became conscious of the impending shift in momentum.

But his arms were not bare. Remo, caught off-guard and lacking anything to grab hold of, lost foot contact with the bus roof and was thrown forward.

Turning in the air, he found his equilibrium and picked a ragtop to alight on. He bounced slightly and came down on the median strip.

Anxiously Remo looked for the off ramp. Maybe there was still time to catch up.

He put all thought of the slippery Dodge out of his mind when a frantic voice cried, "Help me, someone! My wife is trapped!"

Remo jumped over a sedan hood and pushed a man out of the way so he could get to the passenger side of a compact whose engine had been vomited from its shorn hood and was spilling licking gasoline-fed flames.

On the passenger side, a woman was hung up in the straps of her shoulder harness, her head down, a tributary of blood visible in the snarling orange glow washing her forehead.

Remo saw that the driver had escaped through his shattered window. The driver's door had been compacted in place. He was trying to wrench it open, sobbing and crying his wife's name.

Gently impelling him to one side, Remo stepped up to the gaping window and took hold of the jagged frame. He stepped back.

The door surrendered with a lurching groan. He set it aside and crawled in. The straps came free like cobwebs under his swift hard fingers. The woman slumped. There was no time to worry about broken bones. The flames were starting to roar.

Crawling back, Remo pulled the woman out like a dead cat. Only she was not dead. Her heart still beat.

He brought her to the side of the road and laid her there as her husband fell to his knees behind her, sobbing without words.

There were more injured, and Remo went to help them. He had no choice. He had screwed up. Not lying flat on the bus roof had spooked the mafioso. This had been the result.

An hour later, a tired Remo Williams limped back to the Bartilucci Construction Company yard.

"You failed," Chiun said after only a glance at his pupil's bedraggled clothes. His necktie was smeared with soot. Here and there, seams had burst.

"Don't rub it in, okay?" Remo said dispiritedly.

"You should have done your duty, not dallied like an amateur."

"Hey! I was worried about you. Is that a crime?"

"Worry I will accept. Pity is unacceptable. You think I am too old to serve my emperor?"

"No, I do not," Remo said. Chiun glared. "Okay. Maybe a little."

"I will remind you that you were incautious enough to make an alarm sound when Smith sent you on a small errand."

"It was one of those ultrasonic alarms," Remo said sourly. "A fly can't get past them. And I'd like to see you handle one."

"Perhaps you will," said Chiun tightly.

"Great. Then you can teach me. Come on, let's give the bad news to Smith."

"I will leave it to you to inform Smith that the ransom was not properly paid," Chiun said tonelessly.

"Except that I saw you take the envelope. What're you trying to pull?"

"Nothing. Behold. There is no more than forty dollars in this envelope. The remainder is waste paper."

"Only forty?"

Chiun beamed. "Less my finder's fee, of course."

"That's too bad, Little Father," said Remo. "You get only thirty-six bucks."

"Smith will make up the rest, of course. For my fee was based on the ransom to be paid, not the ransom that was delivered."

Remo said, "Chiun, I can hardly wait to be the fly on the wall when you try to work that out with Smitty."

"Smith will not deny me."

"No," said Remo, jerking a thumb at the deceased form of Vinnie (The Maggot) Maggiotto. "If you hadn't eliminated that guy, we would have had a line on LCN headquarters."

"We will not speak of this one to Smith," Chiun said quickly.

"Only if you stop carping."

"I never carp. I enlighten."

"Try enlighting without carping, then," said Remo.

"Only if you will attempt to receive enlightenment," returned the Master of Sinanju.

They left the body to decompose in the dark as they walked to their waiting car parked behind the long shed.

26

Don Carmine Imbruglia was soaking the postmarks off a stack of postage stamps he had steamed off the day's mail when Nicky Kix burst in with the bad news.

"I didn't whack the Jap."

"Scroom, then," said Don Carmine, adding a dollop more Lestoil.

"And I lost the Maggot."

"Screw the Maggot," snarled Don Carmine. "He eats garbage. Tell me somethin' important. What about the fuggin' hard-on disk?"

"Right here, boss," said Nicky Kix, producing the sealed disk unit.

"Beautiful," said Don Carmine, his mood instantly brightening. He kissed the disk. "Beautiful. Now I'm gonna make some money."

"You're already making money."

"Yeah, but I gotta pay tribute on it to Don Fiavorante. This stuff in here is all free and clear."

"Oh, I get it. Guess you gotta let Tollini off the hook, huh?"

"No chance. He don't know about this. And who's gonna tell him? You? Do that and you'll never eat pasta in this town again."

"Don't he gotta install it?" asked Nicky Kix.

This thought gave Don Carmine pause. "Yeah, but he don't have to know what it is."

"What about the Jap? There was a guy with him."

"He look like a fed?"

"No, he looked like a hood."

Don Carmine's disarrayed eyebrows bristled and squirmed in slow thought.

"I wonder who's tryin' to muscle in?" he muttered.

"Search me," admitted Nicky Kix, trying to look innocent. "Maybe it's Don Fiavorante. Gonna make a move on you."

This caused Don Carmine's bristly eyebrows to descend like relays closing.

"If it was, why'd he give back the hard-on disk?" wondered Don Carmine.

"Search me."

"Well, whoever it was, he was makin' a feudal gesture. Completely feudal. We got the disk and we got Boston. Nothin' can stop us now. We're makin' dough hand over fist."

"I am glad to hear this, Don Carmine," said a smooth-as-suntan-oil voice from the slowly opening door.

"Who's that?" growled Don Carmine, starting.

When his eyebrows had jumped up, he could see clearly Don Fiavorante Pubescio's well-tanned features beaming at him.

"Don Fiavorante!" Carmine Imbruglia said brightly, his mood changing from suspicion to forced pleasure. He came out of his seat, wiping sweat off his hairy palms.

"So good to see you, Fuggin," said Don Fiavorante, reaching out to embrace his *sottocapo*.

Carmine Imbruglia returned the embrace, noting the two hulking Pubescio soldiers standing just outside the door. "They don't call me that up here. Up here I'm Cadillac."

"You were always the kidder, Fuggin," said Don Fiavorante. "I like this about you. I always have."

"Yeah, yeah. What can I do for you?"

"I am seeing my rent money come in like it was flowing from a tap, and I say to myself, this Don Carmine, he is one bright boy. I must see his sports book for myself."

"Didn't you get my fax?"

"Perhaps. I do not understand these machines. Many times the machine rings. I get the little light. I hear the loud beeps, but all that rolls out is blank paper."

"Wrong faxes. We get them too. There oughta be a law."

"Tell me, Don Carmine. Your sports book is outperforming Vegas. How do you pick your winners so perfectly?"

"Come on, I'll show you," Don Carmine said, urging Don Fiavorante away from the sealed hard disk with lifted hands that took care not to touch his don. "I got a brilliant new way to pick the winning teams. It's fuggin' phenomenal. Works on the ponies, on football, baseball, anything you want. It's based on a well-known law of human nature nobody but me has caught on to."

They were walking along a curving well-carpeted corridor.

"You use computers?" asked Don Fiavorante.

"Naw. Computers can't do that stuff. Believe me, I tried. First week I had one, I kept typin' in questions like 'Jets or Steelers?' All I got was error this and error that. The fuggin' computer musta thought I was talkin' baseball or somethin'."

"These machines, they are overrated," said Don Fiavorante.

They came at last to a door marked "ODDS MAKERS."

"Watch this," said Don Carmine, throwing the door open. He thrust his bullet head in, startling a quintet of unshaven swarthy-faced men seated around a big-screen TV. They were watching a hockey game.

"Who's playin'?" Don Carmine asked.

"It's the Bruins against the Canadiens," said one swarthy man in a strangely accented voice.

"Who you guys think is gonna win?" asked Don Carmine.

The quintet huddled. When their heads reemerged, the spokesman said, "The Bruins. Clearly."

"Everybody agree on that?" Don Carmine asked.

"Yes."

"Absolutely."

"Of course."

"Great," said Don Carmine happily. "Thanks." He shut the door.

"The Canadiens," said Don Carmine Imbruglia confidently, "are gonna massacre them Broons."

"You are certain?"

"Absolutely," said Don Carmine. He jerked his thumb back in the direction of the closed door. "You see those guys back there? Palestinians, every one of 'em. They're never right. All you gotta do is ask 'em who'll win and then go with the other team. If they don't agree, that means it'll be a tie. I tell you, it's foolproof. Fuggin' foolproof!"

Don Fiavorante Pubescio placed both hands on the thick shoulders of Don Carmine Imbruglia and in his warmest voice said, "Don Carmine, you are a genius."

Don Carmine puffed out his barrel chest. His tiny eyes twinkled like proud stars.

"I know you will go far in Boston," added the don.

"Thanks, Don Fiavorante."

"And because I know great things lie before you, I am increasing your rent ten percent."

"Ten fuggin' percent!" howled Don Carmine.

"Retroactive to last Tuesday. With interest accrued."

"But . . . but . . . but . . ." sputtered Don Carmine, his face turning crimson. "What'd I ever do to you? I do everything you say. I give you no problems. Not one."

Don Fiavorante Pubescio held up a beringed hand.

"Do not consider this modest increase as a painful thing," he said broadly. "Look upon it as incentive. Let it spur you to new heights. You will make more money and so will I. None of us will lose."

"It's gonna fuggin' spur me into an early grave, is what it's gonna do," Don Carmine complained.

Don Fiavorante's genteel expression darkened. "It pains me to hear such ingratitude from one whose markers I carry without complaint. I would dislike having to call in those markers."

"Okay, okay," said Don Carmine through set teeth. "I'll try to look at it that way. But you gotta let me get on my feet a little more. The rent on this dump is killin' me."

After Don Fiavorante had left, Don Carmine Imbruglia stood with his hands dangling down his sides. His fingers hung low enough to almost brush his kneecaps.

When the crimson tinge of his wide face slowly seeped away, Don Carmine growled, "Get that Tony. We gotta make more fuggin' money. Piles of it."

"We need somethin' big," Don Carmine was explaining to a frightened Tony Tollini, who had been hauled from his bed in the dead of night.

"But, Don Carmine, you have everything locked up in this state."

"There's gotta be somethin' we overlooked. Somethin' big. We need a big score. I could knock over banks, but the ones that ain't shut up are carrying our money. We'd be robbing ourselves. These ain't the old days, when you could launder dough through the front door and carry the safe out through the back. Nowadays you hit a bank and it's liable to go under. There's no percentage in it anymore."

Tony Tollini's beady eyes narrowed.

"Come on," Don Carmine urged.

"Well," he said, "there are the Terrapins."

Don Carmine looked stung. "Bowling? Are you talkin' bowling?"

"No, Terrapins. Not Candlepins."

"Never heard of it."

"It's the biggest business operation in this state," Tony explained. "In any state. It's responsible for over a billion dollars a year in fees, licensing, video, movies, toys, and other revenue."

"How come I never heard of this thing?"

"They're global," said Tony Tollini.

"I don't know from fuggin' global," snarled Don Carmine. "I'm from Brooklyn. Come on. You can tell me about it while you're puttin' in a new hard-on disk. I picked up a real nice one on sale. That's the one great thing about this stupid state. Every day's a fuggin' fire sale."

27

In his office at Folcroft Sanitarium, Dr. Harold W. Smith watched the dark computer screen as it displayed a single word in phosphor green letters.

The word was "WAITING."

Smith had been waiting half the night since receiving word from Remo and Chiun that they had delivered the disk. It was impatience on Smith's part that compelled him to stay long into the night, waiting for the hard disk to be installed and reach out through the telephone system via a hidden program he had installed in the disk.

The Boston Mafia would probably wait until tomorrow to install it, he concluded at last. He had been banking on the Mafia's basic psychology of distrust. They would typically check the disk as soon as it was back in their possession.

Smith dragged himself out of his comfortable chair, feeling his knees creak. He reached for his ancient briefcase.

The system beeped once, drawing Smith's gaze back to the dark screen. He sat down hard, his fingers coming up into the backglow of the single word floating in the electronic blackness.

Only now the word was "WORKING."

Smith's lips thinned in anticipation. He had been right, after all.

Then he got a screenful of silent letters. It was an alphanumeric program completion display. Smith tapped a key.

The word "LANSCII" appeared in large letters and Smith allowed himself a tight smile of satisfaction.

He worked swiftly, with assurance, knowing that the LANSCII disk had, once installed, immediately dialed his own computer, thus establishing a dedicated-line linkup.

Smith invoked the password. The Mafia disk had contained the password. It had not been changed.

Every bit and byte of data contained in the Mafia system—presumably a battery of linked PC's—was now at his disposal.

Raw columns of data and electronic spreadsheet programs began to scroll before his eyes.

The headings were varied: "GAMING," "VIGORISH," "CARTING," "BROADS." Smith stopped at "GAMING."

What he saw astonished him. According to the LANSCII files, the Boston Mafia had for over a week been predicting the winners of a wide array of sports events—even to the point of calling tie games. Their point spread was not consistently on the money, but their selections were utterly flawless.

"They cannot be fixing every sporting event in the nation," Smith muttered to his unhearing computer.

He moved on. There would be time to explore that aspect later. He paged his way to the bottom lines. Weekly the Boston LCN was generating a modest six figures of illicit tax-free income. This was unusual only in that its growth rate was virtually doubling from day to day.

"If this goes on . . ." Smith said, his voice trailing off. Smith found names and addresses of contacts in Boston and the Massachusetts state government. Payoff ledgers on crooked officials. Officers on the pad. The tentacles of the Mafia were insinuating themselves into the usual weak societal crevices.

Smith suddenly remembered that he had neglected to check the phone number of the line he had been connected to.

He engaged the back-trace program.

To his surprise, he got a non-working number, but a different one than had previously called in answer to the blackmail ad. The locale numbers were the same, however. North Quincy, Massachusetts. It was a significant clue. One Smith would return to later.

As he poked through the LANSCII data base, he came upon a new file being created hundreds of miles to the north.

As he watched, fascinated, duplicate letters were appearing before his eyes. A strange word completed itself: "TERRAPINS."

"What on earth?"

Silently, letter by letter, a second word appeared beside it: "SKIM."

"Terrapin skim?" said Smith dully.

He had to look the first word up on his electronic dictionary, and when he did, he knew instantly the next target of the Boston Mafia. And he knew how much money was about to pour into the LANSCII files, not merely from Boston, but from factories as far away as Hong Kong and Melbourne.

The Mafia was about to wrap its tentacles around one of the greatest enterprises of modern times.

Harold Smith reached for the telephone, his agile mind instantly recalling from memory the phone number of the Boston hotel where Remo and Chiun were staying.

There was still time to head off this new move.

28

All Jeter Baird ever wanted out of life was to draw comic books.

It was a simple aspiration, a very American one. One which might never have come true for the young artist had an Amherst, Massachusetts, Backgammon pizza shop not been filled to overflowing on the Friday night after finals in late May 1984.

Artist Jeter Baird was balancing a shaky tray containing a provolone-and-sausage pizza and two jumbo Dr. Peppers as he looked about for an empty table. There were no empty tables. Jeter needed an empty table. He was so shy he couldn't stand not to eat alone. What if a girl struck up a conversation? He didn't know how to talk to girls. Jeter also needed the table space to accommodate the sketchpad tucked under his arm.

Since finals at the University of Massachusetts at Amherst were over, Jeter was looking forward to a long sultry summer of fevered sketching. Mostly of girls.

If only he could snag some table space in the tiny pizza shop that was jammed to the counters with his fellow students.

Finally a pair of long-legged blonds evacuated a round corner table.

Jeter Baird lunged for it, his tray held before him like a battering ram carried edge-on.

Simultaneously Devin Western lunged for the identical table, an identical tray slicing the air before him, a sketchpad of his own tucked under his arm.

They landed in their seats together.

"I saw it first," whined Jeter.

"No, I did," insisted Devin.

"Well, I need the whole table for sketching."

"Me too."

The impasse lasted only long enough for each budding young artist to register the fact that he was in the presence of another budding young artist. They glanced warily at one another's work.

"You published?" Jeter asked Devin, getting to the heart of the matter. He knew that no college art student drew comic book superheroes unless he aspired to publication.

"No. You?"

"No."

Silence filled the corner of the noisy room.

"But I'm working on a neat idea," said Devin. "Terrapin-Man."

"What's a terrapin?" asked Jeter.

"Kind of turtle that swims."

"Why not call him Sea Turtle-Man then?"

"Because CD Comics just published *Master Turtle*."

Jeter nodded in sad sympathy. "Yeah, Wonder Comics got *Squirrel Woman* into print while I was still designing the costume for Squirrel Girl."

"I like 'Squirrel Girl' better. It rhymes."

"Her true identity was going to be Doreen Green, because that rhymes too."

"Maybe we could collaborate," suggested Devin.

"Great! Can you write?"

"No. Can you?"

"No."

More silence. Jeter Baird and Devin Western eyed their pizzas with a sad mixture of disappointment and hunger.

Popular culture stood at a crossroads at that moment, although neither artist knew it. Had they fallen to eating their cooling pizza in sullen silence, billions of dollars would never have changed hands, tens of thousands of craftsmen, assembly-line workers, shippers, and truck drivers worldwide would have gone without work, and millions of children across the globe would have grown up with lives somehow emptier and joyless, and no one would ever have known it.

It was then that Devin said, "I know. We'll both write and we'll both draw."

"Great," they said in unison, flipping open their sketchbooks to blank pages.

As their pizzas cooled and congealed, they swapped ideas.

"Terrapin Warrior," suggested Devin. "We'll make him a ninja. Ninjas are hot."

"That was last year. Androids are big this year. Personally, I think androids are too plastic to last. Mutants are good for another five years. We should do mutants."

"Mutants suck. They're always whining and complaining about being mutants. Besides, I don't want to be too commercial. I'm a serious comic-book artist."

"Yeah," said Jeter. "When you're too commercial, no one respects your work."

Marketing philosophies in synch, Jeter Baird and Devin Western brainstormed to closing. The trouble was, they found, all the great superhero character names were taken.

"Cow Princess," Jeter announced, holding up a pencil rough of a voluptuous Amazon with a triple-decker bosom. "She gores her enemies with her forehead horns."

Devin frowned with his mouth and ogled with his eyes. "My mother would kill me if she caught me drawing a girl with six breasts," he said. "Besides, cows don't have horns."

They went back to work.

"Ta-dah!" Devin shouted. "Giraffe Boy."

"How will he get through doors with that neck?" asked Jeter critically, looking at the hasty sketch. "You know how much trouble Flaming Carrot has."

"Good point. Maybe we should get away from animals and fish. Be original. Go with. . . ."

"Fruit."

"The Ultimate Pistachio," cried Devin, sketching up a storm. "See, he wears a giant kevlar-titanium pistachio shell over his face to conceal his true identity as a migrant worker."

"Do pistachios have superpowers?" wondered Jeter.

Devin chewed his pencil eraser. "They're hard and salty," he ventured.

"So's Popeye the Sailor, and he hasn't been big since the fifties."

"I still like my terrapins," Devin said forlornly, scribbling a quartet of happy reptilian faces.

"Mutant Terrapins!" Jeter shouted in triumph.

"No. We gotta be original. Can't call them mutants."

"Transformed Terrapins," suggested Jeter, adding a row of domino masks to his newfound collaborator's sketch.

"Good start," said Devin, grinning with approval. "How about giving them nunchuks?"

"How about Transformed Tae Kwon Do Teen Terrapins?" blurted out Jeter Baird, inadvertently coining a new industry.

"Yeah, yeah. It's fresh, it's original, and most if all it's not commercial."

"Right. No one will take us seriously if we're too commercial."

Little did they dream.

By emptying their tuition funds, Jeter and Devin printed five hundred thousand copies of the first issue of *Transformed Tae Kwon Do Teen Terrapins*, and when the first shipment arrived at their dorm, they ripped open the boxes and reveled in the thrill of being published comic-book artists at last.

Then harsh reality sank in.

"This isn't as funny as I remember," said Devin.

"Maybe we should have hired a writer," muttered Jeter.

They looked at one another, going as slack-jawed as their creations.

"Will anyone buy these?" wondered Devin.

"Will we ever finish our education?" worried Jeter.

Their eyes widened in alarm as they realized that their mothers were going to kill them when they found out.

Jeter and Devin canvased every comic-book store and newsstand in Amherst, trying to sell *Transformed Tae Kwon Do Teen Terrapins* to anyone that would take them.

Where they weren't laughed at, they were spit upon.

"I can't tell my mother," wailed Jeter.

"Neither can I," moaned Devin.

It was Jeter who hit upon the thing that was to enable them to recoup their investment and make them millionaires many times over.

"There's only one thing we can do," he said.

"What that?"

"Get on the Tuckahoe show."

"How will that help?"

"It won't," Jeter admitted. "But both our moms watch him

every day. It's better than having to watch them cry when they learn what we did."

They hitchhiked to New York City, a case of *Transformed Tae Kwon Do Teen Terrapins* number one under each arm.

It was surprisingly easy, they found. The research director of *The Bil Tuckahoe Show* had only to listen to their tale of woe once when she blurted out, "College students who squander their tuition money on comic books!" she cried. "It's perfect, and we can postpone that awful segment on monkey makeovers."

"But we didn't buy them," Jeter started to say.

"We had them printed," Devin finished.

"Don't say another word! Bil likes his guests to go on cold."

The next day, frightened and tearful, Jeter and Devin found themselves in front of a studio audience as the silver-haired Bil Tuckahoe fixed them with his sheepdog eyes and demanded, "You two boys are addicted to comic books, aren't you? Admit it. You'll do anything for a mint copy of *The Fantastic Four*. Lie, cheat, steal, sell your parents into slavery."

They tried to explain. Devin started to cry. Jeter lifted a copy of *Transformed Tae Kwon Do Teen Terrapins* number one up to his face like a felon being hauled before a judge.

A camerman rushed in to capture the cover in his viewfinder, while a studio technician punched up a slugline graphic which read, "Jeter Baird. Addicted to Comic Books."

The image of four fat masked sea turtles clutching Oriental weaponry was broadcast across the nation for the first time, electrifying preschool America.

Jeter Baird and Devin Western never sold a single copy of their comic book. They never finished college or got their marketing degrees.

They didn't have to. The cartoon, toy, and film offers began pouring in before taping ended on that day's edition of *The Bil Tuckahoe Show*.

Soon the images of the four terrapins was unavoidable from Manhattan to Madagascar. The money came in by the sackful. Every toy deal triggered another. Modest TV cartoons led to full-length movie deals. Everything the scaly cartoon creatures touched turned to gold.

It was an American success story of unprecedented proportions.

And, like all American success stories, it had a downside.

Jeter and Devin had enjoyed six years of exponential business expansion, moving directly from their cramped dorm rooms to a sprawling office park *cum* movie studio just outside of Amherst, when they realized the free ride was over.

They realized this when, during the filming of *Transformed Tae Kwon Do Teen Terrapins III: Shell Game*, a sniper killed the star, D'Artagnan.

D'Artagnan was not the actor's actual name. It was Sammy Bong, an out-of-work chopsocky actor running around the TTTT backlot in a polyurethane-and-foam-rubber anamatronic Terrapin costume.

D'Artagnan was about to run an evil ninja through with a fencer's sword when his polyurethane shell was split by a steel-jacketed bullet and the green of his foam chest turned dark with blood.

The demand note came in the morning mail, while Jeter and Devin were still in shock.

The note said: "We get ten percent. Gross. Or Athos is next."

To add insult to injury, the note was made from words cut out of Terrapin toy ads and pasted onto a sheet of official Terrapin kiddie stationery.

"What do we do?" asked Devin in a sick voice.

"We pay. Next time it could be us."

The trouble was, the note forgot to say whom to pay.

They found Athos with his green throat slit and stuffed into a trash barrel on the backlot that very afternoon, his three-toed webbed feet dangling askew over the sides.

Nicky Kix Stivaletta showed up as the private ambulance was hauling the deceased Terrapin away under the wide unblinking eyes of the surviving Terrapins, Aramis and Porthos.

Nicky Kix stepped out of the work car and sauntered up to Jeter and Devin. He was flanked by two goons in pinstripes.

Devin, quicker on the uptake, hissed to the surviving Terrapins, "Swim for it!"

The Terrapins held their ground. They wanted to defend their honor.

"Or you're both fired," added Jeter.

The dejected terrapins slunk off to safety.

"You get my message?" asked Nicky Kix, rolling a toothpick around his mouth as he pushed the hard words out.

"Why'd you kill Athos? We were going to pay you!" demanded Devin, hot tears streaming down his cheeks.

Nicky Kix shrugged. "I like the smell of roadkill."

"Ten percent?" said Jeter.

"Cash. No checks."

"Can we get a receipt?" Jeter and Devin asked in unison, their incomplete business courses coming into play.

"No," said Nicky Kix in a bored voice.

Dejectedly Jeter and Devin led Nicky Kix and his muscular entourage to their joint office, pushing aside plush Terrapin toys, edging past Terrapin arcade video games and cardboard movie-lobby standees.

Jeter cleared a cardboard box containing breakfast—a pepper-and-onion pizza—from a chair so Nicky Kix could sit down.

"I'll stand," said Nicky Kix, eyeing the stained seat warily. He snapped his fingers impatiently. "Now, pony up. I ain't got all day."

In fact, Nicky Kix Stivaletta was destined not to have more than a minute and thirteen seconds remaining in his entire life.

He got an inkling of this when the office door suddenly banged open, upsetting a three-foot-tall plush Aramis doll.

Nicky's bodyguards whirled, hands going into coats, fingers wrapping around hard steel pistol grips.

Webbed three-fingered hands beat them to the draw.

One pair simply swept in for Sal (Toe Biter) Bugliosi's unprotected ears. He heard a thunderclap that kept his eardrums ringing until three days after his embalming. The air pressure scrambled his brain in its skull cavity and opened every fissure in the protective bone.

The other Terrapin—his purple mask and short stature marked him as Porthos—employed a high kick to break Pauli (Pink Eye) Scanga's pelvis like a soda cracker.

Pauli let go of his half-drawn pistol and grabbed his crotch, which was leaking all manner of body fluids, and tried to claw his lower body back into an erect position.

But his legs simply bent at ankles and knees and he made a messy moist pile where he had stood.

"Aramis!" blurted Jeter.

"Porthos?" gulped Devin.

"Bullshit," snarled Nicky Kix as he drew down on the advancing Terrapins with a sawed-off double-barreled shotgun he whipped out from under his coat.

He hauled back on one trigger.

The blast riddled Aramis. Unfortunately for Nicky Kix, it was the plush Aramis in a corner. It also cracked the arcade game screen and made a cheap plastic Terrapin alarm clock jangle discordantly.

Porthos was wide open, however. Nicky sent a blast of buckshot toward his sappy face.

The blast, however, made a kind of black spiral galaxy pattern in the dropped fiberboard ceiling.

Nicky Kix looked up. He saw the peppery hits. He looked down, where he noticed a green three-fingered hand holding his smoking shotgun barrels at an upward angle.

He was thinking: Where have I seen this shit before? when the shotgun was taken away from him rather harshly, and returned, stock-first, into his abdomen.

Nicky Kix said "Oof" and doubled over, still on his feet.

A spongy green hand grabbed him by his Brylcreemed hair and led him over to a microwave parked on a corner table.

"In you go," said a casual male voice.

Nicky thought that he sounded nothing like the real Aramis. He also thought that he was in no danger. Sure, his head was in a microwave oven. But everybody knew they wouldn't work unless the door was closed. And this couldn't happen as long as his neck was in the way.

The male voice asked, "Care to do the honors, Little Father?"

"Normally I do not sully my hands with machines," said a strangely familiar squeaky voice, "but this one is guilty of cruelty to reptiles."

Then came the funny noises. Bangings and crunchings. A piece of the oven wall pierced Nicky Kix's unshaven cheek and he realized that the oven was being compacted. He couldn't imagine how. A steel shard embedded itself in his forehead next. His ears were mashed against the sides of his head. The noises wouldn't stop, and when Nicky reached out for the microwave to pull his head loose, it felt like he had got hold of a crashed sputnik.

"I'd say he's about ready, wouldn't you?" the guy said.

"Let us see if the device still functions," said the squeaky voice.

Despite his predicament, Nicky Kix managed a raucous laugh.

"You guys ain't shit, you know that? It'll never work. There's a contact in the door that has to touch another contact to complete the circuit."

"Thanks for reminding me."

He heard the scrape of a mangled timer dial and the tentative toiling of the timer mechanism itself. Then a sound like a coin dropping into a cigarette-machine slot.

Then Nicky Kix enjoyed the exquisite agony of having every water molecule in his cranium boil under an intense microwave bombardment.

He came erect as if impelled by a cattle prod.

He was dead before a three-fingered greenish hand slam-dunked the compacted microwave, Nicky's head and body following, into a trash barrel, incidentally yanking the plug from the socket.

"I thought those things wouldn't work unless the door was shut," said Jeter Baird, eyeing the dead body partially stuffed into a small Transformed Tae Kwon Do Teen Terrapin kiddie wastebaket.

"They will if you rip the contact off the door and jam it into the other contact," said the tall green figure of Aramis.

"Who *are* you guys?" asked Devin.

"You know how some people have guardian angels?" Aramis asked.

"Yeah."

"You two have guardian Terrapins. Congratulations."

This made perfect sense to Jeter and Devin, who had grown up on a steady diet of comic books.

"How can we ever repay you?" asked a relieved Jeter.

"You are allowed to tip," said the squeaky voice of Porthos.

"Don't listen to him," said Aramis. "We work for free. You won't be bothered again."

"Although we do not guarantee untipped work," Porthos added darkly.

Jeter and Devin hastily brought out their wallets and gave all their personal cash to their guardian Terrapin, Porthos.

"Pass," said Aramis when they offered him a plush D'Artagnan doll. "Just do us all a favor. Don't mention this to anyone."

"Not even our mothers?" asked Devin.

"Of course you should inform your mothers," said the squeaky-voiced Porthos. "One always tells one's mother of good fortune."

After the pair had gone, Devin turned to Jeter.

"You don't suppose it's true . . ."

"If you think about it," said Jeter, "we have been having an unusual streak of luck since this whole thing started."

For the rest of their days Jeter and Devin were never again visited by the guardian Terrapins. But they did discover the Hong Kong actors who usually played Aramis and Porthos. They were snoring, in full costume, in the back of the extortionists' car. They were unable to explain how they got there, nor why Aramis woke up wearing Porthos' head and vice versa.

29

Dr. Harold W. Smith was attempting to do three things at once and was on the verge of succeeding.

He was monitoring the LANSCII file as distant defeated fingers wiped clean the "TERRAPIN SKIM" heading. He was attempting to take his Zantac, a prescription ulcer medicine, and he was listening to Remo's brief report through the blue contact telephone.

"Reptiles everywhere can snuggle in their shells in safety tonight," Remo was saying dryly.

"Er, yes."

"What's next?" Remo wondered.

The office intercom buzzed. Reflexively Smith reached for the switch, inadvertently spilling his medicine.

Suppressing his annoyance, he said, "Excuse me," as he depressed the switch while attempting to swallow a hot splash of stomach acid that had leapt up his esophagus.

"Yes?" Smith said sourly.

His secretary said, "The transfer patient has arrived, Dr. Smith."

"Excellent. Thank you."

Smith returned to the blue phone. "Remo. Please ask Master Chiun to return to Folcroft."

"What about me?"

"I want you to go to New York City."

"What's down there? Besides muggers?"

"Don Fiavorante Pubescio. I want you to deliver a message to him."

"What's the message?"

"Cadillac Carmine Imbruglia is cheating on his rent."

"Who's Cadillac Carmine Imbruglia?" Remo wanted to know.

"The Boston don."

"How'd you find out his name?" Remo asked, interested.

"He foolishly listed himself on a payroll spreadsheet under the title of 'crime minister.' "

"Catchy. And your snooping computers caught him ripping off his own people, huh?"

"Not exactly," Smith said flatly. "Even as we speak, I am doctoring the LANSCII data base to show conclusive skimming of LCN profits for diversion into the Boston don's pockets."

"You play pretty hard ball, Smitty."

"I play to win," said Smith, hanging up. He reached for his Zantac, hoping there was enough left to quell his sour stomach.

30

In his black walnut alcove in Little Italy, Don Fiavorante Pubescio waited for word from his soldier.

"He should have called back by now," he said worriedly. "This thing should have been done by this time." He took a sip of lukewarm ginseng tea. It tasted bitter.

But not as bitter as the taste of betrayal, he reflected.

Don Fiavorante would not have believed it, but the proof lay before his eyes. Computer printouts. Unmistakable computer printouts. They had been laid on the walnut table by a soldier from Boston who called himself Remo Mercurio.

"Check 'em out," had said the soldier, of whom Don Fiavorante had not heard.

He had only to glance over the bottom-line figures to see the truth. Don Fiavorante looked up, his placid gentlemanly expression unchanged.

"You have done me a good turn, my friend," said the don, meeting the hard gaze of Remo Mercurio with his own frank regard.

"Skip it," said Remo casually.

"The contract is yours, if you want it."

"I don't."

Don Fiavorante's manicured hands had lifted questioningly. "That is it? You want nothing in return?"

"You have Don Carmine clipped," Remo had replied, "and I'll have all I want."

"Perhaps you would like to take his place, eh?"

"I'm available," said Remo coolly.

"Ah, now I understand. I will consider this. Once the irritant has been removed from the scene. Go now. With my blessing."

And so Don Fiavorante had sent one of his own soldiers to do the necessary but regrettable.

The plan was perfect. Don Carmine was moving heroin through commercial courier delivery services. The soldier would appear in the guise of a UPS deliveryman, the better to enter the LCN building without difficulty.

But there had been no call. What could have happened? wondered Don Fiavorante in the coolness of his walnut alcove.

31

When Carmine Imbruglia read of the fate of Nicky Kix and his fellow soldiers in the Boston *Herald*, he threw the paper across the room and howled, "They were ready for us. Someone tipped them off!"

"But who?" asked Bruno the Chef, his face characteristically blank.

"I dunno. I dunno. Let me think."

Carmine Imbruglia screwed up his face into a homely knot. He chewed on one knuckle.

"I see two possibilities here," he said, swallowing a fragment of dry skin. "One, it was that Tony. He was the only one who knew we were makin' a move, except you and me."

"What's two?" said the Chef quickly, hoping to steer his don away from the delicate subject of personal loyalty.

"Two is if we can't make more money to pay off Don Fiavorante, we gotta figure out a way that Don Fiavorante gets less."

"Don Fiavorante don't think that way."

"Maybe," said Don Carmine slowly, "Don Fiavorante shouldn't think at all."

Bruno (The Chef) Boyardi's dull eyes grew very, very worried as Don Carmine got to his feet and strode over to a bank of windows along one side of the LCN conference room.

His knotted expression melted into one of open surprise as his gaze went through the dark windows.

"Look what we got here!" he said.

"What?" asked Bruno the Chef, peering out.

He saw a step van the color of dried mud.

"It ain't got no markin's," growled Don Carmine.

"Sure, it has. See the little gold shield on the side?"

"Looks like a fuggin' badge," muttered Don Carmine. "Can you make out the letters?"

"U . . . P . . . S."

"The military! They sent the fuggin' army after us," howled Don Carmine, lunging for his tommy gun. He yanked back the charging bolt and waited.

When a man in a drab uniform identical in color to the step van's paint job emerged from the driver's side, Don Carmine opened up through the windows.

The racket was calamitous. Glass shards cascaded like glacial ice letting go. Smoking brass shell casings sprinkled and rolled about the floor.

Struggling to hold the bucking muzzle on his target, Don Carmine Imbruglia laughed with whooping joy.

"Take that, army cogsugger! You ain't takin' Cadillac Carmine, the Kingpin of Boston!"

"I think he's dead," said the Chef when the drum ran empty.

"Sure, he's dead," Carmine said, smacking the smoking weapon lustily. "This is a tommy. A good American weapon. It kills better than anythin'."

"Maybe we should get rid of the body," suggested Bruno the Chef, watching it bleed with vague interest.

"Get rid of the truck too. Dump it in the river. That's why I picked this joint. The river's a great way to get rid of dead guys."

"Okay, boss," the Chef said amiably, starting for the door.

"But make fuggin' sure you dump it on the Boston side of the river," Carmine called after him. "Let the Westies catch the blame."

"They don't call them Westies up here, boss. They're Southies."

"Westies. Southies. Irish is Irish. Hop to it. And when you're done, get that Tony in here."

"Right, boss."

32

The Master of Sinanju examined the patient in the bed.

He was old. His bone structure whispered of the Rome of Caesar's day. His skin was waxy and yellow as old cheese.

"What is his illness?" Chiun asked Harold Smith.

"Poison."

"Ah, the stomach," intoned Chiun, who in deference to his antiseptic surroundings wore ivory white. He looked about him. A doctor in Harold Smith's employ stood off to one side, looking concerned and even puzzled. They were in the hospital wing of Folcroft Sanitarium.

"He is in an irreversible coma," the physician said defensively. "There is nothing you can do for him. I told Dr. Smith that."

The Master of Sinanju ignored the quack's obvious ravings and examined the machine that forced the comatose unfortunate's lungs to pump, and touched lightly the clear tubes that provided unhealthy potions.

Without a word, he began ripping these free.

This brought the expected reaction from the physician. Seeing his barbaric machines desecrated, he made protest.

"You'll kill him! The patient must have his intravenous liquids."

The Master of Sinanju allowed the lunatic to approach, and with a deft movement snatched up one of his waving forearms and inserted a clear tube into it.

The doctor's face acquired a perplexed dreamy expression and, made docile by the poisons that were supposed to cure the sick, he allowed himself to be seated in a nearby chair.

"Are you certain that this will work?" asked Harold Smith anxiously.

"No," said Chiun gravely.

"Then why are you—?"

"There is nothing to lose," said Chiun, shaking his hands clear of his white sleeves. "This man has been pampered by machines until his will to function has been lulled into a lazy sleep. If he dies, he dies. But if he is to recover, his body must be convinced that this will happen only if it struggles for life."

And before Harold Smith could protest, the Master of Sinanju abruptly plunged his long fingernails into the exposed wrinkled pot belly of the patient.

The man's emaciated body jerked as its spine squirmed and twisted like an electric arc sizzling between contact posts.

Using both hands, Chiun plunged his nails deeper into the sickly greenish flesh.

And into the patient's ear, he whispered a delicate warning.

"Fight for your life, lazy one. Or I will take it from you."

Harold Smith turned away, his teeth set, his eyes closed. In his mind's eye he saw ten eruptions of blood. One for each of the Master of Sinanju's remorseless fingernails.

The next phase of Smith's plan depended upon bringing his patient back to health.

33

"In onore della famiglia, la famiglia e abbraccio," intoned Don Carmine Imbruglia in a corner office at LNC headquarters, lit by sullen candlelight.

"I don't know what the fug it means," he said ruefully, "but they always talk that kinda crap at one of these things."

"What things?" asked Tony Tollini, looking at the dagger and pistol that lay crossed on the table before him. For some reason, the windows were obscured with black crepe.

"Baptisms," said Don Carmine.

"Oh. Is someone being baptized?"

"Good question. You are."

Tony Tollini's eyes bugged out. "Me?"

"Don't be modest. You done good for LCN. We're gonna make you one of us."

Tony started to rise, saying, "I don't—"

Bruno the Chef's meaty hand pushed Tony Tollini back into his seat.

"Show some respect," he growled.

"What . . . what do I do?" Tony asked, weak-voiced.

"Almost nothin'," Don Carmine said casually. "Here, gimme your hand."

Tony Tollini allowed Don Carmine to take up his shaking hand. Don Carmine lifted the silver dagger off the table with the other.

"Okay," said Don Carmine. "Repeat after me, 'I want to enter into this organization to protect my family and to protect all my friends.' "

" 'I want to enter into this organization to protect my family and to protect all my friends,' " Tony repeated in a dull voice.

" 'I swear not to divulge this secret and to obey, with love and *omertà*.' "

" 'I swear not to divulge this secret and to obey, with love and *omertà*,' " Tony added, wondering what an *omertà* was. It sounded like a weapon. Maybe a Sicilian dagger, like the one Don Carmine was waving before his eyes.

A quick pass of the glittering blade, and the tip of Tony's index finger ran red with blood.

"Okay, I cut your trigger finger," said Don Carmine. "Now I cut me." Don Carmine sliced the tip of his trigger finger and joined it to Tony's. Only then did it begin to sting.

"Somebody gimme me a saint," called Don Carmine.

"Here," said Bruno the Chef, pulling a laminated card from his suit pocket.

Don Carmine looked at the face. "I don't know this one," he muttered.

"Saint Pantaleone. He's good for toothaches."

"Toothaches! What are we, dentists now?"

"I got a busted biscuspid, boss."

Don Carmine shrugged like a small bear with an itchy back. "What the fug. A saint is a saint, right? You, Tony, repeat after me," he said, touching a corner of the laminated card to the sickly yellow candle flame.

" 'As burns this saint . . .' "

" 'As burns this saint,' " said Tony, watching Saint Pantaleone begin to darken.

" 'So burns my soul. I enter alive into this organization and I leave it dead.' "

"Do I have to say that last part?" asked Tony, watching the card blacken and shrivel, giving off a pungent stink.

"Not unless you wanna enter the organization dead," said Don Carmine blandly. "In which case that's how you will leave it. The river runs only one way. Get me?"

Gulping, Tony Tollini finished the oath of allegiance.

Beaming, Don Carmine dropped the card into a green glass ashtray, where it curled up like a grasshopper in its death throes.

"Congrats!" he said. "You are now one of us! With all the rights and privileges of bein' a made guy."

"Thank you," said Tony Tollini miserably. When he had

entered the corridors of IDC a decade ago, he had never imagined it would come to this.

Don Carmine spanked the table hard. "Bruno, get us some wine. Red. While I think up a new name for Tony, here."

"I have a name," protested Tony, looking at his Tissot watch.

"What, you in a rush? This is a sentimental moment. Me, when I think back on my baptism, I get all choked up. You, you look at your fuggin' no-numbers watch. That's it!"

"What is?"

"No Numbers! That's what we're gonna call you. No Numbers Tollini."

"Hey, I like that, boss," said Bruno the Chef, setting down several glasses and beginning to pour blood-colored wine from an oblong green bottle.

"No Numbers?" said Tony (No Numbers) Tollini.

"You'll get used to it. Now, drink up."

They drank a toast. Tony thought the wine tasted a little salty until he realized he was bleeding into the glass. He switched hands and started sucking on his trigger finger, which really tasted salty.

It was then that Don Carmine grew serious.

"No Numbers, on account of your quick rise in our organization, we're gonna give you a very important job to do."

"Yes?"

"One that's gonna help you make your bones."

"Please don't break my bones!" No Numbers Tollini said tearfully.

"I said *make*. That means you gotta kill somebody."

"Oh, God. Who?"

Don Carmine Imbruglia leaned into No Numbers Tollini's melted-by-fear features and exhaled sweet wine fumes.

"Don Fiavorante Pubescio, the rat," he whispered.

"My uncle?"

"He's screwin' us. He's gotta go."

"I can't kill—"

"What 'can't'? You took the oath, same as me. Same as Bruno there. If a made guy don't do like he's told, other made guys have to discipline him. It ain't pretty, either. It usually means expulsion from the organization."

"Does that mean . . . ?" Tony gulped.

Running a finger across his throat, Don Carmine nodded sagely. "This ain't IDC, kid. Remember that oath."

Tony swallowed. He tasted the blood on his trigger finger. His blood. He decided too much of it had been spilled already.

"Whatever you want, Don Carmine," Tony (No Numbers) Tollini said hollowly.

34

Antony (No Numbers) Tollini parked his red Miata on Canal Street in lower Manhattan, where the scent of tomato sauce from Little Italy and soy-sauce aroma wafting up from Chinatown commingled into a breathable cholestoral-MSG mix.

He got out, buttoning the lower button of his Brooks Brothers suit to conceal the silenced .22 Beretta that Don Carmine had presented to him with words of fatherly advice.

"It's very simple, kid," Don Carmine had said. "You walk up to the hit, tell a few jokes, make him feel good, and whack him out while he's laughin' with you. He'll never know what hit him."

All during the ride down from Boston, Tony Tollini rehearsed how it would be. He would meet his Uncle Fiavorante in the walnut alcove where he held court. He would surreptitiously pull the Beretta from his belt and fire from under the table. He had seen it done that way in dozens of movies. Uncle Fiavorante would never know what hit him. The threat of the deadly weapon would be enough to get him out of the building alive.

Tony Tollini turned onto Mott Street, nervously wiping his sweaty palms on his gray trouser legs. He had never killed a man before. At IDC he had stabbed a few in the back, corporately speaking. But that was different. It was business. There wasn't any blood.

Tony Tollini decided that he would approach the task before him in true IDC fashion, forthright and unflinching. It would be no different than an employee termination. Besides, how much blood could there be? The bullets were .22's.

Resolutely Tony knocked on the blank panel that served

as the door to the Neighborhood Improvement Association. It opened quickly and the blue-jawed tower of bone and muscle asked, "Yeah?"

"I'm here to see the don."

"Who're you?"

"His nephew, Tony."

"One sec." The guard called back. "Boss, you gotta nephew named Tony?"

A distant voice croaked back, "Sure, sure. Show him in."

Tony was practically hauled inside and marched between two men into the dim black walnut alcove. A figure sat hunched in the gloom. Tony squinted in an attempt to make him out. The figure looked up querulously.

He frowned, "You ain't my nephew, Tony."

"You aren't Don Fiavorante," Tony blurted, staring at the waxy yellow face before him.

No Numbers Tollini realized he had said the wrong thing when the two guards threw him to the floor and pulled his clothes apart. One came up with the Beretta. The other hauled him back to his feet and sat him down so hard in the chair facing the strange old man that Tony felt a bone break somewhere. He thought it was his coccyx.

The old man—he looked like an anorexic corpse—dug a pale shriveled talon into a stained paper bag and extracted a single greasy fried pepper, which he began to chew methodically.

"I don't know you," he said, his voice a dry rattle.

"Cadillac sent me."

"I don't know that name."

"Cadillac Carmine, the don of Boston."

The old man stopped chewing. One eye narrowed in slow thought. The other fixed Tony with watery wariness.

"We ain't talkin' about Fuggin Imbruglia, are we?"

"He calls himself Cadillac."

"He would. How'd that *assassino* get to be in charge of Boston?"

"Uncle Fiavorante gave him the territory," said Tony, figuring only the truth would save him now.

The old man resumed his chewing. "Fiavorante, he is your uncle?"

"Yes."

The old man waved a well-chewed pepper in the direction

of the Beretta, held loosely in a guard's hand. "You come to see your uncle with a cold piece in your belt?" he asked.

Tony said nothing. The other watery eye opened to match its mate. "I see things very clearly now. Can you handle a shovel?"

"Why?" asked Tony.

"Because somebody's got to dig the grave."

"Not Uncle Fiavorante?" Tony asked in horror, momentarily forgetting his mission.

"Naw, we already planted him. I was thinking of giving you the adjoining plot. You'd like that, wouldn't you?"

No Numbers Tollini leaned forward across the scarred walnut table, not noticing the fresh gouge that was the rusty brown of dried blood.

He decided to play his trump card. "Listen. I'm a very, very good friend of Don Carmine's," he confided, trying to sound like Robert De Niro.

"And I got a very, very big vendetta against that rotten Fuggin," returned the old man.

"I'm a made guy, I'll have you know," Tony added, lowering his voice to a sinister growl. "They call me No Numbers. No Numbers Tollini. Maybe you heard of me."

"If I ain't made you, you ain't made. I wouldn't have a guy in my outfit calling himself No Numbers. What kind of name is that?"

"I can get you computers," Tony said quickly. "All you want. I can make your operation as successful as Carmine's. More successful. I swear."

"Fuggin' Carmine couldn't operate a laundry."

"He's getting rich up in Boston," Tony pleaded. "I can make you rich too. Give me a chance to show you, and I'll have you interfacing with every node of your heirarchy. You'll be completely on-line, networked, integrated and paperless. That means no incriminating backup disks."

"What is this you're talkin'? I've been out of action a few years, yeah, but people don't talk like this now, do they?"

"Not that I heard, Don Pietro," said a guard from behind Tony.

Don Pietro Scubisci reached for another fried pepper. His watery eyes narrowed.

"Tell you what I'm gonna do for you," he offered.

"Anything," Tony said, wiping sweat off his mustache.

"I give you back your gun, and I let you shoot yourself in the mouth."

Tony paled. He gripped the table edge. "Why?"

"On account of you talk too much."

Tony blinked. "Why would I do that?"

"Because you do it this way, I don't make you dig your own grave first," explained Don Pietro. "None of my guys gotta take the rap for whacking you out, and you don't die all sweaty and out of breath. Get me?"

"That's an absurd offer!" Tony Tollini said in protest.

Don Pietro shrugged. "It's the best one you're gonna get."

Tony Tollini stared at the old don as a fried pepper like a bright green grasshopper disappeared into his mouth. He couldn't believe what he was hearing. He couldn't comprehend how a simple pilot program, the most brilliant in IDC history, could bring him to this terrible crossroads in his life.

"I ain't gonna wait for your answer till I grow old," Don Pietro warned through his careful chewing.

It was then that Tony Tollini, a former rising star of International Data Corporation, realized that he had been made an offer he could not refuse.

Tremblingly he accepted the offered Beretta. It was cold to his touch. His eyes began to mist over.

Across the battle-scarred walnut tale, the don of Little Italy watched him with vague interest as Tony brought the muzzle of the Beretta into his mouth.

Tony tasted the bitter tang of machined steel on his tongue.

Closing his eyes, he pulled the trigger.

The trigger refused to budge. Tony's eyes popped open.

"Someone help this poor guy. He forgot to release the safety," said Don Pietro in a bored voice, reaching into the greasy paper bag.

And while that cold fact was sinking into Tony Tollini's mind, someone placed the muzzle of a larger weapon to his right temple and splashed the organized receptacle of his thoughts across a dozen hung saints.

Dispassionately Don Pietro watched Tony Tollini slump forward. A dollop of curdlike brain matter oozed out of his shattered forehead. A gleam entered the old don's tired eyes.

Slowly Don Pietro Scubisci dipped the chewed edge of a fried pepper into the matter and tasted it carefully.

While his guards urgently covered their mouths with their hands to keep the vomit in, Don Pietro dipped a fresh pepper into the oozing mass while smacking his lips with relish.

"Needs more garlic," he decided.

35

Harold W. Smith was saying, "If my plan has worked, both Don Carmine and Don Fiavorante are dead by now, victims of their own distrust and greed."

Smith was logging onto the LANSCII files as Remo and Chiun gathered around the CURE terminal.

"Explain it to me again," said Remo, reading the LANSCII sign-on screen.

"You, Remo, have set Don Fiavorante against Don Carmine. Meanwhile, Chiun and I have revived Don Pietro and installed him in Little Italy."

"What happened to Don Fiavorante?"

"Master Chiun eliminated him after you delivered your friendly warning. In the resulting power vacuum, it was a simple matter for Don Pietro to install himself."

Remo frowned back at the Master of Sinanju's tiny beaming face.

"Since when are we in the business of putting Mafia dons back in business?"

"When they are old, weak, and senile," explained Harold Smith, "they are preferable to the likes of innovators such as Don Fiavorante and Don Carmine. It is certain that Don Pietro will not see any advantage to computerization of illicit—"

Smith stopped, frowning.

"What is it?" Remo asked.

"It appears that Don Carmine is still in business," Smith said unhappily. "Even as we speak, he is maintaining his usury file."

"I guess Don Fiavorante's hit didn't go down," Remo said.

"No doubt he employed amateurs," Chiun sniffed.

"Great," Remo said sourly. "We have a direct line to his computer, but no clue to where it is. Usually your computers are more on the ball than this, Smitty. Maybe you need fresh batteries."

"It is obvious that we are dealing with a criminal genius," said Smith unhappily. "He has set up his operation perfectly. Every move we make against him, he counters with the brilliance of a chess player. He may well be the most brilliant criminal mind of our time."

"So we're checkmated?" Remo asked, watching the numbers on the screen change, actuated by unseen fingers hundreds of miles away.

Smith leaned back in his chair. "We know that he is headquartered in Quincy, Massachusetts. But we do not know where. Thus far, the key to thwarting him lies in an understanding of the psychology of the mob. We need to lure him out into the open."

"Any ideas?" asked Remo.

"None," admitted Smith. "I am stymied."

"I have a suggestion, O Emperor," put in Chiun.

Both men regarded the Master of Sinanju in surprise.

"What have you to add, Master Chiun?" Smith asked, his glum voice lifting.

"Merely wisdom," said Chiun smugly, eyeing Remo. Remo frowned but said nothing.

"Go ahead," said Smith.

"Offer this moneylender the thing that most appeals to him."

"And that is?"

"Money," said Chiun, raising a wise finger.

"Do you mean to bribe him?" asked Smith.

"No," said Chiun. "I mean offer this man a generous amount of money, but insist that he accept it in person. Tell him it is in repayment of an old debt that troubles your conscience."

"Never work," said Remo.

"It cannot hurt to try," countered Smith, logging off LANSCII and quickly pecking out a fax message.

He programmed his computer to dial the fax number of LCN. When he was satisfied with the text, he pressed the Send key.

The system hummed.

"What's happening?" Remo asked.

"Emperor Smith is following my wise and brilliant counsel," said the Master of Sinanju in a smug tone.

"I have just faxed my offer to Don Carmine," explained Smith.

"Can you fax straight from a computer like that?" Remo wanted to know.

Smith nodded absently. "It is a common application."

"News to me."

"You have much to learn, round eyes," sniffed Chiun. "Such as how to penetrate so-called secure rooms."

"I'd like to be a fly on the wall watching you get through one of those," Remo said, stealing a worried glance at the reflection of his eyes in the terminal screen.

"You would undoubtedly repeat your earlier error, even as an insignificant fly." The Master of Sinanju beamed. "Heh-heh. Even as an insignificant round-eyed fly. Heh-heh."

When Remo refused to join in the Master of Sinanju's amused laughter, Chiun went on.

"Emperor Smith has explained how the alert machines work. They are very simple. Like you."

"I'm all ears," said Remo.

"One moment," Smith said as his desk fax began to ring.

Out of the port streamed a long sheet a slick paper. Smith tore it off.

"What's he say?" Remo asked.

"He's very anxious to receive the sixty thousand dollars offered him."

"No surprise there. Did he ask what it was for?"

"He did not. I simply said it was an old debt."

"And he didn't question it?"

"No," said Smith, worrying his lower lip in a puzzled way. "But he made a strange request. He asked me to fax him a check." Harold Smith turned to the Master of Sinanju.

"Tell him no," instructed Chiun. "Inform him you wish to tender personal apologies for your slight."

Smith pecked out an answer, transmitted it, and received a prompt reply.

"He has agreed," Smith said after reading the return fax. He looked up. "I do not understand. Why would so brilliant a criminal fall for such an obvious ruse?"

"It is very simple," said the Master of Sinanju.

They looked at him expectantly.
"First, he is greedy."
"What's second?" asked Remo.
"He is no more brilliant than Remo."

36

Bruno the Chef was cooking a simple ravioli when Don Carmine Imbruglia barged into the LCN conference room, waving the morning edition of the Boston *Herald*.

"It's fuggin' on page three!" he chortled, spreading the paper on the conference table.

"What is?" asked Bruno.

"The dope on Fiavorante's gettin' whacked. They found his body last night."

"Guess that Tony pulled it off. So why ain't he back yet?"

"Don't be a mook. He clipped Fiavorante. Fiavorante's guys clipped him back. End of story. Listen, see what it says here." Don Carmine read along. "This ain't right," he muttered.

"What?"

"This can't be."

"What?"

"They say when they found Fiavorante there wasn't a mark on him. What happened to the slugs No Numbers pumped into him?"

"It say who's takin' over?"

"Hold your horses. I'm gettin' to that. Oh, Mother of God," said Don Carmine. "Something is very, very wrong. I smell a rat here. This is wrong. This is very wrong."

"What?"

"Says here that Don Pietro Scubisci has taken over."

"I heard he was in a coma."

"He's out. Maybe he got time off for good behavior. Fug! Now we gotta whack him out too."

"Why?"

"On account of he and I got history together. It's gonna be him or it's gonna be me."

"Who you gonna send? All your guys are dead."

"I'll worry about that later. We gotta protect ourselves first. Lock all the doors. Turn on all the alarms. Nobody comes in. Nobody goes out. We lay low for a while."

"Sure, boss, but what about that sixty G's you was supposed to pick up today?"

Don Carmine looked up from his newspaper.

"That's right. I almost forgot about that." His eyes narrowed craftily. "Okay, so you make the pickup instead. I'll hide out in the computertry room with all the motion alarms running. No one will touch me. I'll be safer than the fuggin' First Lady."

"What if it's a hit?"

"If it's a hit, they won't touch you. It's me they're after."

"If you say so, boss," Bruno the Chef said without enthusiasm.

"I say so," growled Don Carmine Imbruglia, wadding up the newspaper and bouncing it off the wall in frustration. "And on the way back I want you to pick up the oldest, most rotten-looking cod you can scrounge up."

"Why?"

"I'm gonna Fedex it to Don Pietro in the hope that when he gets a whiff of it, he's gonna fuggin' relapse."

37

Bruno the Chef pulled into the Bartilucci Construction yard just after noon.

Getting out of the black Cadillac, he looked around. No one was in sight. He ambled over to the idle nibbler and climbed in. If there was trouble, he wanted to be ready for it.

When they showed up, they were driving a blue Buick. It coasted to a stop beside Bruno's Cadillac. Bruno started the nibbler engine, just in case.

The front doors of the Buick popped out like wings, and two figures emerged with the perfect timing of matched reflections.

Except that the duo bore no resemblance to one another.

Bruno recognized the passenger as the Jap computer expert, Chiun. The other seemed familiar, but the face was not.

They approached with calm assurance.

"How's tricks, Bruno?" asked the man in the silk suit.

"Do I know you?"

"You don't remember your old buddy Remo?"

"Remo!" That was all Bruno the Chef had to hear. It was a hit. He sent the nibbler rumbling forward, engaging the pneumatic chisel, which unfolded like an articulated stinger.

"Let me handle this," said Remo to the Jap. The Jap glowered. "I owe him," Remo added.

Nodding his head, the old Jap stayed by the cars. Remo advanced with an easy fearless walk that was unnerving.

Bruno the Chef maneuvered the chattering blunt chisel until it hovered before Remo's advancing chest. Then he floored the gas.

With seeming ease Remo faded back before the nibbler's angry lunge, the vibrating nib a constant inch away. Bruno sent the nibbler careening until he had Remo retreating in the direction Bruno wanted him to go. When he slammed into the brick wall behind him, he would get it.

Except that Remo didn't get it. He ducked under the nibbler a spit second before it should have turned his rib cage to blood pudding. Bricks cracked and flew. One nearly brained Bruno.

Weaving, Remo stayed one step ahead of the deadly blunt fang as Bruno worked the control levers that kept the nibbler angling from side to side like a noisy scorpion.

He could see Remo's face clearly now. It was different. Like the guy had had his face fixed. And he was smiling a cold smile that made Bruno feel a chill settle in his marrow.

The smile said that Remo could dance with the nibbler all day long without fear. Bruno cut the pneumatic power so he could hear himself talk. The jackhammer sound died.

"What do you want from me?" Bruno demanded hotly.

"Your boss."

"He couldn't make it."

"I'll settle for his mailing address."

"I don't squeal for anybody."

"Suit yourself," said Remo, his back to the well-punctured brick wall.

Bruno saw his chance. He sent the nibbler lurching ahead. The blunt point touched the man's shirt front, pinning him to the wall.

Bruno's hand swept for the on switch. It clicked. Bruno grinned with relief. He had him.

And as the electricity flowed to the jackhammer arm, Bruno the Chef felt the nibbler cab vibrate in sympathy. He closed his eyes because he wasn't interested in seeing all the blood and guts that were about to be spattered in all directions.

Because he closed his eyes, he missed the whole thing.

The pneumatic chisel started to hammer. Bruno found himself holding on to the cab for dear life. The nibbler chassis was really vibrating, like it was going to shake itself apart.

Hearing no screams, Bruno opened one eye.

He saw Remo standing there, his arms lifted, his hands

actually clamped around the nibbler point, as if trying to ward it off. He looked like he was being shaken apart.

The trouble was, Remo was still grinning that cold confident grin.

Bruno the Chef experienced a moment of unreality. The nibbler began to buck and twist. Suddenly he was pitched out of the cab and onto the concrete.

After he had air in his lungs again, Bruno looked up.

His eyes no longer vibrating, he saw clearly again.

Somehow, impossible as it seemed, Remo was holding the nibbler off the ground by its wildly hammering point. He wasn't fazed by this in the least, Bruno saw. He wasn't even vibrating. It was the nibbler that was shaking like a cocktail shaker. It was shaking because Remo was holding the bit perfectly still in his two seemingly irresistible hands.

"Oh, my God," said Bruno, making the sign of the cross as Remo let the bit go. The nibbler bounced on its four fat tires and continued to chatter and smoke impotently.

Casually Remo sauntered up and dropped to one knee.

"Now, that wasn't nice, Bruno," Remo said. "I thought we were buddies."

"The money was just a story, huh?"

"And you fell for it."

"As I knew he would," added a squeaky voice. The Jap, Bruno saw. He had padded up curiously.

"You two were in it together, huh?" Bruno asked.

"All the time. Now, where can we find Carmine?"

"No offense, but I swore an oath never to rat on my don."

"I understand perfectly," Remo said in a reasonable voice.

"You in the life?"

"You might say that."

"What family you with?"

"The Milli Vanilli Mob. Ever heard of them?"

"Yeah," Bruno said vaguely. "I think I so. Somewheres."

"When we talk, people really listen. Now, point us to LCN."

Bruno the Chef started to protest again, but a long-nailed finger simply reached down and seemed to impale his left earlobe.

The pain was instant, extreme, and unendurable. Bruno's eyeballs exploded like hot flashbulbs. At least, that was how it looked to Bruno's brain. He grabbed up a hunk of concrete and shattered several front teeth while biting hard in a vain attempt to control the excruciating pain.

When the seemingly white-hot fingernail withdrew, Bruno was surprised that his fingers came away from his earlobe entirely free of blood.

"That was just your earlobe," Remo said. "I'll bet you have more sensitive parts."

Tears in his eyes, Bruno the Chef violated *omertà*, giving up his don, his familiy, and his honor. After he had answered every question put to him, Bruno the Chef looked up sadly.

"I guess you're gonna kill me, huh?"

"That's the biz, sweetheart," said the one called Remo, grabbing him by the hair and literally dragging him in front of the idle nibbler.

Bruno the Chef, feeling no strength in his still-spasming muscles, and no steel in his bones, simply lay there and begged, "Please don't turn that thing on me. Be a pal."

"I can do that," said Remo, reaching up to take the articulated arm. "After all, what are friends for?" He brought the arm down with cold suddenness.

When the blunt nib silently flattened Bruno (The Chef) Boyardi's throat like a garden hose, his arms and legs flew up and crashed down again. Then he lay still.

"Not bad, huh, Little Father?" Remo asked, walking the Master of Sinanju to their car.

"Not good," said Chiun coolly. "Not anything. It was adequate. But you are young and relatively unschooled. You will learn."

"Bruno said Don Carmine's surrounded by motion-sensitive alarms like the one that ambushed me at his old headquarters. This is your chance to show me how it's done."

"No," returned Chiun. "This is my opportunity to show you up. Heh-heh-heh."

38

Cadillac Carmine Imbruglia was the most secure kingpin in the history of organized crime.

He sat in a windowless room on the fifth floor of LCN headquarters in Quincy, Masachusetts, a fully loaded Thompson submachine gun at his elbow. There was only one exit, a veneer door with a chilled steel core. Beyond the armored door the many terminals of the LCN network glowed in the darkness, their screens like amber jack-o'-lanterns.

Nothing moved in the LCN computer room. Nothing could move because in each corner of the ceiling, boxy devices resembling security cameras looked down. Instead of lenses, tiny wafers of supersensitive quartz silently scanned the room, ready to trigger an alarm at the slighest breeze or change in air pressure.

And in his armored room, Carmine Imbruglia blinked at his personal terminal and stabbed at the keyboard with two stubby fingers, pausing often to correct mistakes, confident that he was as untouchable as Eliot Ness.

It was while updating his ever-burgeoning sports book that he experienced his first brush with computer trouble.

For some reason, the words and numbers on the screen began to duplicate themselves, repeating endlessly until they filled the screen like a million tiny amber spiders swarming behind the glareproof glass.

When the black screen had turned a solid amber, large black letters appeared against the warm brilliant glow.

"What the fug is happenin' now?" snarled Don Carmine Imbruglia, pounding the suddenly dead keys.

39

Remo pulled into the deserted parking lot of the Manet Building and remarked, "Bruno said the don's holed up on the fifth floor with an old tommy gun, no less. There's only one way in or out. So tell me how we're going to sneak up on him? Zip through the motion-sensitive field really fast?"

"That would be too easy," said the Master of Sinanju, arranging the skirts of his sable-and-gold kimono. "For you require a lesson that will stick in your white mind."

"You're too kind," Remo said dryly, looking at the silver-blue building facade and thinking that it looked like it had been faced with old mirrored sunglasses. "How?"

"It is simple, Remo. Instead of blundering in, we will take our time."

"Okay," Remo said good-naturedly. "Lead and I will follow."

They popped a window on the ground floor. It was held in place by a black aluminum frame. No studs or fasteners.

As Remo watched, the Master of Sinanju simply laid one flat hand against the center of the pane. It began to bulge inward.

Just when it looked like it was about to shatter from the strain, the Master of Sinanju spoke a single word and stepped back.

The word was "Catch."

Remo saw the mirrored pane explode toward him like an abstract arrow released from a bow. He faded back, bringing both hands up and held flat before his face.

When the raised surfaces of his palms made contact with the slickness of the glass, Remo pivoted in place.

Surface tension, acting as a glue, brought the glass around with him. When it was at the apogee of its turn, momentum transferred in the opposite direction and the pane let go and knifed into a patch of salt marsh like a square blade.

The Master of Sinanju bowed mischievously and gestured for Remo to precede him.

"Youth before excellence," said Chiun, beaming.

"You made your point," Remo said, hoisting himself in through the opening.

"Perhaps," said Chiun, floating in after him. "Perhaps not."

They found themselves in a room that might have been transplanted intact from Atlantic City. There were roulette wheels and black-jack tables and other gambling fixtures. They passed through this into the deserted lobby.

"Okay," Remo undertoned. "Now we hit the fifth floor. So how do we do it?"

The Master of Sinanju stabbed the up button beside the gleaming steel elevator door.

"By taking the elevator," said Chiun.

Remo frowned. He didn't like the cavalier attitude the Master of Sinaju had been taking to a dangerous situation. He decided to play along, and take control if necessary.

They stepped off on the fifth floor into a nondescript curving corridor, except for the undersmell of garlic.

The room they wanted was clearly marked. It said "COMPUTERTRY."

"Okay, tell me the trick," Remo hissed.

Instead of replying, the Master of Sinanju took hold of the doorknob. He turned to his pupil.

"You must be very, very patient. And quiet. Can you be both?"

"Sure."

"Then we will begin. You will do as I do. Nothing more. And nothing less."

Remo watched the Master of Sinanju. But Chiun did not move, or appear to move. His eyes on Remo, his hand on the doorknob, he simply stood there. Several minutes passed. Five. Then ten. Remo frowned. He opened his lips to speak.

Chiun's free hand came up to his dry lips so fast it seemed

there was no intervening motion. The hand was at his side. Then it was before his lips, admonishing Remo to silence.

Remo held his tongue. His dark eyes darted to the door. To his surprise, he saw that it was open a crack. He kept watching, interest dawning on his face.

Five more minutes passed. The door was slowly being drawn open—so slowly that even Remo could not detect motion. Only a slow elapsed-time result.

When finally the door was open enough to admit them, Chiun beckoned with a quiet gesture. Beckoned for Remo to follow.

It was twenty minutes later before the Master of Sinanju had eased himself through the door. Remo matched his movements, pacing himself to the extreme slow motion of his teacher's body language.

For Remo it was excruciatingly, agonizingly, painstakingly boring. It was so boring, his back started to itch.

But it worked. He found himself inside the room in a little less than ninety minutes. He took no steps. His feet simply crept along the carpet, a micro-inch at a time, neither lifting nor stepping, but achieving a kind of flat-footed sliding locomotion that the ceiling-mounted quartz motion detectors could not detect because although Remo and Chiun were displacing the still air in the computer room, they were not disturbing it.

Remo was glad Chiun had made him remove his silk suit and shirt at the construction yard. The fine hairs along his bare arms acted as sensory receptors, enabling him to pace himself so he didn't trigger warning eddies of air.

Since it was taking them literally hours to cross the room, Remo had plenty of time to take in the computer screens arrayed in work stations on either side of the corridor leading to the blank door behind which Don Carmine labored under a false sense of security.

He noticed that one by one the screens began to fill up with symbols that crowded and overlapped themselves like wire-frame jigsaw puzzles. Like amber cataracts forming on cyclopean eyes, the screens turned a uniform blind amber.

Then big black cut-out like letters appeared.

Remo wondered what a "hard dynamic abort" was.

He had a lot time to think about it. They had entered the Manet Building just after one o'clock in the afternoon. It was approaching six-thirty now and there remained a good twenty feet between them and the blank door. It was dark. The sun had set.

It was like walking underwater, except without the water. So as to keep his metabolism cycled down, Remo had to keep breathing in a shallow way that was almost suffocating. He wanted to scream, to unleash the frustrated pent-up energy that was coursing through his body.

But Remo knew the Master of Sinanju was testing his patience as well as demonstrating his own superior skills. Remo would not allow himself to fall short. Even if he did strongly suspect Chiun of moving even more slowly than neccessary to prolong Remo's ordeal.

As they made their slow way through the computer room, Remo spent most of his time staring at the translucent skin of the back of Chiun's bald head. He thought about all the difficult times that lay behind them. The long months of separation. The terrible battle Remo had fought in the Middle East without the Master of Sinanju by his side. And how badly he had botched his mission, without Chiun there to guide him. And he remembered why he had been so concerned about his mentor. Chiun was a century old. And he looked it, even if he did not act it.

Remo expressed a thought.

I love you, Little Father.

And in the dimness of his mind, he seemed to hear a reply.

You should.

Remo would have grinned, but the mere act of smiling was apt to trigger air currents. He held the warm feeling inside him for the remainder of the passage—it seemed as endless as Magellan's circumnavigation of the globe—across the room.

The door was inching closer. A mere dozen feet away, or less than an hour at their current pace.

Don Carmine Imbruglia would never know what hit him.

They would have made it except that the blank panel abruptly acquired a dozen black eyes created by .45-caliber slugs punching out through the veneer and steel.

Alarm bells began to ring.

Remo lunged forward to pluck Chiun out of the myriad bullet tracks.

He was hopelessly late. The Master of Sinanju dropped in

place, as if a trapdoor had opened under his feet. The bullets snarled over his aged head. Coming at Remo.

Remo slipped off to one side, just in time to evade the outer edge of the spreading spray of slugs.

All over the room, computer screens shattered and gave up smoke and hissing blue-white sparks. Then the long room went completely dark as, in unison, the rows of amber screens winked out.

As his eyes adjusted to the utter lack of light, Remo detected the shadowy form of the Master of Sinanju coming to his feet and sweeping purposefully toward the bullet-riddled door.

He barely paused at the door. His fingers went into convenient bullet holes. Then the Master of Sinanju turned. The door was suddenly wrenched off its hinges and hurled backward, where it flattened a dead terminal to a mass of plastic and mangled circuit boards.

Chiun stepped into the room.

Remo moved in, hard and fast.

And stopped dead at the threshold. Inside, Don Carmine Imbruglia had reared up from his chair, the smoking tommy gun dangling in the crook of one muscular arm. His tiny eyes glared at the ruin of a terminal on the Formica card table before him.

It had been the target of Don Carmine's violent outburst, Remo realized.

"I was robbed!" he was howling. "The fuggin' computer's completely busted."

"Nice shot," Remo said in the darkness.

"Who's that? Who's there?"

"Call me Remo."

"I call you dead, cogsugger," said Don Carmine, yanking back on the charging bolt of his weapon.

"And what do you call me, Roman?" came the squeaky voice of the Master of Sinanju.

In the act of bringing his tommy gun up to bear, Don Carmine turned toward the unexpected sound.

"I know that voice. You're the fuggin' Jap thief."

"Don't call him—" Remo started to say.

Don Carmine Imbruglia never completed his turn. A sandaled foot grazed his kneecaps, turning them to powder. A long-nailed hand took hold of the muzzle of his weapon.

When Don Carmine collapsed, his hands were empty.

The Master of Sinanju made short work of the tommy. The barrel came loose like a pipe being separated from an elbow joint. The drum broke open, raining bullets. Various pieces of the breech and stock were reduced to wood shavings and metal filings under the friction of Chiun's high-speed manipulations.

"What the fug happened?" came the dull voice of Don Carmine, looking at his stung, empty hands.

"You called him a Jap," Remo pointed out.

"Well, he is, ain't he?"

"Oops! You did it again."

Don Carmine felt something like steel darning needles take up his wrist. They squeezed inexorably. Don Carmine screamed. The pain was frightening, like being injected with dozens of acid-filled hypodermics.

"You can't do this to me!" howled Don Carmine through his agony. "I know my rights. You got nothing on me without my computers, and they just took a dive. So there. Go peddle your papers elsewhere. I'm the fuggin' Kingpin of Boston."

"And here's your fuggin' crown," said Remo, picking up the bullet-riddled IDC terminal and jamming it over Don Carmine's head like an astronaut's helmet.

A muffled cursing came from within the terminal.

The Master of Sinanju took hold of the terminal to steady it, Don Carmine's head with it. He separated his hands, then brought them together.

Runkk!

Don Carmine's futuristic head was suddenly two feet narrower and half a foot higher. It hovered in the darkness, balanced on the mafioso's thick neck for long moments.

With a last guttering spark and hiss, it fell across the table legs. Don Carmine's limbs twitched a little, as if feeding off the electricity in the terminal. Then he lay still.

In the darkness, Remo looked up at Chiun.

"We were supposed to find out if anyone else knew how to run the LANSCII program," Remo pointed out.

Chiun shrugged shadowy shoulders. "He called me an unforgivable name." His smile came dimly. "Also, he was the last to labor under that misconception. I could not allow him to slander the Master of Sinanju further. What would my ancestors think?"

Remo searched his mind for an appropriate comeback. He never found it. Instead, he said quietly, "They would be proud of you, Little Father. As I am."

And in the darkness, the two Masters of Sinanju bowed to one another in mutual respect.

From a pay phone in the foyer of a nearby Chinese restaurant, Remo was explaining what had happened to Harold W. Smith.

"Just to make sure, we shattered every computer in the place," Remo was saying. "Believe me, there were a lot of them."

"Thorough but unnecessary," said Smith approvingly. "But they were already useless. I had programmed the LANSCII disk Chiun stole with a computer virus called a time bomb. Once Don Carmine had it reinstalled, it has been silently replicating itself over and over until it filled all available memory in every system in the LCN network, literally paralyzing it."

"Was that the hard dynamic abort I saw?" Remo asked.

"It was."

"Well, it set Don Carmine off. He shot up his own system when he couldn't get it working. He nearly nailed Chiun and me while we were moving in on him."

"Without knowing how much memory we were dealing with," said Smith, "there was no way to predict when system-wide paralysis would be achieved. Besides, you and Chiun are too quick to be stopped by mere bullets."

"Not at that particular moment, we weren't," said Remo, noticing the Master of Sinanju through the glass doors. "Okay, that's a wrap. I've gotta get Chiun back to civilization fast."

"Why do you say that, Remo?" Smith wondered.

"He's found out how cheap real estate is up here. If I don't get him across the state line soon, he's going to have us living here."

"It is not a bad idea, Remo."

"It is a terrible idea, Smitty. Put it out of your mind."

"We have several important matters to address," Smith

said levelly. "Your new face. The disposition of your home. The—"

Remo hung up, saying, "The sheer pleasure of our wonderful working relationship."

He joined the Master of Sinanju outside the restaurant. Chiun was gazing across a busy artery, his eyes fixed on a tall condominium complex with unlighted windows.

"I am given to understand that that entire building is for sale at a reasonable price," Chiun said.

"It must be practically free for you to call it reasonable," Remo said dryly. "It's ugly, too."

"But cheap," Chiun pointed out.

"More ugly than cheap," Remo countered.

"You have not heard the price."

"Tell you what, Little Father. I'll agree to take a look at it if you come clean with me."

The Master of Sinanju lifted his wrinkled little face up to his pupil's own, his expression quizzical.

"Tell me what you had the plastic surgeon do to my face," Remo said.

The Master of Sinanju passed a pale hand the color of a pecan down his wispy beard, his hazel eyes thoughtful.

"You are right, Remo," said the old Korean flatly. "It is ugly."

Remo blinked. "The building or my face?"

"Both."